Cindy,
Thank you for lo
Sexy Alden! ♡
YD Da

by LD Davis

Edited by Kristen Switzer, Switzer Edits
Cover Graphics by Tina Kleuker, Focus4Media
Lyrics by L.D. Davis

l.d.davis478@gmail.com
www.facebook.com/lddaviswrites

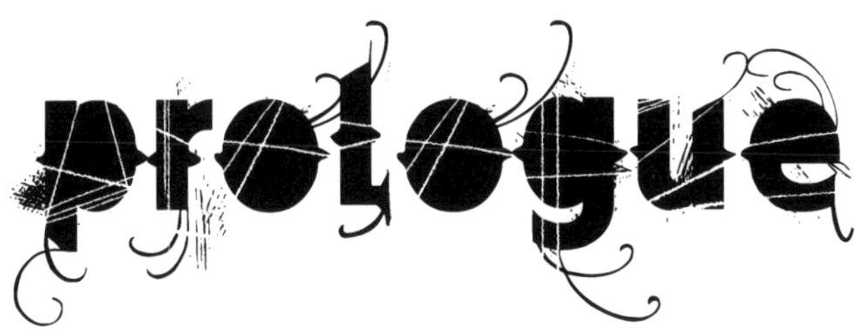

Prologue

I really don't know how I allowed Kristy to talk me into coming to this concert. I was smashed up against the barrier at the front of the stage by hormonal, *crazy*-ass women, screaming, crying, and trying to get the attention of the lead singer on stage. I didn't even like this band that much. I mean, they were okay. Honestly, I didn't listen to Friction. I heard a few songs on the radio, but I never really paid attention to them. Kris was a huge fan, though. When her Friction buddy came down with the flu and landed in the hospital, Kris *insisted* that I accompany her. I couldn't let her go alone, and the fact that she was about to cry was a major contributor to my decision. Manipulative bitch.

So, there I was, suffocating and so not enjoying the show. The lead singer, Alden Breck, was strutting across the stage, grinning and thrusting for the girls, making matters worse for me. When he grinned and thrust in my general direction, I only frowned. Didn't he realize how ridiculous that was? I mean, it was okay when some guys did it, but I don't know…Alden was annoying me. He just seemed so damn cocky. Cocky grin, cocky flirting, cocky thrusting – when the hell was this cock fest going to be over?

Kristy bounced, screamed, and belted songs out at an alarming volume for her tiny stature and voice, all the while reaching out to touch Breck's fingertips. Puh-lease.

After he had taken a few big gulps from a water bottle, he proceeded to fling the rest of the water onto the audience. As I shrieked in disgust, Kris and the other morons screamed with delight. I shook the water off my arms with sheer disgust. I looked up to glare at Alden Breck, but he was already looking at me as he sang. He looked amused, although there was nothing amusing about his song. When he looked away from me, his expression went back to one of anguish while he sang about climbing from the dark, or something equally poetic.

When the band finally disappeared off of the stage, I turned to Kristy. I gave her a look that told her I was ready to get the F out, but she yelled something about an encore. It wasn't until the band reappeared that I figured it out. A freakin' encore? Come on! I sucked in a breath and tried to be patient. I mean, how long could one song take, right? Right, except they did *two more* encores after that one! During the last song, Alden leapt off the stage to reach out to his fans as he sang. He was all the way down at the other end, so maybe I wouldn't have to be too close to him. If he got too close to me, I was gonna hit him for flinging his germy water on me, for taking too damn long to finish the show, and for being a cocky asshole.

The crowd surged forward; people who were impossibly too far back pushed forward to try to touch the musician. The closer Breck got, the harder I was pressed up against the railing. I seriously couldn't breathe. My lungs were being crushed between bodies and metal. I was starting to gasp for air as Breck neared us. By the time Kris got her greedy hands on him and he was standing in front of me, I was starting to panic. I really couldn't breathe, and the people behind me didn't seem to give a shit. Breck looked at me funny as he sang. When he reached for me, the people behind me reached for him, and then I was reaching for him, but out of blind panic because I couldn't even take in a breath. The metal barrier in front of me that had seemed so unmovable and was contributing to my suffocation began to give way. As if he sensed what was happening, Alden stopped singing and his eyes grew wide. He started to yell something to me, but then the barrier was falling and I was falling with it, with thousands of berserk fans behind me rushing forth to get to Alden. I wasn't able to take in another breath again before I was pushed to the floor. I saw feet, heard screaming, heard the bouncers yelling, and I heard Alden Breck cursing at people. My fingers were crushed under more than one foot; people were tripping over and stepping on me. I still couldn't breathe and I knew I was going to die there on the floor, suffocated and trampled to death by Friction fans. I felt a strong hand around my wrist. I felt people being shoved away, and I felt myself being lifted high into the air. As my vision blurred and darkened, I saw the frantic face of Kristy, and then her blonde head was lost in the crowd before I saw nothing. I blacked out.

Patience beyond a virtue, I wait, I watch, I anticipate
Teetering on the edge of possibilities
And so begins the chase
"The Chase"
Friction

I woke up to a light burning into my retinas. I groaned and tried to bat the light away.

"How are you feeling, Noa?" a male voice asked me.

I couldn't get my bearings. I felt like I was on a couch – in an obnoxiously loud and bright room. Male voices boomed around me, sprinkled with a few girlish giggles. The smell of cigarettes and alcohol was prominent. Not just alcohol and cigs – was that weed? And how did this asshat know my name?

I blinked up at a man who looked to be in his late thirties or early forties.

"Who the hell are you?" I asked, surprised at my raspy voice. I reached up to touch my throat, but hell if my fingers didn't hurt. I winced and held my hand up to my eyes. Two fingers were taped and they looked broken. "What the fuck?" I asked no one in general.

"How are you feeling?" the guy asked again.

"Who the hell are you?" I repeated my question.

"My name is Greg. I'm a doctor. I think she needs to go to a hospital," he said to someone standing just out of view near where my head rested on the couch. "She seems confused. She might have a head injury."

Then I remembered being crushed underfoot of maniacal women and it was all Alden Breck's fault! I slowly tilted my head to see who was standing above me and automatically scowled when I saw Breck.

"I agree," he said with a small, cocky smile. "She does seem confused. Women don't usually scowl at me, Greg."

"I'll get the paramedics in here," he said with a sigh. "I knew we should have taken her right away."

"Stop worrying," Alden waved him off.

"No, I won't stop worrying, Alden!" Greg snapped. "If she's seriously hurt and we didn't act hastily enough, you'll have another lawsuit on your hands – hell, I'll have a lawsuit on *my* hands."

"It's fine," Alden waved him off again as he looked down at me. "Little Noa isn't going to sue, are you, Little Noa?"

"How the hell do you know my name – and what the hell am I doing back here?" I snapped and tried to sit up. "Owwwwaaahhh!" I yelled angrily when my ribs ached as I tried to sit up. My head protested with a fair amount of pain, too.

"Lie back down," Alden said impatiently, and then *shoved* me back to a lying position.

"This is all your fault!" I tried to yell, but my whole body ached.

"My fault?" his eyebrows popped up. "Are you serious? I saved your life, Little Noa."

"Stop calling me that! You only had to save my life after you put it in jeopardy with your obnoxious, cocky—"

"Whoa!" He held up two hands. "Obnoxious *and* cocky?"

I made a sound of disgust and looked around for Greg. He was talking to a guy who then talked into a headset. Headset guy nodded, said something to Greg, and left. The good doctor walked back over to us just as Alden was about to start up again.

"Paramedics are on their way," he said kindly.

"Thank you," I muttered. Then I remembered Kristy. "Oh, damn! My friend – where is she?"

Just as I finished saying that, I heard Kris's angry voice enter the room.

"Get your hands off of me! I don't care about the damn band right now! I want to make sure my friend is okay!" Kristy was tiny, barely five-foot-two, two inches shorter than me, but she could be very scary and intimidating when she wanted to be.

"Noa!" she cried, rushing to my side. She had tears in her eyes. "Are you okay? Oh my god, I thought you got trampled to death! How would I have explained this to Warren?"

"Maybe if her boyfriend were here with her, he could have protected her," Alden spat out, glaring at me with his arms crossed.

"Warren is her brother," Kristy said, glancing up at Alden through her eyelashes. She leaned in close to my ear. "He's really smoldering hot, huh?"

I rolled my eyes and attempted a deep breath with my aching ribs. I just wanted the paramedics to get me the hell out of there already.

"Brother?" Alden's eyebrows raised and then a slow smile appeared on his face.

"For the love of all that's good in this world, can someone please make him go away?" I sighed, putting a hand over my eyes to block my view of Alden Breck.

"What is wrong with you?" Kris whispered. "He saved you!"

Before I could inquire after that, the paramedics showed up. They poked and prodded, and then asked a lot of questions as they loaded me onto a stretcher. Before I rolled out, the drummer – Hash – tossed his drumsticks onto my lap and grinned.

"Thanks for falling on your face. I didn't want to do another fucking song."

I looked at the drumsticks. "Umm…you're welcome?"

He sauntered away and Alden appeared at my side.

"Oh, my goodness, do you *ever* go away?" I snarled as I was being wheeled out.

"Your blatant distaste in me has struck a chord," he said with seriousness. "I'm going to be hard to get rid of, Little Noa."

"I'm not *little* Noa," I said. "I'm just Noa – and how do you know my name?"

He grinned and his hazel eyes flashed with mischief. He set my little purse and my phone on my lap next to the drumsticks. "I'll see you soon, Little Noa."

"Not on your life, Breck."

I left Alden Breck behind me as I was wheeled down the long corridor to the exit.

***

"You were turning blue," Kristy was telling me a few hours later as I rested in a hospital bed behind a curtain. "It was funny; I only noticed because Alden was looking at you weird. Then all hell broke loose. I was yanked backward just as I saw you go down. There were so many people all over you and Alden was yelling at people, pushing them off him as he tried to get to you. Finally, the bouncers kept people off him long enough to pull you off the floor. Alden lifted you onto the stage, jumped back up there, picked you up, and carried you offstage. The crowd was nuts – the police eventually had to come in to get everyone under control. It's really surprising that no one else was seriously hurt. But holy shit, Alden Breck saved your life, Noa!"

I rolled my eyes. "I'd rather have been trampled. Alden Breck is obnoxious and conceited."

"I love how he calls you *Little* Noa," she said dreamily.

"Ew."

"You don't have to like him as a musician, Noa," Kristy snapped. "But you should really appreciate what he did for you. You don't understand – he could have been seriously hurt himself trying to save you."

I didn't answer her. I just sulked and fingered the drumsticks that were given to me. Kristy was right, of course. I really could have been dead or close to it if Alden had not saved me. Not to mention, he could have been torn apart by the crowd, but she was also right with her first words. I didn't have to like him. No problem. I didn't.

"When you go home, at least you'll have a story to tell," Kristy said with a small shrug and a smile.

"I don't think I'll be sharing this story," I said softly and yawned.

"You should get some sleep," she said. "Do you want me to stay with you?"

"No." I smiled at my oldest friend. "Go home. It's late. Do *not* call my brother!"

She held up her hands in defeat. "I won't, I won't." She got to her feet and planted a kiss on my cheek. "I hate that you are spending your last full night in California in the freakin' ER."

"A vacation to remember," I sighed.

"Indeed. See you in the morning," she said as she opened the curtain. "*Little Noa.*"

I glared at the curtain even after I knew she was gone. I loved Kristy to death, but if she called me Little Noa again, I was going to drum on her head with one of the drumsticks.

I closed my eyes, feeling thankful that I wasn't any more hurt than a couple of banged up fingers, bruised ribs, and an aching head. The fingers weren't broken, but they hurt like hell. It could have been so much worse, and the doctors feared that I had a concussion, but thankfully not. That may have delayed my trip back to the east coast and I was *so* ready to get back to the east coast.

Kristy and I had been friends since ninth grade. Instead of getting into a catfight about a boy who was secretly seeing both of us, we both dumped him and became friends, and never looked back. Kris and I were complete opposites. She was blonde and I was dark haired. She had blue eyes and a button nose and I had plain brown eyes and an okay nose. My figure was okay, but Kristy's figure was incredible - curvy and just…hot. I sometimes wondered if she just needed a plain friend to accentuate her natural beauty, but after a couple of years, I got over it and accepted myself as I was.

After high school, Kris packed up her life in New Jersey, deciding on the college life at UCLA, and Jersey was something else she never looked back on. She made new friends, found an awesome job after college, and an incredible guy. I was in California for their wedding last weekend, and since they weren't going on a honeymoon right away, I stayed a week to spend some time with my old friend, which was how I ended up at that damn concert.

I couldn't get Alden Breck's smug grin out of my head, and that was annoying me, because I really didn't like the guy. Okay, I didn't know him, but he was actually really good looking with his sandy blond hair, hazel eyes, and a chiseled body; though he still came off as cocky and obnoxious and that was enough for me to dislike him.

After getting used to the noises in the hospital, I started to drift off to sleep. I was almost out of it before my phone vibrated on the table next to me. I hoped it was Kristy telling me she got home all right, but the incoming message was from a name *I did not* program into my phone: **Alden Breck, Musician & Saver of Lives.**

"So obnoxious!" I whisper-yelled.

I was angry – how the hell did he get my number? Then I figured he probably called himself from my phone. I checked that out before I even looked at his message, and I was right. Who does that with an unconscious girl's phone? Unbelievable!

I went back to the text messages and opened Mr. Saver of Lives' message.

Hi, Little Noa. I hope you are feeling better. No hard feelings?

What? Was he kidding me? No hard…*really*?

This move is borderline stalkerish, I keyed in.

I saw a chance and took it, he said. **You weren't awake for me to ask you for your number.**

I pursed my lips as my fingers angrily flew across the keyboard. **I think it is sad and pathetic that the only way you could get my number was while I was unconscious. For the record, if I had been awake and alert, you most certainly would not have my number. Now that you are aware of that, take this opportunity to lose said number. Thank you, Oh Saver Of Lives for not letting me die at YOUR concert. Goodbye.**

Minutes passed, and I believed I had finally gotten rid of Breck. I sat back and started to relax, closing my eyes again, but then my phone vibrated.

Little Noa, Breck said. **I saved you for yourself as much as I did for myself. Sorry, I am not very good at 'losing'. Please get some rest. Almost dying at one of my concerts must wear a girl out. Sweet dreams.**

I could practically hear his smug voice and see his smug face as he said the words. I angrily shut the phone off, put it on the tray, and forced myself into a fitful sleep.

"When did you get that T-shirt?" I asked Kristy, wrinkling my nose in distaste.

Her husband Trent was putting my bags in the car. Kristy and I were standing in the foyer with our umbrellas, getting ready to go out into the pouring rain. My flight left in a little more than three hours. We'd be lucky to get through the stupid San Francisco traffic in time. Kris had picked me up from the hospital only a couple of hours before while still dressed in her pajamas, a pet peeve of mine. It was really no effort at all to at least change into a pair of jeans or even a pair of sweats. Going past your driveway in pants with sleeping cows and quarter moons on them was plain unacceptable.

"Um, well," she said, smoothing the Friction shirt with her hand. It was signed by all the band members, like really signed, not stamped on. "Last night, as I was leaving the hospital, I got a phone call from a number I didn't recognize. I almost didn't answer, but it was late, it could have been some kind of emergency, you know? I answered and it was Alden Breck," she beamed.

"Oh, no," I sighed and hung my head in disappointment. "Don't tell me. You didn't."

"Are you fucking kidding me, Noa? It's *Alden Breck* of *Friction*! At first, I was confused – how the hell did he get my number, but Doctor Greg gave me his number so that I could update him on your condition and Alden got my number from him. Anyway, he told me he had some gifts for you and me because he felt bad about what had happened. So, I stopped at their hotel on my way home and he kept asking me questions about you. Noa, I think he really feels bad that you got hurt. He kept apologizing to *me* about it, and I was like 'dude, she's okay. Don't worry about it,' but he still looked worried. Then I thought about how amazing it was that I was standing in Alden Breck's hotel room, *talking* to him about *my* best friend, and at the same time wishing I didn't just get married last week, know what I mean? I've read a lot of gossip about his um, *skills*."

Kristy had been a long-winded, quick-tongued speaker since the day I first met her. Most of the time, I listened as much as I could. But sometimes, I would honestly just zone out because she tended to throw a lot of unnecessary details into the mix. This time I wasn't brain dead after listening to her speak, but I was appalled that she went to their hotel room alone, and further appalled that Alden Breck couldn't just leave well enough alone. Before I could open my mouth to bitch about it, Trent laid on the horn from the Acura and I had to shut up and go.

At the airport security line, Kristy hugged me fiercely and cried about how much she was going to miss me. Her tears were both moving and irritating. I never had a doubt about how much my friend loved me, but I hated tears. Hated, hated, hated. Finally ready to end it, I pulled away, muttered something about not missing my flight, and started to walk away.

"I put your souvenirs from last night in your suitcase," Kristy called to me as I got into line.

I gave her a look of disgust. She winked, blew me a kiss, gave a little wave, and trotted over to Trent. He gave me a wave and then they were gone.

My ribs hurt, and carrying my carry-on bag wasn't helping. Nor was it easy with two badly bruised fingers. I stopped at a store and got a bottle of water so that I could swallow a few ibuprofen pills for the pain. The doctor prescribed some stronger drugs, but I didn't want to be drooling on my boobs when the last boarding call came for my flight. I carefully sat down in a chair in a corner, trying to stay as far away from other people as possible. I didn't feel like chitchat or overhearing conversations. My head was hurting, too, and I would have screamed if someone got all chatty with me. I put my bag on the chair next to me, tilted my head back, and closed my eyes. I don't know how long I was like that, as unattractive as it was, before my phone vibrated in my pocket.

I cursed at the pain it caused my fingers to pull it out of my pocket and looked at the screen.

Your head hurts, Alden said.

I squinted at the screen in confusion. How the hell did he know my head hurt? Probably just a general statement. Obviously my head hurt. I had a damn shoeprint on it last night for heaven's sake. I frowned, poising to respond with distaste in hopes of chasing him off, but then he sent another message.

You shouldn't keep your phone in your jeans if it hurts your ribs and fingers to take it out.

Oh. My. God. I dared not look up. Alden was somewhere nearby, stalking me. Oh my god, he was a real actual stalker. None of his fans probably knew he was a psychopath.

Stalking again, are we? I frowned as I sent the message. I still didn't look up. I looked to my right and looked at planes moving about on the tarmac, but I didn't look into the crowds of people.

Not stalking. Just passing through to the VIP lounge to wait for my flight. Why don't you join me? You will be able to relax much easier there.

Oh, come on! He wanted me to believe that he was only passing through? That he just happened to be in the same terminal as me? Puh-lease!

Thank you, but no thank you. Now if you don't mind, I am trying to rest my weary head. Goodbye.

I slipped the phone into the front pocket of my bag instead of my jeans and tilted my head back again. I felt exposed and watched, and it made me feel a little anxious, but I refused to open my eyes and look for him. Besides, he was probably incognito. There was no way Alden Breck would have just been able to prance through the airport unseen and unbothered. I tried to put him out of my mind, took a deep, slightly painful breath, and tried to relax. Moments later, I sensed my bag being picked up out of the chair beside me. My eyes snapped first to the chair and then up the legs and torso of the person holding the bag.

Incognito to a point – his hazel eyes burned into mine through a pair of black rimmed glasses, but a hat and the hood of a hoodie covered his sandy blond hair and partially obscured his face. He also had a little bit of hair growth on his face – did he spontaneously grow hair in a few hours like *that*?

"Come on, Little Noa," he said, offering me his hand. "I can't have you sitting here all uncomfortable."

"I'm fine," I snapped, ignoring his hand. "So, you can put my bag down and be on your way."

"Oh, no, sweetheart," he said, and his mouth pressed into a grim line. "It's my fault you're hurt, remember? So, let me help you out. Come on, I'm not going to bite you – unless you're into that kind of thing."

I looked at his hand with skepticism. "If I come with you, it means nothing. I still hate you."

I didn't even know why I was considering it. I really had a strong dislike for this guy, but I'm not ordinarily a nasty person and he was trying to make up for his idiocy from the night before.

"Fine," he shrugged and waved me on with his extended hand.

I ignored his hand and stood up on my own. It hurt, but I bit it back. "I don't need to hold your hand, Alden."

"Hey"—he smiled—"you called me Alden. You actually said my name. We're finally getting somewhere."

He took my hand anyway and led me away.

Once we were inside the lounge, I snatched my hand from his. He walked over to a pair of chairs in the far corner, put my bag down on the floor in front of an incredibly comfortable-looking leather armchair, and gestured for me to sit.

"Drink?" he asked, gesturing toward a bar on the far wall.

I shook my head, feeling a little culture shock at the difference between the common waiting areas and the VIP lounge.

Alden walked over to the bar and I chastised myself when I realized I had watched the way he moved. He had a bad-boy air about him, even in his walk. I hadn't dealt with bad boys since my high school, and all that did was get me into trouble.

"I know you said you didn't want anything, but I brought you something anyway," Alden said, handing me a glass of light amber liquid.

I frowned down at the glass and then at Alden as he sat down in the chair next to mine. "I can't drink anything with alcohol. I am going to take Vicodin as soon as I get on the plane."

"It's just ginger ale, Little Noa," he said, shifting in his seat to hang one leg over the chair.

I refused to recognize his taut muscles pressing against his tight dark blue tee.

"Thank you," I murmured and took a sip before putting it on the table between Alden's chair and mine.

"Relax, Little Noa," he smiled warmly. But even under the warmth, I could see the bad boy lurking.

"I can't relax while you're staring at me," I snapped.

"Fine. I'll read a book to pass the time. Then I won't be staring at you." He reached into his own bag and pulled out a book. *My book.* A book that *I* wrote. It was a contemporary romance novel, so I didn't understand why *he* had it.

Damn that Kristy, I thought as I glared at Alden, who was watching me over the rim of the book.

"Where did you get that?" I asked tightly.

"Bookstore," he said and nodded back toward the door. "Out there. If you don't mind, Little One, I'm trying to read here. Gosh." He let out a phony sound of exasperation and shook his head.

Fuming, I crossed my arms and slid down in my seat until I was comfortable and not hurting my ribs. I rested my head on the back of the chair and closed my eyes. I refused to acknowledge the presence of that asshole.

As I tried to concentrate on taking a little nap, I wondered just how much Kristy had told Alden about me. Okay, so she had told him I was an author, but what else? Did she tell him where I lived? The state, the city? The damn address? Did he know I was just out of a terrible relationship with Larson, a 'safe' boy with a temper? Did he know that my mother was dead and my father may as well have been a pot of gold at the end of a rainbow – nonexistent? What did he know? Kristy was not known for spewing out secrets, but when she was standing in front of her most favorite celebrity on the face of the earth, who the hell knows what she could have said to him.

I didn't remember falling asleep. I only remembered being lightly shaken awake and opening my eyes, finding hazel eyes once again burning into mine.

"Hey, Little One, we're up."

"We?" I asked, sleepy and confused.

"Our flight." He grinned. "We're on the same flight."

Oh brother!

"Why are you flying to Philly?" I asked, slowly pushing myself up out of the chair.

"Believe it or not, I actually have work to do there over the next couple of weeks," he said, picking up my bag with his. He took my hand again, much to my chagrin. I tried to pull away, but he held on to me.

"What kind of work?" I asked with doubt.

"A couple of local news interviews and an interview on a radio show, a big party, and a few other things."

Of course, there's a big party, I thought wryly.

"Which radio show?"

He looked down at me, seemingly happy that I was conversing with him. "Preston and Steve? Ever listen to them?"

"My favorite morning show," I answered.

"Cool. I'll give you a shout out."

"No, no," I said, shaking my head. "Don't do that. Hey," I said as we approached the gate, "they're loading first class before little coach people like me, so…thanks for the VIP seating, but here is where we split ways." I started to pull away from him, but he held fast to me.

He looked down at me with a glimmer in his eyes. "While you were sleeping, I upgraded your ticket. Flying in coach could be very uncomfortable with your injuries," Alden said.

"What?" I stared up at him. "You had no right to do that."

"Just taking care of you since it was *my fault*," he said, eyeing me with a smile, but his eyes looked pretty damn serious. Was it guilt I saw there?

"You don't have to take care of me," I snapped. "I can take care of myself."

"That may be, but I got you this time, Little Noa, so simmer down before the nice security guards think there's a problem over here."

I pushed my anger back some when I realized the security guards were eying us *and* a couple of young girls were looking our way. The last thing I needed was for Alden to be recognized and I get trampled, *again.* I allowed him to lead me onto the plane. I wasn't surprised when after I had sat down in the window seat, he sat down in the seat beside me after pushing our bags into the overhead compartments.

He pulled his hoody off and handed me my bottle of pills. Obviously, he went into my bag to get them, but I didn't fuss over it. I just sighed and held them in my hands until I could get something to drink. Alden had my book out and seemed to be reading it, but maybe it was a trick. It *seemed* that he was on page forty-five already, after only about an hour of reading, which meant he was about to get to a very juicy and erotic part of the book. At that point, I'd rather endure talking to him than for him to read that sex scene while I was sitting beside him. He would know it came from *my* head and he would be curious, and then he would try to use his prowess on me. Gosh, he may even do a pelvic thrust thing.

Before Alden could reach page fifty, where the first big sex scene began, the attendants began their preflight routine. Though he has probably flown more miles in his career than I have driven in my lifetime, he respectively put the book down in his lap and endured the demonstration.

Well. That was unexpected. Bad boy is capable of showing respect?

As the attendant continued on, I couldn't help but to be drawn to the tattoos across Alden's muscular arms. They were elaborate, highly detailed, actual art. One arm was a depiction of Botticelli's *Birth of Venus*, and on the other arm was something that I couldn't see all of because his shirt was covering it, but I knew from pictures that it was a depiction of Atlas holding up the earth. I also knew from pictures that the art piece that climbed up the side of his neck was a fiery clef note, and there were more tattoos on his chest that I never bothered to look at whenever there was a half-naked image of him anywhere. Even if he was on television or in a magazine, I still got the impression that he was cocky, so I didn't care to look any further. At one point on stage, he had torn off his shirt, but I purposely focused on Hash, the drummer, or James, his bassist, instead of the shirtless peacock. Now, Sitting next to him on the plane, I found myself unable to keep my eyes off of his damn arms.

"Do you have any ink?" Alden's sudden question made my eyes snap to his.

I had been so absorbed I didn't even notice that we were moving, picking up speed down the runway, and I had been caught staring.

"What?" I asked.

"Do you have any tattoos?" he asked slowly, like I was dimwitted.

"Yes, yes I do," I said and looked away from him.

"Where?" he pressed.

I shifted slightly as I turned back to him. "On my chest – across my heart. It's…it's small."

"Oh?" he popped one eyebrow and his eyes flickered down to my chest and back to my face. "What is it?"

"Just one word," I said, noticing how low my voice had dropped.

"What word is it? You're killing me here."

"Uhh," I said, swallowing. "It just says 'broken.' That's all."

His brow furrowed. "Broken?"

"Yes." I nodded. "Broken."

He frowned as he stared at me for a moment. When I looked away, I felt him look away, too, and settle back in his seat. When I looked up again, he was holding the book, but his eyes were unfocused. He wasn't really reading, but he seemed to be deep in thought.

As soon as the attendants were able to start serving drinks, I got some water and gratefully popped a Vicodin. I was so sore and my head was starting to pound. I wondered if the doctors were wrong about me not having any brain damage because my head hurt like a bitch. And I was in the company of Alden Breck. With or without trampling tramps, that alone indicated some kind of brain damage.

I covered myself with the small complimentary blanket and reclined my seat as far as I could as I tried to get comfortable. I was secretly thankful that Alden had upgraded my seat. He was right - it would have been very difficult to get comfortable in coach. I closed my eyes, and seconds later, startled when I felt something on me. Alden had put his sweatshirt over me as a makeshift second blanket. I was sure there were extras available had he asked, but I liked the smell of his sweatshirt. My god did I like it. It smelled like expensive cologne, but it also smelled like…I don't know. Like Alden.

Shit!

This wasn't good. I couldn't take my eyes off his tats and then I was surreptitiously inhaling the scent of his sweatshirt. I hated this guy, so what the hell was my problem?

"So…" he started, but looked unsure of his next words. "So, who broke you?"

"That's a highly personal question," I admonished.

"Yeah," he agreed and rubbed his strong jaw. "Yeah, I guess it is. Sorry, Little One."

"Can you just call me Noa?" I asked, scowling slightly. "Just Noa. No Little Noa or Little One or darling or sweetheart. Just Noa."

He flashed me a sexy grin.

Ugh. Now his grin is sexy?

"Sure, *Just Noa*," he said and then resumed looking at the book.

I closed my eyes again, praying to fall asleep quickly.

"But if you're going to have a statement tattooed across your heart for anyone to see," Alden started, making me roll my eyes under the lids before I opened them again to look at him, "then you should be able to explain who broke you."

"I don't have to explain jack to anyone about something written on *my* body," I snapped. "And it's not for anyone to see. Do you see it now?"

"No, but…"

"And you won't see it, either. Ever."

"Ever?" he raised his pierced right eyebrow.

"Ever," I said firmly. "I thought you upgraded me so that I can be comfortable. How can I be comfortable if you keep talking while I'm trying to allow a drug induced coma to overtake me?"

"I apologize, *Just Noa*," he said with an easy smile and turned back to my book.

If I could have stabbed his gorgeous eyes with a sharp object, I would have.

Sometime later, I woke up and looked over at Alden. He was deep into the book, reading and unaware that I was watching him. That meant that he got through at least three big sex scenes. I was a little embarrassed, but not as much as I would have been had he been reading them while I was awake. I pulled the sweatshirt off me, alerting Alden that I was awake, and carefully got up to go use the facilities. As I stepped over his long legs, he put his hand on my hips to steady me. I pretended it wasn't a big deal and continued on my way. On my way back, just as I started to scoot past Alden again, the plane hit an unexpected pocket of turbulence and I found myself tripping over his legs, and then falling backward onto his lap. The seatbelt sign flashed on, the pilot spoke in the speakers about it being a little bumpy for a little while, and a flight attendant asked me to please take my seat and buckle up.

She didn't have to ask me twice, but when I went to move, Alden held me down with his hands on my thighs. I could feel his breath on a sensitive area of my neck and despite my dislike for the man, it was driving me a little batty.

"You do realize that your arms do not count as a seatbelt?" I asked through gritted teeth.

"Just want to make sure you aren't hurt, Little Noa," he purred in my ear.

Dear god, is that what I think it is poking me in the ass? Is that real? How did it grow to be so damn big?

I pushed his hands off me and quickly moved to my seat, ducking my head to put on my seatbelt and also to hide my red face.

With a satisfied smirk, Alden gave me a once over and resumed reading my book. I very carefully pulled my iPod out of my pocket, plugged the ear buds into my ears, and turned up the music. I hated turbulence, and I was sad that I wasn't still knocked out. The best thing I could do was to listen to my music and pretend that the plane didn't feel like it was going to tear apart in the sky.

Amazingly, I fell asleep again. When I woke up, my head didn't hurt anymore and the pain in my ribs was tolerable. I sat up and blinked at Alden. He was staring straight ahead, but his eyes were pinched with discomfort and his leg bounced up and down as if he were nervous.

"What's wrong with you?" I asked before I could stop myself.

"Had to stop reading your book," he said, glancing over at me for a moment before turning back up front.

"It bored you," I assumed.

"Not at all. The exact opposite, actually," he said and then looked at me with *burning* eyes.

Holy hell!

"It turned me on," he said unapologetically. "A lot. We're about to land and I don't want to walk through the airport with a raging hard-on."

I stared at him with my mouth hanging open, and dear me, I couldn't help myself. My eyes dropped to his lap. My book was on his thighs, but above that, an impossible monster pressed against his jeans. It was perfectly outlined in the snug denim. I couldn't believe it. He had to be no less than ten inches of all man.

Oh, my god, Noa! Look away, look away! Stop looking at his cock, for heaven's sake!

Instead of looking away, my mind thought about all of the pelvic thrusts Alden had done on stage, exciting and firing up the women. I had an unwanted image of his hips doing that thrusting while inside of a woman – okay, inside of *me* in particular.

Maybe that was one of the reasons women were willing to kill each other to get to Alden Breck. Perhaps many of them were aware of the monster between his legs, because they read about him or drooled over photos of him, and I was sure it had to come up, so to speak, at some point. But I never paid that much attention to the *cocky* (oh yeah) Friction front man before last night. Now I couldn't peel my eyes away.

"Okay, the fact that you're staring at my boy isn't helping him to go down," Alden said to me, and finally, I snapped out of my haze and looked away, red-faced and dumbstruck.

"My god," I whispered before I could stop myself.

He chuckled. "You're even more gorgeous when you're blushing, Little Noa."

I said nothing. I looked straight ahead at the back of the seat in front of me. As we began to descend toward the earth, Alden had the balls – of course, he did – to run the back of his hand over my cheek. I disappointed myself when I actually shuddered slightly before knocking his hand away. He invaded my personal space, leaned over the several inches between us until his face was close to mine. I felt his breath on my cheek as he spoke.

"I'm intrigued," he said thoughtfully.

"With what?" I responded, leaning away from him before meeting his eyes.

"With you."

I probably looked as flabbergasted as I felt. "*Why*?"

"Because you are trying so hard to dislike me."

I snorted. "I don't have to try at all. It's so easy."

"I want to get to know you better," he said, leaning toward me as far as he could. I plastered myself against the bulkhead and there were still only a few mere inches between us.

"You mean you want to bed me," I corrected him with a scowl.

"Fuck yeah, I want to bed you. I want to pull you into my lap right now and fuck you until you can't breathe. I've wanted to slide into you since I saw your scowling ass at the concert, but I was going to settle for a kiss instead."

"What?" I said a little too loudly.

"I was going to kiss you, but we're not talking about that now. I want to get to know you, and I want to get to know you more than I want to fuck you."

I scoffed. "I'll bet you say that to all of the reluctant women. Smooth, Breck, but not smooth enough."

He reached for me and I flinched so violently, I hit my head. He paused, looking at me with confusion. His fingers extended toward me again, but tentatively. I froze and held my breath, but he only pulled a length of my hair between his fingers and twirled it. My breath came out slow and shaky.

"What if I promise you that I won't try to fuck you?" he asked in a cotton soft voice that made my belly flutter.

Frustrated, and a little scared of the fluttering in my belly, I swallowed hard. "Why? Why are you doing this? Why don't you leave me alone?"

He looked at me for so long, I didn't think he'd answer. I thought he was going to release my hair, give me back my personal space, and give up. But he didn't do any of that. His eyebrows lowered and he looked just as flummoxed as I felt.

"I don't know," he said just above a whisper. "But I don't break promises, Little Noa. I promise you I won't try to have sex with you.

Give me a chance here. Let's be…friends." He said the word as if he had never said it before in his life.

"Friendship must be a foreign concept to a slut like you." It was such a cruel thing to say, but he took it with a shrug of his shoulder and a small smile.

"Yeah, I don't really make friends easily, especially women."

"So, what…I should feel privileged or something?"

"Maybe I'm the one that would be privileged," he said seriously.

We stared at each other for a long time. The plane stopped at the terminal, the seatbelt sign shut off, and people began to stand around us. Yet, we continued to sit there and stare.

"Why?" I asked again, my voice barely audible above all of the other noises around us.

"Fuck if I know," Alden said in the same tone I used. "But I feel it, you know? I feel like I want to know who you are. Come on, Noa. What's the worst that could happen?"

I had a long list of the worst things that could happen, but I swallowed it back. I wrung my hands in my lap, a sure sign of my anxiety. I wasn't anxious because I felt pressured. I was anxious because I knew my answer from the instant he first asked the question.

"Okay," I whispered.

Alden's smile was radiant. And sexy.

Damn it!

three

After we had deplaned, I tried to go my own way, but Alden wasn't having any of it. He steered me away from the line of cabs toward a waiting limo.

"No, no," I said, backing away.

"How are we supposed to be friends if we don't spend any time together?" he chided, shaking his head. Gently, he put his hand on my back and nudged me toward the open door as his driver began putting our luggage into the trunk.

"I just spent *seven hours* with you," I said in disagreement, but I conceded and climbed in. Alden scooted in after me but was kind enough to leave some space between us on the bench seat.

We were awkwardly silent for a couple of minutes. I looked out of the window at the familiar scenery, happy to be back on the east coast finally, but I shivered. I had thoughtlessly packed my jacket in my suitcase, forgetting that I wasn't going to be in eighty-degree weather when I returned home. I rubbed away the goose bumps on my arm just for more to pop up. Alden reached across to the other bench seat to where he had thrown his hoodie. He offered it to me. I stared blankly at it for a moment before taking it from him.

"Thank you," I said quietly. I pulled it on over my t-shirt and pulled my hands into the sleeves in an attempt to warm them. I couldn't help but to breathe in a little slower, getting a good whiff of what was Alden's skin.

I had wondered how he was just going to waltz in to a restaurant without getting mobbed, but his virtual assistant called the little steak house ahead of time and asked them to reserve a private table for two with access to a back entrance and exit. No one would even know we were there.

"Must be nice to be able to get privacy like this whenever you want it," I said after the waiter poured me a glass of wine and placed a tall pilsner glass of beer in front of Alden.

Alden shrugged. "Sometimes, but honestly, most of the time, I just want to sit in the dining area and enjoy a meal like everyone else."

"I can hardly believe it." I smiled over the rim of my glass. "*You* want to be like everyone else?"

He gave another small shrug. "When I started out in this business, I just wanted to make music and entertain my friends and impress the girls. I wasn't shooting to be a superstar. I liked meeting up with my buddies and bullshitting over good food and drinks, or taking a beautiful woman to dinner." He gave me a pointed look. "But I just can't do that anymore. I live this extraordinary life, living the dream, you know? But in order to live this life, I have to be…squeezed into a box."

I stared at him. "You feel squeezed into a box? You have the world at your feet. You have the means to go almost anywhere, anytime, with anyone you want."

He smiled, but I was shocked at how much sadness was in that smile. "The world is at my feet, my door, my window…I can't take a piss without the world knowing about it. When you need something from the store or get a craving for ice cream, you just go out and get it, right? You may run into a few people you know. Hell, maybe you have book fans stalking you, but it's not like my situation at all. I can't pick up a newspaper at the edge of my driveway without someone taking a picture. I can't go into the convenience store and grab a pint of ice cream without having something happen. Someone always wants something from me."

I sipped my wine, letting his words swirl around my brain. I hated going to a certain grocery store because one of the girls there found out whom I was and loved my books. She was a nice girl, but sometimes, I just wanted to get my groceries and be on my way, and not answer ten thousand questions about my books or the characters. Mr. Obnoxious had *millions* of fans worldwide. Going into a different grocery store wasn't going to make a lick of difference. He'd meet with the same result almost every time. We couldn't even get through the airport earlier without him getting stopped several times by fans.

"Don't get me wrong," Alden started a minute later. "I love what I do. I love my fans. I love being at the center of attention, and the women, the parties, the drinking, and luxuries. Sometimes I just want to put it aside. That's all."

I didn't know what to say. I would never have suspected that he didn't always like the spotlight, judging by the way that he thrust across the stage, kissing random women, and stripping off his clothes.

When the waiter appeared, Alden ordered for *both* of us before I could even utter a syllable.

That chafed me, made me feel all prickly-like.

I spent more than three years with a man who outlined nearly every aspect of my daily life, even the meals I ate. I know it was ludicrous that after all of the shit Alden pulled since the concert, that ordering my dinner for me was what triggered unhappy and unsettling memories, but it did. My mind flashed with images of Larson's cruel face and dishes crashing to the floor inches away from my head, all because I didn't eat the meal that had been chosen for me.

An unreasonable fury rose swiftly inside of me, broke out of my mouth, and flew right at Alden.

"Why did you do that?" I flared after the waiter walked away. "I am fully capable of ordering meals for myself." I pushed back in my chair, ignoring his surprised, raised eyebrows. I got to my feet. "You've been trying to control me since the concert," I said as I snatched my bag off the back of my chair. "You didn't like that I didn't like you, so you were going to try to proselytize me into liking you by *kissing* me."

Amusement twinkled in his eyes and a corner of his mouth pulled up. "Proselytize?"

"I am *not* halting my rant to explain to your tiny brain what proselytize means," I snapped. "While I was unconscious, you went through my phone! You put yourself in my phone, like you assumed that I would ever *want* to call you."

Alden sat back in his chair and casually crossed his arms across his chest. I tried not to let my eyes linger too long on the tattooed muscles.

"Do you know how many women would gladly go through what you did to get my phone number?" he asked smugly.

"Trust me, Breck, I'm not one of them. Then you come out of nowhere, force me into the VIP lounge at the airport, and change my seat on the flight."

He snickered. "Yeah, that was so wicked of me, to make sure that you were comfortable after getting hurt at my concert."

I ignored the truth in that and marched on. "I was just going to take a cab home, but you kidnapped me—"

"Kidnapped?" he laughed.

His amusement was only firing my fury. I wanted to slap the grin off his ridiculously handsome face.

"Yes! Kidnapped!" I exclaimed. "And then you *ordered* for me, didn't even give me an option!"

His mouth set in a line. He was no longer smiling. He looked at me for several moments, seemingly deep in thought as his brow creased. I don't know why I didn't just walk away, why I stood there waiting for some kind of response, but when I finally got one, it was simple. Just one word and a nod. "Okay."

I stood there, breathing hard after my crazy diatribe, and clutching the straps of my bag on my shoulder. "Okay," I said snippily.

"Okay," he said again.

"Okay." I nodded and took a step backward. The instant I did, Alden stood up from the table. I watched warily as he took the few steps to reach me.

"Are you finished?" he asked quietly as he towered over me.

I looked up into his disgustingly beautiful, soft hazel eyes with my mouth slightly ajar for a moment before I shook myself and slammed my mouth shut.

"Yes, I am finished," I said insolently. I started to step back again, but I gasped when Alden's hands closed over my shoulders. He bent slightly, so that his face was close to mine.

"I apologize that you got hurt at my concert, due in part to my own actions," he said softly. "I will not, however, apologize for going through your phone. At first, I was going to look for someone to call for you, because I didn't know how badly you were hurt. But the more I looked at you lying there like Sleeping Beauty, waiting for a prince to kiss you, the more I wanted to know about you. Then when you woke up and saw me, you were all claws and teeth. I'm not used to that. I was intrigued. It is rare that I meet a woman who isn't in some way star struck or throwing herself at me – not that I don't like having women throw themselves at me, I fucking love it, but it is…refreshing to meet someone who would rather stab me in the eyes. I just want to get to know you better, Little One. I told you that on the plane, and I meant it."

I was temporarily speechless. I blinked at his chest for a moment. Maybe I was just paranoid. I didn't want to be paranoid. But shouldn't I be cautious? I'd trusted the wrong men before, who's to say I wouldn't do it again?

In addition, befriending a superstar like Alden could put me under a spotlight I wasn't interested in having on me. Being an author had strong elements of anonymity; my hardcore readers may know who I am if they saw me walking down the street, but the normal, everyday citizen would just see me as another nameless face in the crowd. However, if I started spending time with Alden Breck, anonymity would be almost non-existent. I had a past that was mostly silent and in the dark, and I wanted to leave it that way.

But…

I could not disregard that Alden had risked his own life by jumping from the safety of the stage into a pit where he could have been trampled by his own rabid fans so that he could save *my* life. I could not disregard how attentive he had been since finding me in the airport. As much as I wanted to pretend otherwise, I could not un-see the glimpses of the ordinary human man behind his absurdly obnoxious outer personality.

"I can't stand here and tell you that I'm not bossy or dominant, because I am," he said when I remained silent. "I like to take charge, but please believe me, it's not coming from a bad place. Maybe a sometimes arrogant place," he admitted with a small smile. "But never a bad place. As for your dinner, if you don't like the steak and potatoes I ordered for you, we can get them to change the order to whatever you like," Alden said placatingly. "I thought chicks dig that kind of thing."

I deflated. I wanted to crawl under the table and forget the last few minutes happened, that I had not looked like a freaking nut job. Even if the incident at the concert was partially his fault for being a pompous prick, and the fault of the venue for not making sure their equipment was safe, I wasn't completely ungrateful. The least I could do was give him a little bit of my time.

I lifted one shoulder under his big hand. "I like steak and potatoes," I whispered.

I let him lead me back to my chair. After he sat down across from me again, we sat in another awkward silence for a few moments. Well, *I* felt awkward and stupid for my outburst, but Alden looked very comfortable, sitting there, staring at me like his new favorite shiny toy.

"I have a very serious question to ask you," he said, looking very serious indeed.

I waited with my heart pounding in my chest. I wasn't ready to answer the personal questions my behavior had most likely stirred up, and he looked like he wanted to dig deep, to find out what made me tick.

"Why don't you like my music?"

I was so relieved that I burst into giggles. It hurt my ribs, but I couldn't help myself. I covered my face as I laughed. Alden's fingers closed over mine and he pulled my hands away from my face.

He was smiling. "I can't see your face if it's all covered up," he said.

"So?" I said as the giggles subsided.

"So, your face just lit up the whole room while you laughed. Don't cover up," he gently commanded.

I looked down at the table as my heart beat a little bit harder.

"Now," Alden started again. "Why don't you like my fucking awesome music?"

I laughed again, but I was careful not to cover my "lit up" face.

We had talked about music for a long time. Alden had repeatedly referred to himself as a "lyrical god" and other egotistical titles, but I had to give him *some* credit. He had written more than three-quarters of Friction's songs, and of the six albums they had released, four had reached platinum status, and the other two gold. Three years ago, he had created the Frictitious record label, which currently had over a dozen signed bands or artists from different genres, and almost all of them had at least one hit playing on the radio at any given time. Along with a designer friend, Alden had also created the Friction Merchandising Company. They sold all things Friction – hats, apparel, keychains, posters, action figures, and even guitars, and more.

Then there was the reason he was in Philly. Alden organized a series of galas to benefit a particular charity. When children are put into foster care, it tends to happen quickly, and they often are placed without necessities, like clothes, shoes, and personal hygiene products. Furthermore, they are often thrown into a new school and lack the supplies they need. The charity donates bags to foster kids that contain all of those things and more. There were six galas planned across the country over the course of ten weeks. Friction would be playing at every one of them, along with at least two or three other performers that would vary city to city.

If Alden hadn't told me all of that, I would have continued to assume that he was a pretty face that happened to be able to sing.

Okay, so he was interesting, but he was still an arrogant, bombastic, *horny* windbag. My god was the man a horny bastard. He transuded sex from every pore of his body. A light gaze from his hazel eyes spoke a myriad of things he'd like to do to my body. The way his fingers delicately caressed any inanimate object was a promise of what those fingers could do to my flesh. His swagger as he approached even from a few feet away was an admonition of the things he could do with his hips and drew my attention to the monster that always seemed to be at least half awake. Even saying the most ordinary things, Alden's voice dripped with salacity. Being friends with him was going to be difficult, because even I was affected by his blatant, potent, aura of sexuality, even if half the time I felt like punching him.

It wasn't just his sexual dexterity that was the problem, nor his bigger than life personality. Regardless of how very little I paid any attention to Friction, they were known *worldwide*. There was nowhere Alden could go where he wouldn't be known. Over dessert and coffee, Alden told me several stories about situations when fans got out of control. The stories were meant to be funny, but the half smile I had worn on my face was a smile of disbelief and horror. It was true that I didn't want to share in any of his spotlight because of my own insecurities, but it was also true that the thought of being in situations like San Francisco *repeatedly* was not appealing.

Fortunately, Alden would only be in the Philly area for the week before moving on, and our "friendship" would probably soon thereafter be forgotten. He admitted that he doesn't really do friendships with women, that the few he had, he had for a long time already. And even if we were able to avoid the complications that came with a sexed-up rock star, his schedule was insane enough to leave no time for friendships with the nerdy little girl from Philly that didn't put out.

The next day, I slept late into the morning. It had not been too late when Alden helped me carry my luggage up to my apartment the night before, but being trampled by tramps and resisting the sexual static that crackled from a rock star takes a lot out of a girl. I had taken a Vicodin and slept like the dead. The only reason I got up a little before noon was because of the insistent knocking on my front door. As I stumbled out of bed with my eyes half closed, I had forgotten all about my injuries and twisted the wrong way. I cursed all the way to the door. I stood on my toes, peeked through the peephole, and sighed. I stood there for a moment, trying to decide whether I should answer the door or pretend I wasn't home.

"I know you're standing on the other side of the door," Alden said. "I heard you cursing before you got here."

I blew out a breath and opened the door a little. There he stood, dressed in a snug cable knit, dark blue sweater and a leather jacket. Looped through the belt of his dark jeans was a leather belt with a large gold buckle that spelled out "Rock Star." The jeans were also snug, hugging his long legs and his long…

Oh, my god! Does that thing ever *go down?*

While I was busy looking Alden over, he was busy looking me over. When I blinked up at his face, his eyes were moving slowly up my body, lingering long on my breasts and lips before stopping at my eyes. I crossed my arms over my chest. I had forgotten that I wasn't really dressed. I had on a pair of lavender silk sleeping shorts that barely covered my ass, and a matching camisole, and no bra.

"Why are you here?" I asked as a greeting.

"I came by to say hello," he said. He crossed his arms and leaned against the side of the doorframe that was closest to me.

"Hello, and goodbye."

I started to close the door, but Alden put out a hand to stop it.

"Little One," he said admonishingly. "Is this the way you treat your friends?"

"We're friends, but we're not *friends*."

Alden's smile was the kind of smile that would make an ordinary girl's toes curl, but my toes were curling because the hardwood floor was cold, not because of the gorgeous man in front of me.

"You know," he said conspiringly. "If you renege on your end of our deal, I get to seduce you into bed."

"What are you talking about?" I asked irritably.

"You said you'd let me get to know you, that we could be friends. Without the friendship in place, I'm free to take you to bed."

"You would be free to *try*, and fail." I smiled sweetly.

"Are you reneging?" he asked, tilting his head and looking entirely too hopeful.

I forgot about covering up my chest and put a hand on my hip. "What if I am?" I challenged.

Alden's eyes started at my toes and again, climbed my body. His voice was soft and sensual, and I could almost *feel* his words.

"Before you would even have a chance to close the door in my face, I'd have my hand on that silk between your sexy legs, rubbing it against your clit, pressing it inside of you. Your shorts will be soaked with your arousal. While my hand is busy sending you toward a climax, I'll bend over and nip at your nipples through your cute little shirt until they're painfully hard. Then I'll put my hand in your soft hair, wrap it around my fist, tilt your head back, and kiss you. My tongue will stroke your mouth slow and precise, so you'll have an idea of how it will feel on your clit later. While I'm kissing you, I'll slip my other hand *inside* your shorts, push two fingers into your soaked entrance, and make you come so hard your pretty knees will give out and the only two things that will be holding you up are my fingers inside of you and my hand in your hair. Then, when you think you just might die from pleasure, I'll carry you to your bed and the real show will begin, because…" He shrugged, licked his lips, and smiled. "That first orgasm was just a preview."

Stunned, I stood there, gaping at him as he openly adjusted his package.

"So, Little Noa," Alden said in that same sensual tone. "Are. You. Reneging?"

For a second, for one serious second, I almost threw open the door and shouted, "I renege! I renege!" But that second passed, and common sense and my propriety settled in.

"You wish I'd back out," I snorted, pushed the door open further, and stepped aside. I made a wide sweeping motion. "Come in…*friend*."

Alden's self-confident smile as he moved past me made me want to kick him in the teeth.

"Sit there," I demanded, pointing to the couch as I moved across the room. "I need to get dressed."

"I'm perfectly fine with what you have on," he said sweetly as he sat down on the center of my couch.

I gave him a derisive smile before slamming the bedroom door.

I came out a few minutes later, dressed in jeans, a T-shirt, and Alden's hoodie that I had 'forgotten' to give back to him the night before. His eyebrows rose slightly when he saw it, but he didn't comment.

"Your neighbor came by, dropped off all of your mail from last week," he said and pointed to the small dining table across the room.

My eyes widened. "You answered my door? Why did you answer my door?"

"Because someone knocked on it and you were unavailable."

"It's a good thing that Mrs. Q is an old lady and doesn't know who you are. The last thing I need is for random groupies showing up at my door."

"She may be old, but she still wants me," Alden said haughtily.

"What did you do? One of those pelvic thrust things?"

"Do you like my pelvic thrusts?" he asked as he got to his feet. To my horror, he did one slow motion thrust in my direction.

I gave him a bland look. "I don't like your pelvic thrusts. Don't you ever pelvic thrust me again."

"Little Noa, if you ever renege, I will pelvic thrust you *all night long*."

I ignored his statement. Ignored everything about it. What it implied, the prickling sensation that it sent down my neck and straight to my center.

"So, what did you want to do, *friend*?" I asked him. "Braid each other's hair and talk about boys?"

"How about we go to the art museum?" he suggested as he came to stand beside me.

I looked up at him. "Really?"

"What? Because I'm a rock star – an awesome, good-looking, brilliant rock star – I can't be interested in art?"

Rolling my eyes, I said, "Well, I thought maybe you would want to go to the bar, start drinking, and maybe have a brawl. Isn't that what you rock stars usually do?"

"I don't brawl," he said indignantly. "I kick ass, and I can do that shit any day, any time, in any place. I'd rather do something…substantial while I'm getting to know my new friend."

"Okay," I said after a moment. "We can go to the art museum." I threw the rest of the mail back onto the table. "Let's go."

I was halfway across the room before Alden stopped me.

"Wait, don't you have to like, go put on makeup or whatever?" he asked.

I stared at him. "Do I need to put on makeup?"

I knew that I was plain, but that was a little harsh.

Alden gave me an apologetic look. "That's…that's not what I meant, Little One. For the record, no, you don't need to put on any makeup. You're beautiful without it, but I don't know of any woman who would go out with me without makeup. Like none."

"First of all, no one 'goes out' with you," I pointed out. "You pick them up while you're already out. Secondly, if you haven't figured it out yet, I'm not like other women. I'm not saying I'm better, but I'm not like the women that you're used to. I'm pretty low maintenance."

"Thank god," he said, looking truly relieved. "Because it takes forever for women to cake that shit on their faces. Let's go."

He grabbed my hand, plucked my keys off the key ring by the door, and pulled me out of my apartment.

***

We strolled through the museum slowly as Alden told me about all of the exhibits he'd been lucky to see around the world during his travels. He didn't know a lot about art, but he had a deep appreciation for it, especially for impressionism.

"I love Renoir," he murmured as we stood before Renoir's *The Large Bathers*. "This is my favorite of his works, though he caught a lot of flak for this one. Do you know why?"

"This is very…defined," I said. Alden looked down at me, seemingly surprised that I was answering. "In impressionism, the brush strokes aren't smooth. The objects or people in the paintings may look…blurry. Maybe that's not the right word, but in this painting"—I gestured—"his strokes are smooth. Even his use of light seems different from his other works. I don't know a lot about art, so I don't know how right or wrong I am on that," I added hastily.

Alden smiled at me, not his "I'm going to eat you alive" smile, either. It was an appreciative smile.

"Good answer, Little One."

"Why is this your favorite?" I asked him. I fully expected some long, boring artsy answer I wouldn't get, but he surprised me.

"It's a real portrayal of real women," he said with a shrug. "They look so…soft and warm. They're not thin; they're not all angles and edges. Curvy. Smooth. Perfect."

I looked up at him, expecting to find his eyes on the painting, but his eyes were on *me*, wandering slowly over my body.

Suppressing a shiver, I said, "Stop looking at me like that."

"Like what?" he asked, his voice low and teasing.

"Like I'm dinner."

"Maybe I'm hungry."

"Take your appetite somewhere else, Breck," I said, moving away from him. "You're not biting here."

***

Over the next few days, I tried to get back to my normal routine. After hardly writing at all while in California, I cracked down on myself and spent almost two whole days lost inside of my made up worlds of love, lust, and angst. I didn't leave the house; I cooked whatever was left in my freezer and fridge and sucked down coffee like it was going to save my entire life.

About half way through the third day, my fingers started to cramp. When I went to my fridge to get something for lunch, all I found was old milk, one cracked egg in a carton, and condiments. The freezer had ice-cubes and an ice pop left over from the summer. My cabinets weren't much better. I had no choice, I had to venture out into the real world and go to the grocery store.

I sniffed in the vicinity of my armpit. I also needed a shower.

As I started across the apartment toward my bedroom, someone knocked on my door. I paused and stood stock still, looking at the door. I didn't have the kind of friends that just dropped by, and my brother didn't even know that I was home from California yet. Besides, Warren had a key and after the first knock, would have let himself in. The only other person it could have possibly been was…

"I know you're there, I can hear you thinking about whether or not to open the door," Alden Breck said.

I scowled as I marched over to the door. I threw it open and put a hand on my hip.

"You can't just drop by here whenever you feel like it," I said.

Hazel eyes peered through the black rimmed glasses he had worn at the airport in California. A Minnesota Vikings stocking cap was pulled down over his blond hair, and he wore a hood of another hoodie over that.

"If you're trying to be incognito, you should probably wear an Eagles or Flyers hat," I suggested.

"Good idea," he nodded and then pushed past me to enter my apartment.

"I didn't invite you in," I said irritably, but closed the door behind him.

He turned around to face me with a small grin. "Yeah, but you wanted to."

Cocky bastard.

"What are you doing here, Alden?" I crossed my arms and leaned back against the door.

"I wanted to see you," he said simply, as if it were really that simple. "You weren't answering my texts."

"Because I was busy," I said pointedly. Alden had indeed texted me several times, but I had only answered him maybe two or three times. "I try not to let anything or anyone distract me when I'm writing."

He nodded. "I can understand that. It's the same for me when I'm writing new songs. Am I distracting you now?"

"No, but I am about to shower and head out to the store. I think I've eaten every edible thing I had."

"I'll take you."

"No," I said slowly. "I can take myself."

He took a few steps toward me until he was only inches away from stepping on my bare toes with his booted feet. I was completely unaffected by his nearness. Completely. Really.

"Friends go shopping with friends, right?" he asked quietly.

"Yeah, but—"

"So, are we friends, Little One? Or are you reneging?"

I rolled my eyes and let out an exasperated sigh. "I'm going to go shower." I slid away from him and started toward my bedroom. "Stay out here and don't answer my door, and don't touch my stuff."

With an amused smile, he inclined his head once before I shut the door. Even though I was going to lock the bathroom door, I decided that it wouldn't hurt to lock the bedroom door also.

Thirty minutes later, I was in the passenger seat of a Maserati Gran Turismo that Alden had retrieved from his home in New York. I had been proud of my new Camaro, but Alden's car made my car look like a dollar store discounted toy. I even felt underdressed for the car, like my forty-dollar jeans, fifteen-dollar Old Navy T-shirt, and my pretty black and pink Reeboks weren't fit to sit on the black leather. Alden's sweatshirt, which I not only didn't give back, but had the nerve to put it on before leaving my apartment, cost almost two hundred dollars – I looked it up! That was more than everything else I was wearing in combination with whatever I would wear the next day. The hoodie was the only thing making me worthy to sit in the car.

"What kind of car do you drive?" Alden asked, as if he knew where my mind was.

"A Camaro."

He nodded slowly. "That's okay, you know, for the price."

Car snob, I thought.

"Yeah, your car is okay, too; you know, for the price," I said mockingly.

"Little One," he said seriously. "This is a Maserati Gran Turismo."

"Mmm hmm. It's cute."

"Cute? Cute?" Alden was appalled. "Baby, this car is not 'cute,' okay? Your car is cute; my car is manly. Zero to sixty in under five seconds, 453 HP, with a max torque of 460. You don't call a car like this cute."

I snickered. Alden shot me a look.

"Your Camaro can't beat my car," he said haughtily. "So, I don't know why you're snickering."

"You're right. My Camaro can't beat your car, but my Bugatti Veyron Grand Sport can."

Alden stared at me in shock for so long that I had to yell at him to put his eyes back on the road.

"You're shitting me," he said after a minute.

"Zero to sixty in *two point six seconds*," I said with a sly grin. "Over a twelve hundred BHP with a max torque of a thousand. So, is your car cute in comparison? Yes. It's cute. But the Bugatti trumps all."

Alden whistled and shook his head. "What the fuck is a little girl like you doing with a car with all of that power?"

"Little girls and their toys and all of that," I said sweetly.

"You know, when they have half naked women in front of cars at car shows, they don't do anything for me. But picturing you driving a Bugatti is making me hard as steel."

Somehow, I managed to avoid looking into his lap this time.

"I'll take your word for it."

"So, where is this Bugatti?" Alden asked as we turned into the parking lot of a busy Wegmans grocery store.

I sighed long and deep. I opened my big mouth just to tease him, forgetting that I'd have to give some kind of background story.

"My ex bought it for me as an engagement gift," I said quietly. "When I left him, I left the car."

"You had an ex with enough money to afford a car like that?"

I rolled my eyes. "Yes, believe it or not. I know I don't look like the type of woman who could have driven a 2.4 million dollar car. I don't look like the type of woman that used to walk around with a half a million-dollar rock on her finger, or the type of woman that used to wear designer clothes every day, all day, right down to my undergarments and sleeping clothes. But I *was* once that woman. I was her for three years, and for six months out of those three years, I got to drive the fastest street car in the world. Now I drive a Camaro and shop at normal stores, and instead of giant diamonds on my fingers, I wear tiny ones in my ears and a simple bracelet of gold linked hearts that my brother gave me when I was fourteen." I held up my wrist for emphasis.

Alden pulled into a parking spot and put the car in park, but he didn't turn it off right away. He looked out of the window with his brow furrowed as he gently bit down on his bottom lip. I unbuckled my seatbelt and put my hand on the lever, waiting for him to unlock the doors.

"I didn't mean it like that," he said after a few seconds. He turned his head and looked at me. "I actually have a Bugatti in L.A., and if I were boyfriend material, I wouldn't mind being your boyfriend. I didn't mean to suggest that you wouldn't be good enough. I told you over dinner that first night that when you were knocked out backstage after the accident, you looked like Sleeping Beauty. I wanted to be your prince, you know? At least for a little while. Drive you around in my fast car, take you to nice places and maybe buy you some nice things, and serenade you, but you already have a prince."

I could have laughed at him and told him that was the most ridiculous thing I'd ever heard and teased him for hours, but honestly, it was probably the sweetest damn thing anyone has ever said to me. But I didn't want to tell him that, either.

"Larson was…was many things," I said softly. "But he is no prince. He is a villain. But…" I smiled a little. "I don't need a prince."

I found the button to unlock the door and let myself out of Alden's cute car.

five

Shopping with Alden had been like shopping with a four-year-old. He wanted everything he saw, especially junk food. I wasn't opposed to junk food, but he was putting it in my cart as if he was going to be around enough to consume it.

He had kept his hat, hood, and glasses on the entire time we were in the store, but once one person recognized him, it was almost as if Wegmans had made some kind of announcement that Alden Breck was in the store, in aisle five in front of the oatmeal. I was just glad that it wasn't later in the day, or the small crowd that followed behind us to his car would have been much bigger.

I kicked him out of my apartment soon after he finished helping me put away groceries so I could get back to work. He had gone without too much of a fight, but he had returned early the following morning with breakfast. He didn't stay long, because apparently, he had his own things to do. He went back to New York for a couple of days, but after again using the whole "friends or fuck" thing against me, he convinced me to have dinner with him on Sunday night.

Unlike the first time I had dinner with Alden, we didn't get a private dining room. I was acutely aware of the many stares and whispers focused our way. I had learned quickly that being in the presence of a superstar almost always earned nothing less than stares and whispers. I didn't like being under the scrutiny of a whole bunch of strangers, but I reminded myself that I only had a week to go before Alden would be out of my city and on to another one.

"So, *friend*," Alden said, leaning on his elbows on the table. "I want to ask you something, though it's just a formality because I won't take no for an answer."

I frowned but said nothing and waited for him to continue.

"I want you to be my date for the galas."

Ignoring the fact that he didn't actually ask a question, I said, "You want me to go with you this weekend?"

"I want you to go with me to *all* of them."

"You want me to go on the road with you for two months?" I asked incredulously. "Even though you *just* met me, like five minutes ago?"

He took a long sip of his coffee and nonchalantly raised a shoulder. "It's a little more than two months all in all. We have some other shows in between."

I didn't miss the fact that he failed to address the last part of my statement.

I shook my head. "I can't go."

"Why not?" he looked truly perplexed. "You're a writer, right? You don't have a stationary job, and you don't have a secret kid and husband I don't know about, do you?"

"If I did, they would be a *secret*," I pointed out derisively. "Look, it's just…it's just not a good idea," I said, dropping my eyes back to my chicken marsala.

"Give me a good reason why it's not a good idea," Alden demanded, leaning forward.

"We barely know each other."

"Irrelevant. I often have to work with strangers."

"You often have sex with strangers," I said caustically.

"I can have sex with you, too. You only have to say the word."

"Which word is that? Puke? Gross? Repulsive? Odious?"

"All you have to say is 'fuck me, Alden' and I'll gladly comply," he said with a smile that may have undone other women, but Alden Breck couldn't undo me. No way.

I ignored the way my spine tingled just below my neck as a sarcastic half smile pulled at my lips. "That's three words, and they are three words you'll never hear from me. I know you find it hard to believe, but not every person with a vagina wants to spread her legs for you."

His grin was dangerous. It was sweet on the surface, but if you looked close enough, you could see all sorts of wicked things hiding behind it.

"If that's how you really feel about me, Noa, you should come with me to the galas. Since I won't break my promise, I won't try to slide my cock inside of your pretty little pussy. And since you aren't at all attracted to me, you'll never have to worry about succumbing to any of your desires."

I crossed one leg over the other and squeezed, just once. Just because. It wasn't because of him.

"You're not doing a very good job convincing me to go," I said with an air of disinterest.

"Kristy thinks you should go. She thinks it will be good for your career."

I narrowed my eyes. "You talked to Kris about this? Stop talking to my friends!"

"She's my friend, too." He smiled smugly. "And *our* friend thinks coming with me will be good for your career and good for *you*."

"What else did Kris say?" I demanded. When I got a hold of that brat, I was going to kick her ass.

"Not much, except that you had a rough few years and that you need this."

"I don't care what she thinks," I said crisply. "You two had no right to be talking about this – about *me*. I'm not going with you, Alden."

He leaned forward even more, locking his eyes with mine. I wasn't even sure if his butt was still in his seat. "What are you going to do for the next two months, Noa? Hmm? Sit in your apartment writing? Maybe run out to Starbucks for a latte? You would rather stay here, stationary, staring at the same bleak city sidewalks every day while you try to come up with your next good story?"

His voice had been mild, but the words stung.

"I can't just pick up and leave and follow Friction around the country."

"You're twenty-five years old, childless, unmarried, no boyfriend, no fiancé, and you haven't really mentioned having anyone in your life besides Kristy and your brother. What's holding you here? Where is your sense of adventure?"

Again, his voice had been mild, but his words seemed to have slapped me right in the face. How could I tell him that the last time I had a sense of adventure, things went very wrong?

How could I tell him that I was terrified of what he could do to me, of the things he could make me feel…

Instead of answering him, I asked my own question.

"What made you choose this charity?" It came out a little snippy, but at least I wasn't trying to gouge his eyes out with my fork.

He sighed, disappointed that I didn't respond, but he answered me anyway.

"I've had some experience with them. People tend to go with the charities for childhood illnesses and things like that. This one gets overlooked – a lot – because the kids in the program are overlooked – a lot."

I nodded my understanding. "So you've donated before. Have you been able to see the results of what you've donated?"

"Yes, but more than that, I *am* a result of someone's donation."

It took me a moment to catch that. Then my eyes narrowed with understanding. "You…you were a foster child," I concluded.

"Yep," he said, meeting my eyes. He smiled, but his words came out with a bitter edge. "My mother never wanted me, you see. She wasn't on drugs and she didn't drink, she was just plain evil. When I was taken from her 'care,' I was undernourished, dirty, beaten, and scarred. My mother 'home schooled' me, but when I first left her at the age of nine, I could barely read or do simple math, and I had no social skills. I was in and out of trouble growing up after that, always in a fight."

He took a long pull on his beer before gesturing to our waiter for another. My heart was in my throat as I waited for him to continue.

"When I went into foster care, I had nothing. I mean *nothing*. Just the shitty clothes on my dirty ass back. On my first night, I was given two bags. The first bag had a blanket, clothes – *new clothes* – sneakers, socks, and underwear. In a little travel bag inside of that bag I had deodorant, a toothbrush, toothpaste, and a few other things I would have needed. The second bag contained items that were just as much life-changing as clean Spiderman underwear."

"What was in it?" I asked as I imagined a small version of Alden Breck, scared and damaged.

"Inside the second bag were a few school supplies and a few toys, but the person who put that bag together did something a little differently. Taking up far too much space in the bag was an acoustic guitar. *That* changed my life, Noa. I was still a little badass, in and out of trouble, but I taught myself how play that damn instrument, and I studied really hard in school so that I could write my own songs. I taught myself how to play the piano and drums, too. I don't know where I would be if I never got that guitar. So, I personally donate a thousand bags a year, at least, but I always include a guitar, or drumsticks, or a keyboard. I also ask others to donate something that means something to them – whether it is art supplies or books."

"That's amazing," I said with a genuine warmth. "But why a gala? Why not a concert or a festival or something? Wouldn't you raise more money that way?"

"Well, those venues are usually much more money than say, renting the grand ballroom of a hotel for the night. I want to be able to put as much money as possible into the charity and not make up for the costs of raising the money. Does that make sense? I mean, yeah, it can be done, but rich people and politicians like to dress up and walk a red carpet, and they're important to have around. I hold the politicians accountable for making sure foster kids and other kids in the system are safe. Most importantly…" He paused for effect. "I look damn good in a tux."

I smiled, my irritation from earlier gone. "What you are doing is…it's truly amazing, Alden. I'm impressed."

He chuckled. "Still think I'm an obnoxious and conceited ass?"

"Yes," I said without having to consider it. "Are you an only child?"

His facial expression changed. It was strange. It seemed to harden and soften at the same time.

"Twelve years ago, my piece of shit mother met a guy, married him, and moved to Minnesota of all places. She got pregnant, probably thinking that this could be a child she could actually love and care for, but as it turns out it wasn't just something she had against me personally. Tammy just isn't meant to be anyone's mother. Her husband was the only defense the kid had and he died. Peyton was taken from her a little over a year ago. I didn't even know about him until late last year," he said with some sadness. "Had I known about him sooner, maybe I could have saved him some serious hurting."

Alden looked like he was blaming himself, and he wasn't to blame. His detestable egg donor was to blame.

"How did you find out about him?" I asked.

"He knew about me," Alden said, rubbing his jaw. "He knew I was his brother. Tammy must have said something at some point. Of course, the authorities there didn't believe him at first. Who's going to believe that a poor little kid in foster care has a big rock star brother? So, he wrote me." Alden smiled. "Every day for two months. It's impossible for me to read every piece of fan mail that comes in, but I trained my assistants to pay close attention to any mail from kids. Sometimes the kids I give bags to write me, and even though I never require a thank you, I like getting their letters of gratitude. It makes me feel like I really made a difference in their lives."

"It took your assistants two months to realize that the same child was writing you every day?" I questioned.

"Little Noa," Alden said with a big grin. "I'm Alden Breck. I am a popular guy. I get a lot of mail that has to be sorted through."

I rolled my eyes. "Continue with your story."

"I read Peyton's letters. I followed up on them and found out he was writing the truth and I immediately flew out to Minnesota to meet him. Noa, he is such a good kid," Alden said with pride. "He's not anything like me. He's not mad at the world and he does well in school and gets along well with other kids. He's smart as hell and he's funny. I don't know how we turned out so differently raised under such similar circumstances."

I smiled warmly at Alden's obvious affection for his brother.

"Do you talk to him often?"

"I try to talk to him at least twice a week," Alden said, and then quietly added. "Noa, I'm trying to adopt him."

My eyebrows shot up. Was he serious? Alden Breck adopt a kid?

"He's living in a foster home right now, but it's not permanent. He can move again anytime. I want more for him. I can give him everything he could ever need and want and I *want* to, but I have to get my act together first," he said with a heavy sigh. "After I got arrested in New York, my lawyer made it clear that I wasn't helping my chances of adopting Peyton if I was getting arrested for fighting, or if there were always pictures of me drunk off my ass and passed out. You would think that with all of my money and resources that I would be able to adopt him fairly quickly, but since my life is on public display all of the time, it's only making it harder."

"Well, then," I said. "I guess you better stay out of trouble."

"What about you?" he asked as his eyes quickly flickered over my entire face. "I know you have a brother, Warren, right?"

"Yes. He's four years older than me. He doesn't live too far away from me."

"Are you close?" Alden asked.

I shrugged. "We're okay."

I wouldn't describe my relationship with my brother as a *close* relationship. He took care of me when I was younger, but the truth was that he really didn't know me very well at all, but I didn't want to get into that with Alden.

"What about your mom and dad?"

I poked at my chicken with my fork. "I don't know my father. I mean, I kind of remember his face, but he left when I was maybe three and he never came back. My mom…well, let's just say that you and I have something in common there."

Please don't ask questions. Please don't ask questions.

I could feel his eyes burning into me, and I could practically taste the questions that he wanted to spit out, but to my surprise, he didn't. He cleared his throat and said, "Yeah, well, sometimes mothers are assholes."

Relieved, I smiled again and raised my fork to that. We ate in silence for a couple of minutes, though I felt Alden's eyes flickering to me every few seconds, assessing me. I kept my eyes cast down, ignoring his glances and the buzz around the room that often carried his and the band's name. I ignored the obvious flash of cameras and the girlish giggles of a group of women a few tables away.

"Say yes," Alden said so quietly I almost didn't hear him.

I looked up and met his gaze. "What?"

"Say yes," he repeated, a quiet command.

"Why?"

"Because you want to say yes."

I *did* want to say yes. I would be stupid to say no. The only things holding me back were my own fears and anxieties – and having to deal with a pelvic thrusting, arrogant blowpipe, but I could handle him.

Of course, it would be great for my career. I would have plenty of writing material after hanging out with a band for two months. Kristy would kill me if I said no, but more than anything, I wasn't sure how *I* would feel about myself if I said no.

And *that* was what made up my mind in the end. I knew if I said no, I would wonder "what if" for the rest of my life, and I had enough of those to live with. I didn't need any more.

Wringing my hands, I said the one word that would change the entire course of my life. I said, "Yes."

Oh god, I realized right after I gave him my answer. *I just agreed to spend nine weeks with the most pompous, oversexed man on the planet. How will I survive his ego?*

How long will it take me to renege on my promise?

A tiny, tiny, TINY voice way, way back in my head whispered *Hopefully, not long at all.*

Sometimes you have to take a leap of faith
Even if it doesn't end your way
No one will ever tell me I didn't fucking try
"Try"
Friction

I had to wonder if Alden Breck ever slowed down, if he ever slept. After dinner, I was ready to wilt, but Mr. Rock Star wanted to go to Atlantic City for the night. I fought him on it for a half hour before I finally gave in. I made sure that the room he booked had two bedrooms before I packed an overnight bag.

Later, I sat beside Alden at a high stakes poker table. I wasn't much of a poker player, but Alden was apparently damn good. He was up twenty-five grand, which felt like a staggering amount of money to have earned in a couple of hours, but then again, Alden makes money sleeping. Friction's albums and songs stay in the top 50.

Women hung around close by, trying not so discretely to get Alden's attention. Every time he won a hand, they'd clap and cheer him on, bounce their boobs around, and say things like "Nice job, Alden. My room number is 234," or "Alden, can I show you my poker face – in my suite?"

Puh-lease.

The nice thing was that Alden didn't pay them any mind, not really. He'd flash a smile, maybe say something a little flirty, but otherwise, he focused on the game, and on me. After every hand he had won, I got a chaste kiss on my cheek and – god help me – every now and then, he'd run his knuckles over my cheek and down my neck. I put on my own poker face and pretended that it didn't matter, but it affected my unused sexy parts dramatically.

After a couple of hours of basically sitting in the same position, I was beginning to feel a little sore. I slid off my stool, and Alden reflexively wrapped his arm around me.

"I need to take a walk and stretch a little," I said quietly to him.

He looked at me with concern. "I'll wrap this up then."

I waved him off. "Play on, player. I'll be okay on my own for a little while. I'll be upstairs."

He was just dealt a hand and couldn't focus on both the hand and me. So, the bastard folded. Just folded and threw away I don't know how many thousands of dollars.

"You're a fool," I said, astonished.

He gave a nonchalant shrug. "You are more important than the money, Little One."

After Alden had collected his winnings, we made our way up to our suite, which, of course, was on the top floor and the biggest they had available. It was ridiculous, because we were only staying for the night. We didn't need such a huge space, but I guess when you have more money than you can count, you can do whatever you want with it.

"How's your pain?" he asked after we stepped inside.

"Tolerable. It's not the worst physical pain I've been in," I said but then wished I hadn't.

"What's the worst?" he asked, his brow furrowed.

Damn. I opened this can of worms and now I had to find a way to close it back up before too many got loose.

"My arm was broken last year," I said as I went to stand by the large windows.

"How did you break your arm?"

A ghost of a pain shot through my arm as if it could remember the incident that broke it. I wasn't ready to talk about that, and I didn't know if I'd ever be ready to talk about that with Alden.

I started to tell him I didn't want to talk about it, but I didn't have to. My cell phone started ringing, my brother's ringtone, and I practically ran to my bag to get it.

"Hello?"

"Why didn't you call me when you got home from California?" Warren demanded.

"I'm sorry," I said meaningfully. "I got…distracted…" I glanced at Alden. "And I forgot."

I sat down on the couch, propped my feet up on the glass and pewter coffee table, and gave my brother ten minutes of my time. I gave him a brief rundown of my visit to Kristy, sans the trampling tramps incident, and reassured him that I was fine and that I didn't need anything. I knew I would have to tell him about Alden and the galas, but I wasn't sure how he'd take it, and I wanted to be alone when I discussed it with him.

"Your brother?" Alden inquired after I ended the call. He had kept his distance from me throughout the call, but then he joined me on the couch.

"Yeah." I nodded.

"He's very protective of you. I was under the impression you weren't close."

"He tries," I admitted with a shrug. "It's really only been this past year that he's kept dibs on me like this. He feels bad about…" I trailed off when I realized I was about to give up too much information about myself.

"What?" Alden asked softly. "What does he feel bad about?"

I looked at him, studied his face, searching for…what was I searching for? Some sign that I could give him this piece of me and it would be okay? Would it backfire? Would he use it against me later? Would I wake up one day and find my story in some gossip magazine?

I was going to spend a lot of time with the guy. I was going to have to learn to trust him.

"My mother didn't want us, either," I said softly. He looked confused, since he didn't ask about my mom, but he said nothing and let me continue. "One of my earliest memories is from when I was about three or four. My mom couldn't keep a job – she blamed my brother and me. Without a job and no way to pay the bills, our electricity had been shut off. We were at my grandmother's for the night. I had an accident. When my mom took me into the bathroom to clean me up, she was so angry. She said, 'Noa, this is all your fault. I wish you were never born. I should drown you in this toilet.'"

Alden's gaze darkened as he frowned. His hands on his knees balled up into fists, but still, he remained silent.

"There were periods when things were okay, or seemed okay," I continued quietly. "I guess they were never okay. Warren stopped giving a shit after a certain age, but I was always trying to please my mom, to prove to her that I was worth more to her than being drowned in a toilet." I gave a small shrug. "It was all for naught. Warren is four years older than me. He moved out when he was sixteen, leaving me with my mom. He blames himself now, but I never blamed him. He did what he needed to do to survive."

"Blames himself for what?" Alden asked again, his voice rough and tight.

Maybe I had revealed *too* much. I could have given him a short and sweet answer, but I had told him things that no one else knew. Not even Warren knew what my mom had said to me in our grandparents' bathroom that night.

Alden's face softened and he put his hand over my twisting hands in my lap as he said my name with compassion. "Noa…"

"He…he blames himself for…for the things that happened to me after he left."

His fingers caressed mine. "Like what?"

"There are some things I'll never speak about, Alden," I managed in a whisper. "My mom died when I was sixteen, but I had already left her and her string of boyfriends by that time." *Again,* I gave away too much information. Alden cringed when I mentioned the string of boyfriends. I hurried on before he could say anything. "By the time I got into college, I was all fucked up. I dated all of the wrong guys, did too many drugs, and drank way too much. After I was arrested for possession and lewd conduct, I straightened myself out, with a lot of help from a friend. About a year later, I ended up in a bad relationship for three years. Warren blames himself for that, too," I said, frowning deeply. "But none of it's his fault – not my mom, not Larson. But he's trying to make up for it all anyway."

Alden's awesome hazel eyes bored into me.

"You went through a lot of shit," he said quietly. "I'm guessing that the string of boyfriends added to your problems." When I shifted uncomfortably, he rushed on. "I won't push you on that one, but my point is…you endured a lot of shit, but none of that broke you. Larson was the one who finally broke you."

I had this amazingly large lump in my throat. I put my hand to my neck as I nodded. "You could say he was the straw that broke the camel's back."

"He broke your arm," Alden concluded.

I gave a quick nod. Alden closed his eyes for a beat. I watched him anxiously. I had never revealed so much about myself at once to anyone, and I suddenly felt very stupid for doing it.

"Okay, we need…" He looked at me with a thoughtful expression and then jumped up. He went to the phone on the counter of the kitchenette and dialed. "I want one enormous hot fudge sundae with two spoons. I don't really care if the kitchen is closed. Get someone to make it."

He hung up the phone and turned back to me grinning. "We need ice cream."

I managed to smile back at him as I got to my feet. I couldn't help the wince that followed, though, as my hand shot to my aching ribs. Alden was immediately at my side.

"You've done way too much today," he said, frowning. "That's my fault. I'll make an icepack for you. Go in your room and get comfortable."

"It's okay," I said, though I was still wincing. "I'll be fine. Besides, you need someone to help you eat that ice cream."

Alden carefully turned me around with his hands on my shoulders. "To your room, Little Noa," he said and then smacked my ass! "I will bring the ice and we will eat ice cream in your bed."

"You're a bully," I said over my shoulder with my bottom lip poked out.

"Thanks," he beamed.

I went into my room and closed the door behind me. I stepped out of my heels and peeled off my jeans before pulling my shirt up and over my head. That part hurt the most. I was going to change into a pair of pajama bottoms and a T-shirt, but I stopped in front of the mirror to assess the bruising on my torso. I seriously looked like I had the shit beaten out of me. I would know what that looks like…

I had just decided to move away from the mirror and get dressed when my door swung open.

"I have your…holy shit," Alden cursed softly as he stopped in his tracks and openly gawked at me.

My face must have turned a million shades of red, but I tried to play it off. It wasn't my first time semi-naked in front of a man. It was just my first time semi-naked in front of someone like Alden.

"You have seen Victoria's Secret before, haven't you?" I teased and extended my hand for the icepack.

He took a few steps toward me until he was close, too close. With his eyes locked on mine, he placed his hand over my heart where my tattoo was. He didn't say anything, and he didn't have to. I understood the significance of that moment immediately. I had told him that he'd never see it, and he was up-close and personal with it.

"Fuck," he said and took a step back. He ran a hand over his face and put the icepack in my hand. "I can't bring ice cream in here with you dressed – or undressed like this. You'll fucking melt it, Little One."

"Don't worry," I said, turning my back on him to show how nervous I really was. "I'm about to put clothes on. The ice cream will be saved."

"Shit. You know, it's a good thing that I promised not to fuck you. You'd be a lost cause right now, girl."

I pulled a T-shirt over my head. "Yeah, because my bruised ribs are so sexy," I said, rolling my eyes.

"You have a beautiful shape under those bruises, but I wasn't looking at your ribs, sweetheart," he said with a heart-stopping smile.

"You're a pig."

"I'm a man."

"Same difference," I said with a snort.

I gave up on the pajama bottoms because I just wanted to lie down. Alden rearranged the pillows on the bed and held the blankets up for me. I slid into the bed and made some minor adjustments until I was comfortable.

Alden opened his mouth to speak again, but someone knocked on the door. Reluctantly, he left to answer it. He returned a couple of minutes later with the biggest sundae I had ever seen in my life.

"We'll never finish that!" I laughed.

"Maybe not, but we can damn well try," Alden said and settled down on the bed beside me.

We ate ice cream and talked about books, movies, and art. Alden didn't ask me any more awkward questions or go on about my looks. We just talked like normal people, not ridiculously famous Alden Breck and the mousy N.H. Eddington.

I only had a few days to find my first dress. I was surprised when Alden said he'd take me shopping himself, and insisted on paying for everything I'd need. We argued about it for almost two days, mostly in text messages because we were each busy with our own things. Eventually, I gave in because I got tired of arguing about it.

When I got into the limo early Thursday morning, I expected a trip into Philly to one of the boutiques. What I could not have even dreamed up on my own was being ushered into a helicopter not far from my apartment.

I was so nervous. So fucking nervous. Flying on an airliner was one thing. Flying in a little metal cage was another entirely. Alden strapped me into my seat, chatting loudly about getting to New York faster. When he finally looked up at my face, he frowned and held my face in his hands.

"Are you afraid, Little One?" he asked.

"Terrified," I admitted. I recalled an interview he did on the radio the previous week where he said he wasn't afraid of flying, but he was afraid of falling. "I thought you had a big fear of falling? Helicopters fall. A lot."

"I can't not live my life because I fear something, baby," he said. "But that's just me. You have a choice. We can get off this thing right now and just drive up. Anything you want, Little One."

First of all, he called me baby. *Wow*. Second of all, he was willing to throw all of his plans out the window for me.

I sighed and said, "No, I'll be okay."

"You sure?" he asked, ignoring the guys telling him he had to sit down.

I nodded. Alden did the most remarkable thing. He gently planted a kiss square on my lips and then took his seat beside me. After he was all strapped in, he put a pair of those headphone things on my head and put on his own. He held my hand in both of his and we were off. Or…up.

***

I spun around in a slow circle, feeling utterly ridiculous as Alden lounged in a chair, letting his eyes roam over me. I was in a beautiful emerald green dress that reminded me of something Scarlett O'Hara would wear. Even though she was my most favorite fictional female character ever, I couldn't pull off her look.

"No." Alden shook his head. He had kicked the sales lady out a long time ago. She wouldn't focus on her task at hand, only on Alden. "I'll go get you a few more. Try on the red one."

"You're really picky," I said and turned around so that he could unzip me. Every time he zipped me up or unzipped me, his knuckles would trail slowly along my back. I shivered every time. I knew the bastard just enjoyed watching my body tremble.

"I'm not picky. You look great in anything you wear, Little One, but this is too much dress for you."

"You should take a part-time position on the Style Network," I said, walking back to the curtained off section of our little room.

While he was gone, I added the green dress to the four previous. Alden had only liked one dress, a white one with a scoop neck and an open back. It was really long, but with a pair of heels, I was able to manage. I just hoped I wouldn't trip in it, or hell, spill anything on it. I slipped into a nude colored dress next. I gasped when I saw myself in it. It hugged curves I wasn't really aware that I had. Though I had a substantial amount of breasts, this dress made them look far better than I could ever recall them looking in anything. It had spaghetti straps, but the neckline plunged down between my boobs and ended just above my belly button. It covered enough so that no one could really see the bruises on my torso. My ass looked amazing, and for the first time ever, I appreciated the little extra ba-donk-a-donk.

"Need to be zipped up, Little One?" Alden's voice sounded as he walked into the room.

I shoved the curtain aside and rushed out to meet him, my eyes aglow. He stopped walking, the dresses in his hands held high as if he were going to hang them up, but he was frozen. The only thing moving on him was his head and eyes as he looked at me from head to toe, and back up again.

"This one is a keeper," I said excitedly.

"My god," he whispered.

"I know, right?" I asked, moving over to the three-way mirrors. "I think this is the first time in my life that I've ever thought I looked hot."

Alden hung the dresses up and walked over to me.

"Every dude at the gala is going to fuck you with their eyes," Alden said, scowling. "You can't have this dress."

"What?" I put a hand on my hip as I glared at his reflection "You're kidding me, right? I look great!"

"You look more than great," he said. "You look like a fucking goddess and I don't know if I want to see other dickheads worshiping at your feet!"

He let out a growl of frustration and then…I don't know why I was so surprised…but then he actually reached into his jeans and adjusted his sea serpent. There was the compassionate, sweet Alden, and then there was *this* Alden, the one I wanted to kick in the face.

"Shit," he growled.

"I finally look hot and you want me not to?" I gasped and spun around to look at him. "You bastard – you've only been choosing dresses that don't…I don't know…flatter me."

"Yes! Okay? Yes!" he put both hands in his already naturally messy hair. "Because after only four days, I already consider you to be *mine* and I don't want anyone else to even think about going near you!"

"Well…I'm not yours!" I snapped. "Besides, you don't do relationships anyway."

"I didn't say it was a commitment." He scowled. "I just said I consider you mine."

"Are you serious?" I laughed without humor. "You consider me to be yours while you're still picking up women?"

He shifted from one foot to the other. "What are you talking about?"

"Oh, just because you're not doing it in front of me, doesn't mean that it's not happening. You're Alden Breck. You have a sea monster to feed. Oh, don't look at me like that. Last night, you spent the evening at a club stuffing your tongue into a Main Line socialite's mouth, and no doubt stuffing your one-eyed monster into her after that. Philly's a small town, Alden, don't look so surprised that I know."

The image of Alden slobbering into the woman's mouth was all over social media when I woke up early in the morning. It had irritated me and put me in a bad mood for the first part of my day. It wasn't until I saw the helicopter that I had forgotten about why I was so pissy, but now I remembered and I was ready to throw something at his head.

He let out a loud growl of exasperation as he stormed toward the door.

"Get whatever dress you want then!"

"I will!"

He slammed the door and I went back behind the curtain and tried to slam that shut as well.

***

Alden and I barely spoke for the rest of the day. I left the shop with three dresses. To be spiteful, I tried to pay for them with my credit card, but he scowled at me and knocked my hand away. In the end, I was glad I didn't pay for them because together they cost almost as much as a new car.

A limo took us to an apartment that Alden owned in the city. Lunch was already waiting for us, spread out across a table that was situated in front of a wall of glass that had a beautiful view of the busy city and Central Park. Alden spent the entire meal on the phone with his manager and publicist. I didn't really pay attention to what he was talking about, but every now and then, he'd raise his voice to get his point across. When I finished eating, I left him at the table and just stood at the window for a long time, watching people move along with their lives. I wondered if any of their lives had changed as quickly and significantly as mine had.

When I got tired of standing at the window daydreaming about other peoples' lives, I walked around the living area. I looked at the guitars hanging on the walls, the artwork, and pictures of Alden with various influential people. I stared a long time at a picture of him with a gorgeous Hollywood starlet he had rumored to spend a lot of time with a couple of years ago. I wondered how far their relationship had gone. Was it just sex? Just friends? Or friends with sex? Or were they in a full-on committed relationship that he no doubt destroyed when he was unable to keep his dick in his pants?

"Noa," Alden called my name.

I turned around. He had the phone on his shoulder, obviously still busy with work. He held something out to me. I took the credit card but looked at it with confusion.

"Al will drive you to Jimmy Choo's. They know you're coming."

"Okay," I said slowly. "But I can buy my own shoes." I tried to pass the card back to him, but he refused to take it.

"Victoria's Secret is also expecting you, just tell them your name," he said with a straight face. "When you're all finished, just hang on to the card and I'll see you in a couple of days. Al will drive you back home."

I could practically feel the coolness radiating off his body. Alden was looking right at me, but he was withdrawn. There was a wall between us that had not been there before, at least on his side. I didn't understand it, and I especially didn't understand why it troubled me so much.

This is your own fault. You just let him walk right in with all of his smooth talking.

I didn't say anything to him. I pushed the card into my back pocket and moved away from him. I got my coat out of the closet by the door and put it on.

"Noa," he called my name as I pulled open the door, but I kept walking and pulled it shut behind me, even though he was still calling me.

I punched the button for the elevator as Alden came out of the apartment, but to my surprise the cab doors slid open and someone was already inside.

"Oh!" the beautiful starlet started as she stepped off the elevator and almost ran into me. "I didn't realize anyone else was up here." Trisha, I remembered. Her name was Trisha Livingston. Her gorgeous red hair was swept up away from her creamy, lightly freckled skin, and even under her winter coat, I could see how curvy her body was. She reminded me a lot of the actress Scarlett Johansson. Beautiful and timeless.

She walked over to Alden, who was now looking very tired as he put a hand in his hair as he looked from Trisha and back to me.

"No one else is up here," I said dryly and stepped onto the elevator.

"Noa," he said, moving toward me. He stood on the threshold, holding the doors open with one hand.

"The elevator won't move until the doors are closed. The doors won't close until you move," I said in a very tight voice.

I could hear someone yelling on the phone and Trisha was calling for him. But he stood there, staring at me as if he wanted to say something.

I reached into my back pocket as I said, "Seems like you're wanted by everyone – but me." I pushed the card into the front pocket of his jeans. As he reached for it, the doors started to close and I pushed him backward. The last thing I saw before the doors closed was his startled expression.

When I got home from New York that night, I found my brother, Warren, sitting on my couch. I nearly had a heart attack before I realized who it was. I still had nightmares from time to time that I would come home and find Larson sitting in my living room or hiding in my bedroom closet.

"I almost pepper sprayed your face," I told him as I released the trigger on the spray and dropped my keys onto the hook. "What are you doing here?"

"One of my friends shared a video on my Facebook page today. Would you like to guess the content of the video?"

I didn't have to guess. I *knew*. I just didn't know where and when the video was shot. It could have been anywhere – the museum, the grocery store, any of the places we'd gone to eat.

"I'm sorry," I said, wincing. "I was going to tell you soon."

"Tell me which part exactly? That you're screwing one of the biggest womanizers on the planet or that he's whisking you away for two months."

"I'm not—"

He cut me off when he stood and held up a hand. Then he marched over to the small closet by the door and threw it open. He gestured madly inside.

"It's a closet," I said slowly.

"Come see what is in the closet, Noa," he demanded.

Confused and curious, I joined him at the entrance of the closet. What I found there were the dresses I had just tried on hours ago. They were each inside a thick, black garment bag, but I knew what they were without having to investigate. I was wondering how the hell the dresses made it into the closet when Warren spoke up.

"Some guy just dropped these off a little while ago. Why is he buying you dresses if you're not fucking him or going with him to the galas?"

I closed the closet door. I really didn't know if I was still going with Alden to the events. He had not called me after I left his apartment, which was just as well. I got way too close to him in too little time.

"I really don't know if I'm going with him," I told Warren as he followed me back into the living room.

I stretched out onto the couch as he stood over me, looking pissed off. "You're the girl that got trampled at his concert, aren't you?" he demanded.

"Yes, I'm the girl that got trampled at the Friction concert. You've figured it out. You should be a detective. But like, somewhere else."

"Noa," he said tiredly, wiping at his eyes. He must have come to my place right after work. He was still wearing his work clothes, minus the suit jacket, which was strewn over the back of the couch, and his tie was loosened around his neck.

"It's not a big deal. I'm fine," I said.

He looked at my hands, eyeing the bruised fingers. I still had a small bruise right at my hairline on my head, and by the way I was laying, it was obvious I was in some amount of pain.

"Kristy said your ribs were badly bruised," he said.

"I told you I'm fine," I said irritably.

"Noa, why don't you ever tell me when you're hurt?" Warren asked. I could tell he wasn't just thinking about recent days, but he was thinking about Larson and my teenage years when I was still at home with our mom.

"You can't change what happened in the past by knowing every time I fall down and scrape my knee in the present, Warren," I said and closed my eyes.

"You kept me in the dark every time, Noa." He said it as if he still couldn't believe it. "For some reason, you thought you had to endure it all alone."

"Warren, you left me alone with her," I flared. I had told Alden it wasn't Warren's fault, but there was this part of me that I didn't like to see, this part of me that blamed him.

"I was just a kid myself, Noa, but if you had just come to me—"

"Forget it," I said in exasperation. "Can we please move forward?"

"Not until you promise to talk to me when you're hurting or when someone is hurting you."

I was hurting right then, and not just physically. I didn't know how to tell him about my current pain because I couldn't really describe it myself.

"I promise," I said, more or less to get him out.

"I guess I'll be talking to you very soon then, because Alden Breck is definitely going to make you hurt," he said dryly.

I felt his lips on my forehead and then he was gone, leaving me alone with my thoughts and the pain I was unwilling to admit I had.

***

Fifteen minutes after my brother left, someone knocked on my door. I was tempted to ignore it, but the person on the other side was persistent. The knocking wasn't only annoying me, but it was most likely annoying my neighbors. I got up and looked through the peephole. Alden stood on the other side, looking right into it.

"How long are you going to keep me waiting out here, Little One?" he asked in a slightly irritated tone.

"How much time you got?" I countered.

"Just open the door so I can properly apologize," he commanded. "I'm giving you the opportunity to open the door yourself."

"If I don't, are you going to break it down?" I asked doubtfully.

"No, I will use this," Alden said and held a key up to the peephole.

"Impossible," I gasped. "You never had the opportunity to copy my house key."

Alden rolled his eyes and muttered something about me doing shit the hard way. "Always have to be complicated," he said.

I looked down at the doorknob when I heard a click. I took a few steps back and watched with astonishment as Alden let himself into my apartment.

"Where did you get that!" I demanded, reaching for the key in his hand.

"You'd be surprised what fame and fortune can get you, Little Noa," he said as he locked the door behind him.

I crossed my arms defiantly and narrowed my eyes at him. "Maybe I don't want you here."

"I'm me," he said as he stepped toward me. "Why *wouldn't* you want me here?"

I backed away from him, rolling my eyes. "What are you doing here anyway? I thought you had business and Trisha to take care of."

"Are you jealous?" he asked with a smirk.

"Not on your life," I said, trying to push him away from me, but he continued to advance and I continued to walk backward to get away from him.

"Why are you running from me," he sang.

"You're unpredictable. Why wouldn't I run from you?"

"For the love of all that's good in this world!" Alden yelled and grabbed my shoulders to keep me still. "Stop moving! I don't feel like chasing you around this apartment."

"Then don't, you ass-hat. Go home or to your hotel room or to hell."

"Are you going to fucking let me say I'm sorry or what?" Alden snapped, shaking me lightly.

"Well, get it done and over with so I can go on with my life. I have plans tonight," I said, raising my head a little higher. I so didn't have plans, but he didn't need to know that.

Alden growled in frustration and looked up at the ceiling for a moment.

"You are exasperating, Noa Harlow Eddington."

"You don't exactly set the bar for non-exasperating personalities," I snapped.

He closed his eyes for a moment. When he opened them again – holy shit – his eyes were – he was…*smoldering.*

I'd written about smoldering gazes, and I always thought that I imagined them just right, just how they would be, but I was totally unprepared for the severity of a real life smolder. I felt as if his hazel eyes were radiating pure, lava-level heat. If I had been wearing pearls, I would have clutched the hell out of them.

"I apologize for my cold behavior earlier today," Alden said in a quiet voice.

"Okay. Apology accepted. Thank you. See you tomorrow," I said as I tried to get away from this *hot,* smoldering man.

"I'm not finished," he growled. He snaked an arm around my waist and roughly pulled my body against his.

Oh boy.

"You can't finish from…say the armchair while I sit on the couch?" I asked in a small voice. My torso ached from being forced against his body, but I hardly noticed because I could feel how hard his body was. And not just the sea serpent – which seemed to be waking up – but also the muscles in his abs and chest were hard.

"No, I can't," he scowled. "Stop being difficult, will you?"

I sighed noisily. "Carry on," I said in a bored tone, looking at his shoulder instead of his face.

He tilted my head up to look at him. "That's better," he murmured and then stroked my cheek.

Aw, shit.

"You have such beautiful eyes, Little Noa," Alden murmured.

I rolled my "beautiful eyes" and said, "Yeah, okay. Plain brown eyes are so attractive."

"Your eyes aren't brown," Alden said disdainfully. "They're like…burgundy, with little specs of green."

"I think your contacts are drying up or something. You can't see right," I said.

I squeaked when Alden suddenly picked me up in his arms and carried me into my bedroom. He stood me up in front of my large floor-mirror and turned on every light in the room. He moved the mirror to a brighter spot and then pulled me over. He stood behind me, his body flush with mine as his hands rested on my hips.

"Look at those eyes, Noa," he whispered in my ear. "Move closer and really look at those eyes."

"This is ridiculous," I started to argue, but Alden shut me down.

"Look!" he commanded and moved me forward until my toes touched the mirror.

I sighed and moved forward to look at my damn eyes. At first, I didn't see anything more remarkable than my usual plain brown eyes. I looked a little closer, and then closer still until I saw what he saw. Little dashes of dark green against dark, dark burgundy.

"Oh," I gasped, widening my eyes.

"You see it now?"

"I do." I frowned. "I never noticed before. How could I not have known?"

"I'm under the impression that you don't really look at yourself – I mean *really* look at yourself."

I stood upright again and met his eyes in the mirror. "I never wanted to," I admitted quietly. Then hastily added, "Besides, it's not like there was much to stare at. I don't think I'm ugly or repulsive, but I'm not in the same league as Kristy…or Trisha."

I hated that I sounded jealous when I said her name.

"Baby," Alden whispered, his lips moving softly against my ear. "You're above them all."

My brow creased with irritation. "Now you're just fucking with my head, Alden." I began to pull away from him, but he held me there.

"Noa, look at yourself. Really look at yourself. What do you see?"

With narrowed eyes, I looked at my reflection in the mirror.

"I see a vertically challenged woman with plain brown hair, okay boobs, and I can stand to lose a few pounds."

Alden looked at my reflection's face with what could have been…sadness? Pity?

"Hasn't anyone ever told you that you're beautiful, Noa?"

Yep, it's pity.

I shrugged. "Not with any sincerity."

Right, because telling me I was beautiful while I was sucking a cock or after leaving bruises on my face just didn't make the statement ring true.

Frustrated, humiliated, and anxious, I shrugged him off me. "I'm so over this. I thought you came here to apologize, not to have a heart-to-heart about my body image."

When I tried to move away again, Alden held me there with his hands on my hips. Once I was still again, his hands moved to the top of my shirt and he started to unbutton it.

"What the hell are you doing?" I asked with my eyes wide and my heart pounding. I slapped at his hands. "Stop. Stop!"

Alden's hands stilled on my shirt as he watched me carefully. I was breathing heavily and my pulse beat wildly in my throat.

"I'm showing you your body," he said gently. "You need to see yourself how I see you, how countless of other men probably see you. I promise that I'm not going to hurt you. Don't be afraid of me, Noa," he whispered close to my ear. "Please, don't ever be afraid of me. I'll never hurt you. Do you trust me?"

I stared at him in the looking-glass. I shouldn't trust the pelvic thrusting, womanizing, arrogant son of a bitch, but I did. There was no explanation for it, but I felt it in my chest.

I nodded once, and he made quick work of removing my shirt, stripping me down to my bra.

In a state of shock, I watched our reflections as he unbuttoned my jeans and pulled the zipper down. He kneeled behind me and pulled my jeans down over my thighs and down to my feet. With a trembling hand on his shoulder, I stepped out of the jeans. Alden stood back up and splayed his hands across my midsection.

I shook violently against him, but I didn't make him stop.

"Tell me again how you see yourself," he said, his voice low and rough.

"Vertically challenged woman, with okay boobs, plain brown hair, and I could stand to lose a few pounds," I murmured awkwardly.

"Vertically challenged, maybe so, but I would say you are petite." He smiled in my hair. "Your hair…" he said, running his fingers through it. "Is what other women *pay* for: wavy, soft, and naturally highlighted. I love how it frames your face and I love the way it looks when you just wake up. It smells…" He took a long whiff of my hair. "It smells intoxicating."

I swallowed hard as his hand returned to my midsection. "Now, let's discuss your few pounds." His hands caressed over my belly, over my hips, and over my thighs before smoothing up to my waist.

"Where you see a few extra pounds, I see curves," he murmured as his hands began traveling again. "Exquisite, sexy curves. This flesh on your belly…" he said, running a hand across my stomach. "Makes me want to lick it, bite it, and kiss it."

Oh. My. Goodness.

"And these breasts…" his hands cupped my breasts and I just about died. To my shock and horror, I felt my nipples pucker and harden under his touch. Alden groaned as he gave them a squeeze and I had to bite my bottom lip to keep myself from groaning, too. "You have perfect tits, Little Noa. There's nothing petite about these. They're firm, but soft at the same time, and they are a perfect fit for my hands." He squeezed again and I couldn't help the light moan that escaped my lips.

"You see, you're beautiful," Alden said and gave me a light kiss on my neck. "Hasn't anyone ever made you *feel* beautiful?"

I shook my head, unable to find my voice.

"Really? Many women feel that way after a good orgasm."

"I guess I'll never know," I managed to whisper.

Alden's eyes widened. "You've never had an orgasm?"

"Only if I give one to myself," I said and swallowed hard. I couldn't believe the turn the conversation had taken. I needed to steer it back on track, back to his damn apology. I opened my mouth to speak, but I gasped when I felt Alden's fingertips in the top of my panties.

"That bastard Larson couldn't even give you an orgasm?" he questioned, watching my face in the mirror for a response.

"No."

"What about any of the other guys you dated?"

I shook my head. Nope.

"How the hell do you write such hot sex scenes if you can't ever remember having an orgasm?" he asked in astonishment.

"A girl can dream," I said softly.

"Okay," he said after a moment. "Okay." He took a deep breath. "I promised I wouldn't try to fuck you, and I won't. I mean, technically I will, with my hand."

I started to object and pull away, but he held me fast and told me to be quiet and listen.

"I will make you feel good and I will make you see and feel beautiful when you come. This is about you, not about me. Understand?"

It didn't matter if I understood or not. It wasn't up for discussion at that point. He was going to do it – or try, and my god I wanted him to try. I didn't want to admit it out loud, but I was turned on by our display in the mirror. I was still afraid and anxious, but I was more aroused than anything.

"Before we start, I need to tell you why I was being such an ass," Alden said, brushing my hair away from my neck.

"Which time?" I snorted.

"While we were arguing about your dress, I realized how strongly I feel about you after only a few days," he said in a very soft voice.

I met his eyes in the mirror, but his eyes were so bright and effecting, I had to look away.

"Okay," I said slowly, looking off to the side, away from the reflection of our bodies together.

"I didn't know how to handle what I was feeling, so I just turned my emotions off," he said and left a single, gentle kiss on my neck. "I can't promise that I won't act like an ass again – it's in my nature, you know, but I will *try* to behave more sensibly."

"It's also in your nature to be the whore that you are," I said, meeting his eyes again. "So, make sure you get your emotions under control. You wouldn't want to take either of us in a direction that would just end badly."

"Agreed," he said and left another kiss on my neck that left me sighing.

"So maybe you should let me get dressed now." I attempted to pull away from him, but I don't know why I bothered. Alden wasn't going to let me go unless Alden wanted to let me go.

"Oh, no, Little One," he smiled sexily and mischievously. "I still have a few lessons to impart on you."

"It's going over the line, Alden," I said firmly.

"I always go over the line, sweetheart," he said with a big grin. "Consider this a thank you for agreeing to do the gala tour with me." His smile faded and he looked serious once again. "I want you to see yourself as I see you."

With his last three words, his hand slipped into my panties and before I could react, his middle finger made contact with my clit. I pulled in a sharp breath when I felt it.

"You're warm," he murmured in my ear as his fingers stroked over my clit. "And *wet*."

I tried to breathe normally as he touched me, but I was having a very hard time with it. I bit back a moan when he pressed down a little harder.

"Noa," he growled lightly in my ear. "Look at yourself, baby. Look at my hand in your panties. You see that? Mmm…" Alden moaned. "You see my hand moving around under your pretty panties? Stroking you? Spreading your moisture all over your hot cunt?"

Dear me, I couldn't help myself when I moaned. His skilled fingers felt incredible on me.

"Your face is turning a light shade of pink because of your arousal," Alden breathed, stroking a finger over my cheekbone. His fingers stroked over my slightly open mouth. "And look how your lips part as you try to control your breathing. You look so fucking hot right now, so *beautiful*."

His fingers pressed harder on my clit as he moved them in a slow circle. My head fell back against his body. When my eyes began to close, Alden scolded me.

"Keep your eyes open, Noa," he commanded. "Watch *everything*," he whispered. "How do you feel?"

"G…good," I managed.

"But you don't feel *great*," he said. "You don't see yourself the way I see you yet. Don't worry, I'm not finished with you yet, sweetheart," Alden said as his fingers easily found a nipple through my bra.

I groaned. He was rolling it and squeezing it between his fingers. The material of my bra was adding to the pleasure that was now shooting through my nipples and to my core.

"Yesss," Alden hissed in my ear. "Look at your face now, Noa. See how it's burning with desire?"

He released my breast, grabbed my hand, and put it just above my panty line near his other arm.

"Run your hands over your body a little bit," he demanded before reaching for my breast again. "Touch your body."

I stroked my fingers over my belly just above where his fingers were pleasuring me. I traced a lazy trail that went around my navel, over it, and then up to the swell of my breasts.

"Mmm…" Alden groaned and pressed his groin into my ass. "Now move your hand back down and push it into your panties under my hand."

I did as I was told, trying hard not to close my eyes as he moved to the other breast and began to assault that nipple as well.

"Get your hand down there," he commanded roughly when my fingers lingered near my sex.

I pushed my hand down until it was under his and over my clit. He pressed on my hand with his, adding more pressure than ever to my aching clit.

"Oh, god," I breathed as he made me touch myself.

"Do you feel how wet you are, Noa?" he murmured as he kissed my neck. "Do you feel how hot you are? Look at your face, baby. Look how turned on you are. Your eyes look like they're on fucking fire. So fucking beautiful." His tongue flicked at my earlobe.

My moans were getting louder and longer as Alden touched me and made me touch myself. He slipped his hand inside my bra and palmed my breast. I pressed forward a little and he growled as he squeezed me hard.

"Look at your hips rocking against our hands," Alden said in awe.

My eyes trailed down to our hands working together toward one common goal. I hadn't realized it at first, but I *was* grinding gently against our hands.

"Keep touching yourself," Alden warned as his hand slid farther into my panties. A second later, I felt a finger thrust inside of me.

"Oh!" I cried out as his thick finger invaded me.

"Your panties are getting in my way," Alden growled and before I could stop him, he tore them away from my body. Then his finger was back inside of me, pushing in and pulling out, and pushing back in again. "Look at that, Noa," he groaned. "Look at my finger going in and out of your tight pussy – keep touching yourself!"

He pulled out of me completely, but I didn't have time to miss his touch before he was pushing *two* fingers inside of me. I watched in the mirror as his fingers repeatedly disappeared into my damp sex. My own fingers were frantically rubbing my clit and Alden's thumb was stroking over my nipple under my bra.

"Use your other hand and squeeze your other nipple," he demanded.

When my fingers closed over my nipple, I felt like my whole body turned into one big exposed and sensitive nerve. Watching both of our hands on me and in me was making me feel so…*hot*. I felt like there was something quickly building inside of me and I vaguely wondered if this is what it felt like to climb toward an impending orgasm with someone else's hands on me.

"I know you're about to come," Alden breathed in my ear. "Your pussy keeps squeezing my fingers. You're going to come so damn hard, Noa."

My cries echoed off the walls of my bedroom. Alden's moans and growls sounded in my ear, making me climb even higher. Suddenly, Alden's teeth sunk into the sensitive flesh on my shoulder and I peaked. I stopped touching myself and wrapped my arms around Alden's neck.

"Alden!" I screamed his name as I started to come.

"Look at your beautiful face, Noa," he moaned.

He pushed his fingers farther into my cunt and then squeezed my nipple harder as he sucked and licked my skin. He growled and grinded harder against my ass. The sensations I was feeling were almost too much to take. I wanted him to stop touching me, but I wanted it to keep going and going. My body convulsed, trembled, and tightened. I watched my face as he told me to, and saw how flushed and bright it was. I looked like a different person, like a different Noa Eddington. I looked…beautiful…

As my orgasmic high began to descend back down to Earth, Alden pulled his fingers out of me and stopped thumbing my nipple. I let my arms slip away from him and down to my sides. He laid gentle kisses on my neck and I shuddered, still feeling very sensitive.

"Look at your reflection," he said softly. "Your whole body looks like a live wire. Your face looks even more beautiful than it did before. You *feel* sexy and beautiful, don't you?"

I nodded weakly.

"Good."

He withdrew from me suddenly, leaving me feeling cold and, well, half-naked. I watched as he covered his face and groaned near my door.

"I gotta go," he said in his hands.

"What? Seriously?" I asked, watching him.

"Yes!" he yelled and glared at me.

"Why are you mad at me? I didn't do anything to *you*," I pointed out, feeling a little angry myself.

"You drive me fucking crazy!" he countered, and then stormed out of the room yelling, "I need to go take a fucking cold shower or go find some pussy! This is ridiculous!"

By the time I got to the doorway, he was walking out of my apartment, muttering about keeping promises. Just like that, he was gone. I didn't know how to feel about it. I couldn't say he used me. Clearly, I used him, but I felt…awkward.

As I turned to go back into my bedroom to pick up my torn panties, Alden walked through the door again. He stormed over to me, planted a rough kiss on my cheek, and angrily said, "I'll see you tomorrow."

Then he left, again.

Holy cow, he's a fucking nut.

I woke up the next morning feeling sore and couldn't remember why at first. Then I recalled the whole sexual scene in front of the mirror, the way my body shuddered and trembled. I didn't feel the pain then, but fuck was I feeling it in the morning. I wasn't even sure if it was worth it. Alden had very skilled hands, but how much credit could I give him if my own hands were just as involved? It made me question whether or not a man could really give me an orgasm.

I carefully got out of bed to use the bathroom. I thought about the things I needed to accomplish during the day. I still had to find shoes for Saturday, and maybe make an appointment for a manicure for Saturday morning. I was supposed to have lunch with a friend at one, but after that, I really needed to focus on getting some work done. As a rule, I usually wrote no less than ten pages a day, even if I had to burn it like crap the next day. The important thing was to keep working, and since meeting Alden, I didn't think I wrote ten pages in the entire week.

With my day planned out in my head, I got into the shower. Afterward, I wrapped myself in a towel and combed the tangles out of my damp hair. I really needed something mild to take the edge off my pain, so I left my bedroom with the intent of going to the kitchen for some ibuprofen, but I almost pissed myself as I covered my mouth and muffled a squeal. Lying on my couch, stretched out and sleeping was Alden.

What the hell – I wish I knew how he got a fucking key to my apartment. He looked dead-ish. Actually, he looked a little beat up. I leaned in for a closer inspection and realized that he did indeed have a nice bruise under his left eye and a couple of other cuts and bruises on his neck and face. His knuckles looked a little torn up, too. One thing I knew about Alden Breck before our chance meeting, was that he was always fighting. He had been arrested countless times for getting into fistfights. I wondered where and with whom he was fighting this time – and why. Did he blow off sexual steam by pounding someone's face? That's dumb.

I sighed and backed away. I had to continue on with my day despite the infamous, bad boy, hard rocker lying on my couch. I went into the kitchen and took something for my pain. When I turned around, Alden was standing in the doorway. I screamed and threw the bottle of pills at him.

"Why the hell are you sneaking up on me?" I yelled at him.

He squinted sleepily at me and grinned. "I was going to pull your towel off and run away," he said.

"Ass hat," I muttered. "Why the hell are you here?"

"I was tired," he said to me as if I should have known the answer to that. He stretched and I couldn't help but watch as his muscles seemed to pop out all over the place.

"So? Don't you have a hotel room?" I asked, moving past him.

"Yeah, but there were girls in there," he said with disgust as he followed me into the bedroom.

"So, why didn't you kick them out?" I asked as I started pulling out clothes to put on.

"Too much trouble." He waved a hand.

"So, I guess you got your pussy last night."

"Maybe too much," he said, dragging his hands over his face.

Alden was probably the only guy I knew who could have his fingers inside of me, screw around with other girls later that night, and then have a casual conversation about it the next day. I had to question my own sanity since I was an active participant in said casual conversation.

"What happened to your face?" I asked, leaning against my dresser.

"Nothing much." He shrugged it off as inconsequential. "Just a fight. I'm going to take a shower," he said and started toward my bathroom. "When I am finished, we will go to breakfast."

"Umm…"

I didn't know which thing to address first, the fact that he was going to use my shower or the fact that he just assumed I was some loser with nothing else to do but to wait for the big rock guy to take me to breakfast.

"Umm?" he asked, leaning in the doorway to the bathroom. He filled the space with his arms stretched above his head as his hands gripped the top of the doorframe. I swallowed back my drool.

"I have to go to DSW to find shoes and then I'm meeting a friend for lunch at one. Then I have to get some work done."

"A friend?" His brow furrowed. "A guy friend?"

"Yes, a guy friend," I said casually.

Alden looked like he just tasted something terrible. "I don't like it."

Oh boy.

"Okay, you don't have to like it." I shrugged. "It's not going to change anything."

"Is this a date?" he asked, walking toward me with his bad bad-boy walk.

"No, it's a lunch, but for the record, if it were a date, it wouldn't be any of your concern."

Alden moved in close to me and I felt forced to take a step back, but he only closed the distance again.

"I regretted my behavior yesterday, not what I said," he said quietly.

"I'm afraid I don't know what you are speaking about," I lied as I looked up into his hazel eyes.

He put a finger under my chin and leaned in so close I could smell his breath. I never thought someone's morning breath could smell so…I don't know…manly? He smelled like cigarettes, beer, and something sweet. Maybe it wasn't the most attractive smell, but it rather added to his bad-ass-ness.

"Mine," he said just above a whisper.

Dear Lord.

I batted his hand away and moved away from him. "I'm not your shiny new toy, Alden. We're friends – kinda, and that's about it."

"After what I did for you last night, we're only 'kinda' friends and 'that's about it'?" he asked incredulously as he stalked after me.

"Actually, I more or less did *that* myself, and you whore around enough to know that one orgasm doesn't signify anything," I said, pulling myself up onto the bed in an effort to get away from him. I walked across it to the other side, but then Alden was standing on my bed, following me.

"*I* did that to you!" he said, all full of himself. "And I'm not saying we're in a committed relationship or anything but hey, there's something going on here."

"There's nothing going on here," I said, moving into the living room. "How can you even suggest that when you just banged god knows how many women last night?"

I moved around the couch, trying to put it between us, but the bastard just followed me.

"Three. I banged three women last night," he said haughtily. "And let's get back to the orgasm."

"You mean the one I gave to myself?" I snorted, still walking in circles to get away from Alden. "I should have known you couldn't give me one yourself. Too much hype around the great Alden Breck and his sexual prowess. It's okay; I don't blame you. I'm just the only one who knows how to get me off."

Alden looked angry now. I guess I didn't blame him. I basically just told him he sucked at one of the things he thought he was best at, but Alden was also done chasing me around the small apartment. I realized that he was just *letting* me walk away from him, maybe it was fun for him to watch me scurry away, but he was done chasing. As I went into the bedroom with the full intent of closing and locking the door, my towel was torn away from my body. I yelped and turned around with my arms crossed over my breasts and the junction between my thighs. Alden stood in the doorway holding the towel. He looked like a lion about to attack his prey. If I moved, he would attack. If I didn't move, he would attack. I was shit out of luck.

"Fuck," I muttered as he took the few steps to close the distance between us.

"Little One, there are many things I'm good at, but there are three things especially that I am a beast at," he said, inching me backward toward my bed.

"I'll bet one of those top three things is throwing yourself onto women who don't want you," I said snottily.

"They *always* want me, Little Noa, and even though you act like you don't want me, I suspect that you really do."

The backs of my knees hit the bed and with just a tap to my shoulder, Alden made me sit. To my surprise, he got on his knees in front of me.

"One," he started as his hands smoothed over my thighs. "I'm one hell of a musician. I'm the best I know. Two," he put his hands under my knees and yanked me forward until I was sitting on the very edge. "I'm one hell of a businessman. I've built my band and brand into an empire." His hands pushed at my knees to make me open my legs. I resisted, but that was pointless. Alden forced my legs widely apart. "Three, I'm a beast with all things sex, Little Noa. No one leaves unsatisfied."

"Except me," I said dryly.

"You are mistaken – that was all me last night, but I guess I have to further prove myself because you're so damn difficult."

"You have to do no such thing," I snapped and tried to move away, but he hooked his arms under my thighs and pinned me there.

"You're so cute when you try to be tough," he grinned. "Feel free to pull my hair and grind yourself on my face. It will be that good, I promise."

Before I could object, Alden's tongue was pushing into my entrance. I tried not to react.

"You probably won't do it right like all of those before you," I said to him.

Roughly, he yanked me forward. My ass was barely on the bed and I had to brace myself by grabbing onto the bedding.

Alden's tongue dipped inside of me repeatedly and I couldn't deny that it felt good. My breathing changed slightly and I felt myself relaxing.

"Your pussy is so sweet," he murmured and nipped at my inner thigh.

With a low groan, he went back to work, this time, running his tongue from my entrance all the way up to my clit. I groaned when his tongue flicked hard over my clit. He did it again, his hazel eyes burning into mine to gauge my reaction. After a few more flicks, his lips closed over the nub and he sucked it into his mouth.

"Oh, god," I groaned as Alden sucked on my clit.

At first, the sucking was gentle, but he progressively sucked harder until I found my hands in his hair, pressing his head to me. Alden moaned as he sucked and licked my cunt. He hooked my legs over his shoulders and pushed two fingers inside of me. His other hand found its way to my breasts where he randomly alternated between squeezing and tugging at my nipples. I groaned loudly as I grinded into Alden's face and fingers.

"Feels so good," I moaned as I threw my head back.

I cried out when I felt Alden's fingers hit my g-spot. Expertly, he massaged the bundle of nerves, applying just the right pressure as his mouth worked on me outside.

It started in my lower belly, this feeling of enormous lethal butterflies, fluttering throughout my body, making me extra sensitive. My hands pulled hard on Alden's hair as the sensation fluttered through my breasts and hard nipples that Alden was still manipulating. My toes began to curl and I felt my inner walls squeezing and releasing Alden's fingers. Then it happened.

"Oh my god!" I screamed as my orgasm tore through my body. "Alden! Oh…"

I grinded hard on his face and fingers as my pussy contracted. Alden pulled hard on my nipples and moaned loudly as he continued to push me over the edge. It was suddenly too much. His mouth, his hands – I tried to push him away, but he wouldn't release me, wouldn't stop licking, sucking, and finger fucking my cunt or terrorizing my nipples. I was over-sensitized, but he kept going until another orgasm hit me suddenly and hard.

"That's it," he grunted as a new sensation hit my pussy. I felt like I was…well I felt like I was releasing…something. I couldn't explain it even to myself at the time.

As Alden's fingers continued to move slowly inside of me, I could hear how wet I was. I mean, I sounded soaked, *literally*. When I opened my eyes and looked down at Alden, his mouth was *so* wet, and my god, so was his shirt. *What the hell!*

My eyes must have just about fallen out of my head because Alden grinned up at me as he finally pulled his fingers out of my sensitive channel. He held up his hand. Soaked.

What. The. Fuck.

"Was that your first time?" he asked with a big grin.

"My first time what?" I asked, breathless.

"I guess it was – and damn, *I* did that for you," he said and lazily ran a finger through my vaginal lips.

"Did what?" I demanded. "Oh my god, did I fucking pee myself or something?" I nearly yelled, as mortification began to set in.

"Calm down, Little Noa," Alden said softly, his tone reassuring. "You ejaculated."

"I what!" I yelled.

"You squirted," he said proudly.

"No, no, no, no," I said, pulling away from him and retreating onto the bed. "I've never done that. I can't do that."

"You *did,* and *I* made you do it," he said, getting to his feet.

I looked at the bed where I had been sitting. It was wet there. Cautiously, I crawled back to the edge of the bed, careful not to touch the wet spot and looked on the floor.

Oh. My. Gosh.

There was a small puddle on the floor.

"I did that?" I asked in a small voice.

"Yes, baby, you did. And *I*—"

I cut him off. "Yes, *you* did it to me, I know!" I snapped.

"I have to go take that shower now," Alden said, backing up with one hand on his crotch, on the sea serpent. "Or I'm going to fucking burst."

"I need to shower again," I said distractedly as I got up to find something to clean up my…mess.

"Want to join me?" He wriggled his eyebrows.

"And interrupt your jerking off time?" I asked dryly. "No thank you."

"I'm so fucking hard," he whined. "It's not fair that you do this to me!" he yelled and the bathroom door slammed.

I got some paper towels and cleanser. I really didn't know how to clean it up, but that was the best I could think of. I cleaned up the mess on the floor and then stripped the bed. I marched the bedding straight to the little laundry room off the kitchen and put the blanket in first. I went into the powder room and cleaned myself up again using the sink. After cleaning the sink, I went back into my room to get dressed.

I stood in the middle of the room then and let what had happened really sink in. I smiled and covered my mouth as if anyone could see me. Those were the best two orgasms of my life. I wanted more – well, not right that moment – but in the future. I was sure Alden would be up for it, but then again, I didn't want to rely on him for that – for anything really. Maybe when I was ready to date again, I could teach the guy to do what Alden had done. Though it was pretty hot to look down and see Alden's hazel eyes gazing up at me while he worked on bringing me to the brink.

Okay, Noa. Get your shit together now. You have a busy day ahead.

I shook myself from my little daze and finished dressing. I needed to brush my teeth. I decided I'd just go into the bathroom and grab my toothbrush and toothpaste and take it to the powder room, but I had barely cracked the door open when I heard my name.

"Fuck," Alden said, his voice just barely audible above the shower. "Noa…" he moaned.

I couldn't mistake the sound of him jerking off. It's just one of those sounds that you know when you hear it, a hand sliding up and down the shaft, and from the sounds, it was pretty soapy.

So, Alden was fantasizing about me? Okay, I guess I could understand. He did just make me…squirt, but I was sure there were better women to fantasize about.

Suddenly, he growled out my name; again, his voice barely heard over the sound of the shower. I had a feeling he was trying to be quiet on purpose, like he didn't want me to hear him fantasizing about me.

"Oh, baby," he groaned and then grunted several times. Then I could only hear his soft pants as he tried to catch his breath.

I knocked hard on the door and walked in.

"Just grabbing my toothbrush," I said quickly.

I heard the shower curtain open. When I looked up in the mirror, Alden's head was poking out.

"You sure you don't want to join me, Little One?" he asked with a wicked smile.

"As you can see, I'm already dressed," I said, heading toward the door.

"Your loss," he teased.

"I'm sure."

I closed the door behind me and breathed a sigh of relief. What the hell were the next nine weeks going to be like?

***

Tucker Barry was the boyfriend that almost-but-never-was. I first met him in my first semester of college. I thought he was a pretty good-looking guy with his dark hair, caramel skin, and grey eyes. We ran in completely different circles then. I was a too flirty, drank entirely too much, and smoked too much weed and snorted too much coke. Tucker hung out with the good kids; he rarely drank and didn't do any drugs. He dated nice, good, clean girls and he was always very respectful to them, even if it didn't work out. We would chat in class, but that was about it. Once we walked out the door, he went his way and I went mine. I didn't think anything of him until after I was arrested.

The night I was arrested, I was having sex in the backseat of a car. A police officer banged on the window and told us to get out. The officer later told me he was just going to give us a speech about our actions, but as I was climbing out of the car, my bag of weed fell out of my pocket, right at his feet. I only spent that night in jail, but it was a wakeup call for me. Did I ever want to go back to jail again? What was I doing with my life? I broke away from my mother and her boyfriends all of those years ago for what? To screw my life up on my own?

I thought about all of the 'friends' I had at the time. None of them were really doing too well. Most of them were failing the classes they bothered to show up to. More than half were usually stoned or drunk out of their minds. They had no real hopes or aspirations. They were headed to one big fat dead end. If anything, I needed to prove to myself that I was worth more than sex in the backseat of a car with a married man. I needed to prove to myself that I was worth more than being drowned in toilet water. It didn't matter if my mother was dead and gone. I still had something to prove and I wasn't going to do it with my usual company.

The morning I got out of jail, I barely made it to class on time. Tucker passed me notes as he always did, making fun of the professor and the girl that used to pick her nose subtly in class, but this time I didn't say much back. I was so focused on getting down my notes and paying close attention to the professor. I wasn't failing any of my classes, but I was fully capable of doing much better than I had been doing. I had one week left of the semester before winter break and then a new semester would begin. I needed to get my shit together.

After class, Tucker asked me if I was okay. I remember looking at him, opening my mouth to speak, and bursting into tears. Tucker could have walked away from the crazy, crying girl. Tucker could have patted me on the back and told me to man up. He could have stood there and stared at me – there were so many things that Tucker *could* have done since he was just my classmate and we had no relationship outside of that, but Tucker surprised me.

Tucker hugged me. He hugged the trashy, druggy, drunkard girl under watchful eyes, and he didn't stop there. After a few minutes of saying nothing and just holding me, he took me by the hand and led me to an empty lecture room. He sat me down in the very front seat and then he sat on the desk in front of me. With a little prodding, I spilled my heart out to him. I told him about my mom, gave him enough information about her boyfriends for him to form his own idea of what had happened to me. I told him that I had started drinking at the age of thirteen and drugs soon followed. I told him my life had been out of control since I was very young and I needed to get myself together. I needed to be a different person.

Again, Tucker could have put his hands up in defeat and walked away. He could have judged me. Instead, he stepped up to the plate and offered to help me beat down my demons. He was there for me every step of the way. With Kristy on the other side of the country, Tucker was all I had to keep me grounded and steered straight. He was more than a savior and supporter; he was a friend.

One night, a few months later, hc kissed me. He was a little drunk after a big frat party. I didn't think he meant it, but the next day when he was sober, he kissed me again, but I was afraid of corrupting him. I was afraid I would never be good enough for him. So, I told him we should only be friends. I soon regretted it when he started dating another girl, but after that, he became the template for all of the men I dated. They had to be good, safe guys, but I never found anyone like him. I discovered the hard way that I couldn't replicate him.

I was very fortunate to still have him as a friend all of these years later. He didn't live too far away from me, but he worked a lot and traveled often for his work, but since I left Larson, we always made sure that we were able to meet up at least once a month.

As I hurried to meet him for lunch, I tried not think about the fact that we were both single. No point in getting my hopes up.

“Sorry I’m late,” I said, hugging him.

“It’s fine,” he said. “I just got here.”

I threw my shoe bags and coat into the booth, and then slid in. Tucker waited until I was seated before he sat down. Nice guy, right?

“I ordered you a mudslide,” he said. “I ordered your lunch, too.”

“Thanks.” I smiled at him, but his return smile didn’t hold its usual warmth.

Tucker wasn’t a motor mouth or anything, but he was a great conversationalist. Even though he apparently already ordered, and he knew the menu by heart, he stared at it as if he had no idea what the place served. We always ate at the Cheesecake Factory. It was our go-to place.

“Okay, spill it,” I said after sipping my water.

“Spill what?” He looked up at me, but not for long before his eyes darted to some point beyond my head.

“Tucker,” I said his name softly.

He looked at me again and then sighed. “Alden Breck,” he said simply.

“What about him?” I deadpanned.

“Are you…with him? I’m still in shock that you somehow ended up anywhere near a rock star, let alone a superstar prick like Breck.”

“I’m still in shock, too,” I said dryly. “I’m not ‘with’ Alden. I know some of the gossips think so, but I’m not. We’re…friends.”

He looked at me dubiously.

“Tucker, would I lie to you?” I asked.

He sighed. “No, you wouldn’t.”

I simply omitted the fact that Alden had had his fingers inside of me twice within the last twenty-four hours.

“Are you really going on the road with him to all of those charity events?”

I took a long sip of my Mudslide. “Yes. Kristy and Alden both think it will be good for my career. Even my agent is all over that.”

"He's unpredictable, sometimes volatile, and he's a sex maniac," Tucker said pointedly. "How do you plan on handling all of that over a nine-week period?"

"I don't know," I said truthfully. "He is a handful, to be sure, but I'm hoping other things will distract him."

"You mean other women." Tucker smiled faintly.

"Definitely." I smiled back.

We were sitting in a secluded corner of the restaurant and my back was to the door. I looked up to say something to Tucker, but he was staring open-mouthed at something behind me. Confused, I turned my head to see what he was looking at.

What the hell?

Alden was ambling down the aisle with that walk of his, wearing a pair of dark sunglasses and a cap on his head. If no one was paying attention, they might have missed whom he was, but that damn swagger and cocky-ass smile gave him away to anyone who knew who Alden Breck was.

Without being invited to do so, Alden slid into the booth beside me, forcing me to move over the few inches between the shoes and me. He swung an arm around me, which I immediately attempted to shrug off, but it was like a fly stuck to flypaper.

"Hey, I'm Alden," he said, reaching across the table to shake Tucker's hand.

"What the hell are you doing here?" I asked him, knocking their hands apart with my own hand.

"I wanted to have some lunch," he said nonchalantly. "I'm hungry. Funny how we ended up at the same place, huh?" He flashed his sexy smile, but I just grimaced.

"You're a stalker and you know it," I growled, trying unsuccessfully again to knock his arm off me. "How did you find me?"

"I am not stalking you," Alden said innocently. "I just happened to be passing by the only DSW within ten miles of your apartment and I got hungry. After checking out the other five restaurants in this lot, I decided that I really, really wanted some fried macaroni and cheese and cheesecake. And I just happened to see you after wandering up and down a couple of aisles. Now, are you going to introduce me to your friend, Little Noa?"

"Little Noa?" Tucker looked at me with amusement and equal disdain.

"Tucker, Alden. Alden, Tucker," I said really fast. "Now that you have met my friend, you can go away."

"Why are you so uptight, Little One?" Alden asked, flipping his sunglasses up so he could peer at me. "I thought after this morning, you'd be a little less…uptight."

Tucker's eyes widened and then narrowed. I could practically read his mind. I had just said that I wasn't with Alden and now Alden was making it seem like I was. I shook my head at him, and then rolled my eyes in Alden's direction to imply that he was crazy.

"Made her come twice," Alden said, leaning across the table to speak confidentially to my friend.

Tucker's mouth fell open.

"Alden, stop," I said, shoving him.

Oh goodness. He thrust two fingers in the air obscenely. "Made her squirt the second time," Alden said proudly. "Her first time."

I angrily knocked his hand down and shoved him again.

"What?" Alden asked, actually looking confused by *my* behavior.

I ignored him and looked at Tucker pleadingly. He was eyeing Alden with a blank expression.

"Tucker, it's not what you think," I started, but he cut me off.

"The girl I'm dating swears that she can't squirt," Tucker said to Alden. "What's your trick?"

Oh. My. Shit.

Wait.

"What girl?" I demanded. "You didn't tell me you were dating anyone."

"I was going to tell you today," he said dismissively before turning back to Alden. "So, what's the trick?"

I stared at Tucker with an open mouth as Alden explained the proper way to make his female partner ejaculate. Tucker had just jumped all over my shit about my relationship with Alden, and then out of nowhere, he seemed to be crawling up the man's ass so that he could get his girlfriend off.

I rested my head in my hands on the table while the men talked. When my lunch was set on the table, Alden started eating it and then had the nerve to offer me some. I only glared at him before asking the waitress for a cranberry and vodka, extra vodka.

The next hour passed with Alden and Tucker yapping like old friends while I drank more than my fair share of alcoholic beverages. I didn't participate in the conversation, but the couple at the table across from us listened intently, and then Alden talked to them as if they were sitting at our table, too. When Tucker said he had to get back to work, the men exchanged numbers.

"We'll have to get together sometime," Alden said, shaking Tucker's hand.

"Absolutely," he grinned before finally remembering my presence. "Noa, see you at our next lunch. Have a safe trip." And he was gone.

"I was really worried about that guy," Alden said, taking a sip of my drink. "But I don't really have anything to worry about. He's cool. You may see him again, Little One."

"I hate you so much right now I can't see straight," I mumbled with my cheek smooshed against my hand as I leaned on one arm, looking bored.

"Baby, it's not me, it's the alcohol," Alden said. "Come on. Let's get you home." He started to pull me out of the booth with him.

"I drove here," I said. "And I'll drive myself home. You will go…somewhere else that isn't my place."

"Damn, you're cute," he said giving me a final tug.

I got to my feet and swayed. Alden helped me into my coat, grabbed my bags from DSW, and reached for my hand.

"I don't need your hand!" I snatched my hand away and stumbled slightly in the process. I held my head up high and started to walk as straight as I could down the aisle. One older woman looked at me disdainfully. I narrowed my eyes at her and gave her the finger as I passed by.

"Okay, enough of insulting old ladies," Alden said and steered me out of the restaurant.

Al and the limo waited at the curb. Alden ushered me into the backseat as half a dozen people started calling his name.

"What about my car?" I whined as I put my feet up on the seat, hoping to keep Alden at a distance.

"I'll have someone get it for you later," he said. He lifted my legs, moved over, and rested my legs on his lap.

"I hate you," I said as I let my head fall back against the seat.

"I missed you," he said simply. "So I joined you for lunch."

"Why didn't you just find some tramp to keep you company?"

"Why have a tramp when I can have you?" he asked, running his hands over my legs.

"You stole my friend," I complained.

"I didn't steal him. I borrowed him."

Alden's hands were moving higher and higher until he was rubbing me through my jeans.

"Stop," I said weakly.

"Why?" he asked huskily.

"Because I said so, and because you'll just get all horny and angry like it's my fault that you can't keep your hands to yourself."

"I said I wouldn't fuck you. That doesn't mean you can't jerk me off or give me head."

I tried to pull my legs out of his lap, but he held me there. So, I settled for punching him instead, except I did it with the wrong hand and then howled in pain.

"Poor silly baby," Alden said and kissed my fingers.

I wanted to yell at him some more, but the alcohol killed my energy. Within seconds, I had fallen asleep, and Alden still held my hand.

"Why are you so nervous?" Alden asked me as he helped me into the limo. "Haven't you ever been to a charity function like this?"

"Yes," I said. "But not with A-list celebrities. And you."

"Little One, there aren't going to be *that* many celebrities in Philly tonight. They like to wait for places like New York and L.A."

"Whatever. It makes me nervous."

"You weren't this nervous when you met me," he frowned.

"What was there to be nervous about?" I snorted. "I didn't like you. I barely like you now."

"You *love* me, Little Noa. The sooner you realize that, the happier I'll be."

"What? Do you mean the happier *I'll* be?" I gestured to myself.

"No, I meant me."

I rolled my eyes and looked out the window as we pulled away from my apartment building.

"Does my hair look okay?" I asked suddenly as I turned back to look at him.

"Everything about you is beautiful, Noa," he said soothingly.

"I don't feel beautiful," I said. "I feel frumpy and raggedy."

"You feel frumpy and raggedy in a three thousand dollar dress?" Alden asked doubtfully.

"Yes?" I half asked.

"You don't look frumpy and raggedy, Noa," he said. "Why don't you ever believe me when I tell you you're beautiful?"

"Because you would say anything to a girl to put your dick in her."

"Well, since we agreed that I am not to put my dick inside of you that does not apply to you."

I fidgeted with the little gold sequined purse in my hands. I was really, really nervous. What if Tom Cruise showed up? What if Will Smith showed up? It *is* Philly. I could get jiggy with Will Smith anytime, anywhere – if his wife allowed it. What if Bon Jovi showed up? What if the three remaining Boys II Men showed up? Oh, my goodness, what if Trisha was there?

"Noa," Alden said my name, snapping me out of my thoughts. "Hey," he said, putting a hand under my chin. "What are you worried about?"

"I'm not cut out for the A-list world! I'm just *me* and they are *them* and I can never be *them* because I'm just *me*!"

Alden cupped my face in his hands. "You are *amazing* and any of those bastards would be lucky to be anything like *you*. Okay?"

"Maybe?" I looked at him doubtfully as I bit down on my bottom lip.

Alden sighed and motioned for me to get up.

"What?" I asked him, confused.

He took my purse and threw it on the seat across from us. He hit the button for the privacy window and we were separated from Al up front. He reached down and started to push my dress up my legs.

"What are you doing?" I cried out, smacking at his hands.

"Noa," Alden said firmly, making me pause to look at him. "I'm going to make you relax, okay?"

"How?" I asked skeptically as he continued to push my dress up.

"Put your knees on the seat facing me," he commanded without answering me.

I looked at him with doubt, but his face was stone serious. Hesitantly, I got on my knees, facing him, and he pushed my dress up over my thighs. He moved to the center of the seat and simultaneously positioned me on his lap so that I was straddling him. My eyes were wide as he pushed my cape off my shoulders and tossed it on the seat beside him.

"What are you doing?" I whispered and swallowed hard. I had my hands on his chest and my god did I like the muscles under my hands.

"I'm going to make you relax," he said again in a husky voice.

He spread his legs, which made my own open wide. He pushed his hand between our bodies. I inhaled sharply when I felt knuckles drag over my clit. He pushed my panties aside and pushed two fingers into me. His thumb found my clit and I almost collapsed.

"You just need to relax, Little One," he breathed on my neck.

As Alden's fingers pumped in and out of me and his thumb caressed my clit, his other hand pulled the straps of my nude colored dress down my arms.

"Take your arms out of the dress," he whispered hoarsely.

With my brain muddled with lust, I obeyed and slipped my arms out of the dress. Alden pulled it down, setting my breasts free, and my goodness, right at level with his mouth. Looking up into my eyes, the tip of his tongue slowly went over one of my nipples. I moaned louder and grinded my hips lightly on his fingers. He then used the flat part of his tongue to lick my nipple and my fingers curled in the lapels of his tux. Alden's hand smoothed up my bare back and then pressed me forward. I wrapped my arms around his neck as he pulled a nipple into his mouth.

We were locked into place, my arms around his neck, my tit pressed into his mouth and his fingers pressing into my core. I rocked my hips as he fingered me, and ran my fingers through his hair as he sucked and nibbled on my rock hard nipple.

"Alden," I breathed as I felt my orgasm building. "Please…" I begged.

He moaned and switched to my other breast as his fingers moved faster and harder inside of me.

"Oh my god…" I groaned. "Make me come."

His hand tangled in my hair. He released my breast and pulled me down so he could sink his teeth into my neck just under my ear. I came hard, groaning out his name as my hips rocked on his hand.

As my orgasm died down, Alden left kisses along my neck and shoulder until my body stilled. Without a word, he pulled his fingers out of me and helped me slip the dress back into place. He took the cape from the seat and wrapped it around my shoulders. Carefully, I rose in a half-standing position as he fixed my dress. I sat down beside him and looked out the window at the passing cars' lights. Alden ran his fingers through my hair and arranged it on my shoulders as it was before we started.

We didn't speak again before arriving at the gala. Alden's plan worked. I was no longer worried about the ball. I had a whole new worry: Alden Breck was getting under my skin.

***

He was right. There weren't that many A-listers there. A small handful really, and the rest were city and state officials from Philadelphia and a few from the surrounding states. There was also a fairly large amount of young people. They paid thousands of dollars to get in the door to mingle with Friction, the other two bands, and the few celebrities. From the moment we walked into the ballroom, women shamelessly threw themselves at Alden, and Alden being Alden, shamelessly flirted with them. It didn't seem to matter to him or the women that I was on his arm.

I was introduced to important and famous people. I smiled, shook hands, accepted kisses to the cheek, and answered questions as best I could. I tried to pretend I cared enough to participate in the conversations, but I wasn't really focused on the people at the party. My mind was in the limo when Alden was gently kissing my neck and shoulder.

Sex and sexual acts aren't always…intimate. Sometimes they're just mechanical, a need that needs fulfilling, and doesn't have to include lust or love or a general giving a shit. Alden could have thrown me off him when he was done and made some cocky comment about his skills, but he didn't. He kissed my skin tenderly and helped me get myself together. We were both quiet after that, but for him, that was unusual. As he held my hand at the gala, his thumb lightly stroked over my knuckles; that was definitely intimate.

As we made our way across the ballroom to our assigned table near the front, I decided right then that I needed to find a boyfriend. If I was beginning to think of Alden as 'intimate' after only a week in his presence, I really needed a man. It had been a year since Larson. I was ready to leave that part of my life in the past and move on.

"Hey, Face Plant," Hash, the drummer, called to me as we approached him and the doctor, Greg.

"Hello, Hash, Greg," I said, smiling.

Hash openly ogled me, his eyes lingering at the low neckline of my dress. "Well, don't you look pretty," he said approvingly.

"If you don't stop staring at her tits I'm going to put my fist into your mouth," Alden warned Hash.

"If you don't want anyone to admire your toys, you shouldn't bring them out to play, Breck," Hash said and walked away laughing.

Great. Even Hash thought I was a shiny new toy.

"How are you feeling, Noa?" Greg asked.

"Sore, but getting a little better," I assured him. "Thank you for your help that night. I really do appreciate it."

"I didn't help you enough if you're stuck here with Alden," Greg muttered.

"She *loves* me," Alden snorted.

"I really don't," I said to Greg. "If I do not hate him with every bone in my body, I am only tolerating him. Right now we are in a tolerant phase, but that can change moment to moment."

Greg chuckled at first, but my straight face told him I wasn't kidding.

"Very funny," Alden said. "I have to go make sure everything is running on schedule. I'll be back shortly. Stick with Greg. He's the only one I trust not to eye fuck you, or literally fuck you."

"And here's the hate part," I muttered, taking the seat in front of my place card.

Greg sat down beside me and gave me an understanding smile. "He's hard to handle sometimes."

"Sometimes?" I rolled my eyes. "I would say that twenty-three out of twenty-four hours in any given day I feel like body slamming him. I can't believe I agreed to do nine weeks of this."

"I'm actually surprised that he asked you," Greg said as he looked at me with curiosity. "This is the fifth year that we've done this and this is the first year that Alden has asked someone to stay with him the entire time."

"Let me guess," I said sourly. "He picks up some whore bag in each city."

Greg nodded and said, "Less mess that way."

"Well, there won't be any mess here, Greg. I am not sleeping with that sack of STDs."

He scratched his head as he looked at me. He looked like he wanted to say something but was hesitant.

"What?" I pushed.

"Well…I mean, I guess I'm more worried about the fact that you're *not* sleeping with him. That's just…not like Alden. If he falls in love with you, I'm not sure—"

"Whoa!" I said, putting my hands up. "Whoa…there is no *love* here. Alden Breck is incapable of falling in love – that would mean monogamy and we both know that Alden Breck doesn't do monogamous relationships. Less mess, right? So I'm not like the other girls? Can't a guy and a girl just be friends?"

"Not if that guy is Alden," Greg said flatly.

I frowned. I felt like Greg was trying to dissuade me from going.

"Maybe I shouldn't go then," I said, trying not to sound putout.

Greg's eyes widened and then softened as he smiled. "No, no, please don't misunderstand, Noa. I want you to go, and moreover, Alden wants you to go. I've known him for many years and I've never seen him this way. I guess I'm just a little worried because it's only been a week and he is very taken with you. I'm afraid he's going to rush into something and get hurt, or hurt you."

"I won't be hurt because I won't be rushing into anything with him," I said firmly. "He just likes me because I hate him and Alden can't fathom that anyone could possibly dislike him."

Greg laughed warmly. "Okay, maybe that's it after all." He held up his hands in defeat. "I promise I won't mention it again."

"I've been meaning to ask you," I said. "Why the hell is a doctor on tour with Friction?"

"Alden doesn't like hospitals," he said with a shrug, as if that explained it all. When I simply raised an eyebrow, he continued. "Alden fights – a lot. I stitch him up or bandage whatever needs bandaging, but when I first came on tour with the band, it was to keep an eye on Hash. He was going through withdrawals and the withdrawal symptoms were a bitch. I really liked being with the guys and they really liked having me around, so I became a permanent fixture. I do physicals and prescribe meds and all of that when they're sick. "

"I don't think there's enough medicine in the world to cure Alden of his big head," I said with a sigh as I watched him amble across the room toward us. Even in a tux and a bow tie, he looked badass.

"Thanks for not fucking my date," Alden said, sitting down and slinking an arm across my shoulders.

"No problem," Greg said. "But next time, I can't make any promises."

Soon, the table began to fill up with the other members of the band and their companions if they had any. Hash had some trampy blonde with him who kept making eyes at Alden. James didn't have a date, but was married with a kid on the way. His wife was at their family home in L.A.

The first forty minutes of the event consisted of a lot of boring speeches by the mayor and other important people in the area while we ate dinner. When Alden wasn't eating, his arm was across the back of my seat and his thumb caressed my bare shoulders. The first few times he did it, I had given him a dirty look, but this was Alden. He was going to do it anyway. After a while, I was so used to it that when he stopped, I actually missed his touch. When I realized that I was missing his touch, however, I wanted to drown myself in my glass of wine.

The first performer was a pop diva, a young woman who had won one of those televised talent competitions. I didn't really follow her career, but I did like a few of her songs. When she played one of her slow songs, Alden looked at me with his cocky expression.

"Would you like to dance with the sexiest, most talented fucker in the room?" he asked.

"Why, yes." I smiled. "Yes, I would."

I turned away from Alden and looked at James across the table. "J, will you dance with me?"

The table erupted into noisy laughter and taunting as I got up and took James's arm. I looked back at Alden, who looked so angry I swore I saw steam coming out of his ears. He was snapping at his friends and glowering at James and me.

"You must really enjoy insulting his ego," James said with a big grin as he put his hand on my waist.

"It's entirely too big," I said haughtily. "He needs to be knocked down a peg or two."

"He's going to kick my ass for dancing with you," he said. "But it's worth it. The look on his face was priceless."

"How can you stand him?" I asked. "He's such an asshole sometimes."

James shrugged as he settled his blue eyes on me. "He's the biggest asshole I know, but he's the biggest asshole I know with the biggest heart. So," he said slowly, "you should be very careful with it."

I couldn't help the burst of laughter that bubbled through my lips. "That's just ridiculous. Alden barely means anything to me and he knows it. Trust me. It's not like that."

James looked at me thoughtfully. "If that's the case, why did you agree to go with him?"

"My friends and agent think the experience will help my career," I said, unashamed.

He sighed and looked away for a moment. When he looked back, he was all seriousness.

"It's none of my business, but that asshole is one of my best friends. You are different to him."

"It's only been a week," I objected.

"I don't care how long it's been," he pushed forward. "You're different. Maybe at first, you were just a challenge because of the way you reacted to him that first night, but now it is more than that. Alden doesn't…keep girls around, and he's been with you just about every day this week."

"What about Trisha?" I found myself asking before I could think about it.

"She is in love with him," James said with a sigh. "He cares about her, but he doesn't want her like that, but that doesn't keep her from repeatedly trying. She'd rather get hurt ten times over for even the smallest glimmer of hope that he may want her back someday."

"That's kind of sad," I said, frowning.

"It is, and I don't want to see Alden reduced to that, Noa. Ever."

"So…" I bit my bottom lip. "Maybe I should back out of going on the road with you guys?"

"No." He shook his head. "No, don't do that. Then he'll be impossible."

"You mean he's not now?" I smiled a little.

James chuckled. "He'll be even more impossible. Just be careful. Don't fuck with his head."

"I'm really not that kind of girl."

"Don't accidentally find yourself being that kind of girl," he warned and then his eyes flickered to something behind me. "Oh, he is *pissed*."

I looked over my shoulder and saw Alden storming over to us. He roughly grabbed my arm and shoved James away.

"You have a girl to dance with, fucker," Alden growled, forcing me into a slow dance stance with him.

"Stop being a fucking baby," James said, smacking Alden in the back of the head. Then he leaned in close to us and said, "By the way, you smell fucking delicious, Noa."

He quickly moved out of the way and Alden's fist hit the air next to his head. He walked away chuckling.

"That was mean," I said.

"What you did was meaner," he objected as he scowled down at me.

"You asked me a question and I answered. You asked me if I wanted to dance with the sexiest, most talented fucker and I did just that."

"You are a wicked little one, aren't you?" He suddenly smiled. "I am so going to punish you later."

I snorted. "I'm feeling punished *now*."

Sunday morning, Alden stood in my kitchen. He was leaning against my counter, reading the newspaper and drinking a glass of orange juice. He was only wearing a towel and his body was still moist from his shower. I had stopped short as I entered, gawking at his muscular, inked body. I tried to keep my eyes from looking down at his towel, but I just couldn't stop and—

Holy fucking shit.

That thing was barely contained under the one hundred percent Egyptian cotton towel. One false move and I'd be playing peek-a-boo with Alden's one-eyed monster.

"Umm…" I said and cleared my throat. "Maybe you should put some clothes on."

"If I did that, you'd have nothing to stare at," he said with a sly smile without looking up from the paper.

"I wasn't staring," I said quickly and then walked into my own damn kitchen as if it didn't bother me that he was standing in there more than half-naked.

"Okay, then. Prolonged looking."

"Shut up, Alden," I snapped.

"Better watch that mouth," he said, suddenly behind me and talking in my ear. "I'll have to punish you again, but then…you might like that."

I elbowed him in his hard gut, but he didn't seem to notice as he chuckled and then planted a kiss on my neck that left me trying hard not to drop my coffee.

After we had returned from the gala, Alden took me out of my dress. He kissed my back as he released the zipper, and he left a trail of kisses on each shoulder while he pulled the straps down my arms. I had objected and called him names, but it didn't count much since I was panting. By the time the dress and my undergarments were pooled on the floor, my snarls and jabs at his manhood turned into begging for release as his fingers manipulated my clit and nipples. Every time I got close, he would pull back just enough to keep me on edge. He did this repeatedly for a half hour until I was almost sobbing, begging for an orgasm.

"Now," he had murmured, his lips moving against my sex. "Who was the sexiest, most talented man at the party?"

"You!" I had cried, trying to press his head down so I could fuck his face.

"That's a good girl." He grinned. "I guess I can let you come now."

Oh my word, did I come. Alden worked his magic and had me gushing all over the place.

Now, just the idea of him making me come like that again sent a small ripple of want through my body and to my core. Ignoring the ripples and whatnot, I started to leave the kitchen with my cup of coffee, but Alden grabbed a fistful of the back of my shirt and gently tugged me backward.

"Alden," I huffed as he pulled my back against his bare chest.

"Look, Little One," he said, once he had me enclosed in his arms with the paper in front of me. "We made the paper together."

"Again?" I sighed. Since our first outing, my face had made it into a couple of the tabloids, but more than that, there were pictures of me with Alden, and me alone all over the internet. It made me uncomfortable because I was sure someone somewhere was digging into my past, and I wasn't sure how Larson would react to it. I hadn't heard from him in months, but could my arrangement with Alden bring him out of the woodwork?

I finally focused on the picture in the paper. It was a color picture of Alden and me on the dance floor. His arms were around my waist and my hands were on his shoulders. I was smiling up at him and he had a big grin on his face. I remembered the moment, because he had just told me a stupid joke, one of those jokes that were *so* stupid that you couldn't help but to laugh.

"That's a nice picture," I admitted quietly. I don't know why, but looking at the picture while in Alden's arms put me on edge.

"I haven't been able to take my eyes off it," he said quietly. "Until you walked into the room anyway." He kissed the top of my head. "Looking at this, one could assume we were a happy couple."

Oh! Stupid heart – why must you beat so hard and fast?

I swallowed hard and forced myself to look away from the photo. "I need to go pack for New York," I said lightly.

Alden was quiet for a moment, but then he kissed my head again before releasing me.

"We're not leaving until about two," he said, following me out of the room. "You have plenty of time to pack."

"Yeah, but I need time to clean before I go. It's getting a little raunchy in here. You can go…do whatever you need to do so you're not in my way. I'm sure there is some hussy somewhere in need of a sea serpent."

"I'll help you clean," Alden said as he pulled clothes out of his bag on my bed.

I laughed. "When was the last time you cleaned something? Besides your dick – I'm assuming you clean it."

A big sexy grin appeared on his face and he gestured lewdly at me, making the sea serpent…*bounce.*

Good god.

"You want to do an investigation and find out?" he asked.

"Ewww," I said, screwing up my face.

"For your information, Little One…I clean. Sometimes."

"Like when the maid is on vacation?" I asked, quirking an eyebrow.

He looked at me nonchalantly. "Yes. When the maid is on vacation."

I snickered. "I'd love to see you scrubbing a toilet, but you'll just be in my way."

"No, I want to help," he said, looking sincere.

I studied him for a moment. I could get him to reach all of the high places I rarely got to dust, and it *would* be amusing to watch him scrubbing a toilet. The great Alden Breck – writes, produces, and plays music, does charity work when he's not boning desperate women, and scrubs toilets. Hell yes.

"Okay then, Mr. Breck." I smiled at him from across the bed. "I will assign you a few tasks."

He winked a hazel eye at me and smiled. "Thank you, ma'am."

And then he dropped his towel.

Fuck.

I spun around just as the monster came loose. I didn't get a very good look at it; I only saw the enormity of it and *holy cow*!

Fortunately, I really did have to turn my back on him while I went into the bathroom closet to check the status of my cleaning supplies. I busied myself with this task a little longer than necessary until I was sure that the sex god with the tattoos and piercings was dressed.

I grabbed an armful of cleaners and closed the closet door. When I did, Alden was standing there – dressed. I squealed and smacked him.

"Stop sneaking up on me!"

He chuckled and then leaned in the bathroom doorway, displaying his powerful forearms as he crossed his arms.

"What tasks have you for me, Miss Eddington?" he asked.

I put the cleaners down on the sink and then handed him the toilet bowl cleaner.

"I want you to clean the toilet," I said with as serious of an expression as I could muster.

"With what?" he asked.

I pointed to the toilet brush behind the toilet. He looked at it for a moment before plucking it out of its holder.

"This is used for cleaning the toilet?" he asked and then suddenly pointed it at me. I shrieked and jumped back. "I thought it was used for brushing hair. Come here, let me brush your hair."

He teased me, making me laugh and shriek as he pointed the thing at me. Finally, he backed off and I gave him a list of shit to do, which was just hilarious. I was giving Alden Breck a list of common house chores to do.

We both got to work a few minutes later. I plugged my iPod into the stereo in the living room and blasted the music. After about a half hour, while I was mopping the kitchen floor, Alden came up behind me and scared the shit out of me again when he put his hands on my waist.

"I haven't heard any Friction off that thing yet," he said with a raised eyebrow.

"Friction? Who's that?" I asked. When he gave me a murderous look, I dropped the mop and ran away, but Alden caught me around the waist, careful not to hurt my ribs.

"If you don't get some of my music on that iPod right now, I'm going to spank your ass," he growled in my ear.

"Okay, okay," I breathed as I felt his breath on my neck.

"Hop to it, Little One," he said, smacking my ass once and giving me a gentle shove in the direction of the stereo.

I walked over to the stereo and stopped a Justin Timberlake song. Damn, I really liked that song, too. I picked up the iPod, made sure it was locked and then I started to rub it between my hands.

"Babe, what the hell are you doing?" Alden asked.

"Putting some *friction* on my iPod," I said, trying not to laugh.

"Your ass is mine," Alden said as he began stalking toward me.

I ran away, even though it hurt to run at all, but I was having fun, and so was Alden, and it actually didn't involve a sexual act. Eventually, we did get back to the cleaning, this time while listening to Friction on Alden's iPod.

***

I loved Alden's New York apartment. Now that he wasn't being a cold-hearted bastard, the place felt warm and homey and I couldn't get enough of staring out of the large windows at the city below us.

"Do you like it?" Alden asked as he stepped up beside me and handed me a glass of wine.

"I do." I smiled. "Your whole apartment is rather awesome, but I really love this view."

"I'll give you a key," he said, leaning against the glass to watch me watch the city. "You can come here whenever you like – when you're not already with me, of course."

I snorted. "I'm 'with you' for nine weeks, Alden. Then you'll go your way and I'll go mine."

"I've decided that I want you in L.A. with me while we're writing and recording." His expression was serious, but I couldn't help but to think he was joking.

"You've decided?" I laughed. "Funny. Thanks, but no."

I sipped my wine as Alden's eyes watched me with calculation. He must have been off his nut if he thought I was going to stay with him in L.A. for however long it took them to put an album together. Seriously. I honestly didn't know how I was going to get through all of the charity events and the other appearances in between with his cocky self.

It didn't matter that he gave me the best orgasms of my life. Or that he sometimes made me laugh so hard that I snorted. Or that he really was sexy – though I'd never tell *him* that. No way. And it didn't matter that under his very, very thick, cocky exterior he was actually very sweet and compassionate, especially where his younger brother was concerned. It *definitely* didn't matter that he was actually kinda nice to cuddle up to. None of that really mattered. It wasn't enough to make me want to spend any additional time with him. Period.

"I think you'll change your mind," Alden said with a small, but actually kinda sweet smile that made my toes wiggle.

"What makes you think so?" I asked with doubt.

"You're going to fall in love with me," he said with absolute confidence. Total, unshakeable confidence.

I stared blankly at him for a moment. "Are you on drugs?" I asked seriously.

He had to be on drugs. Because seriously, what he said was just plain absurd.

"I don't do that shit," he said, clearly offended. "You think just because I'm an awesome rock star with tattoos and piercings that I'm on drugs?"

"I'm not that shallow," I said, rolling my eyes. "I'm simply looking for a reasonable explanation for your delusions."

"There is your first problem, Little One," he said and then caught my chin with his finger. My goodness he smelled good.

"What is my first problem?" I asked in a bored tone.

"I'm not delusional," he said with that same pure confidence. "You're going to fall in love with me, and when you do, I will have no qualms telling you I told you so."

I batted his hand away from me, gave him a contemptuous look, and said, "You're crazy. Definitely delusional, and don't touch me."

In my back pocket, my phone vibrated and then burst into the song "U Can't Touch This" by MC Hammer.

"Hey," I said to Kristy when I answered. "Aren't you on your honeymoon? Why are you calling me?"

"Nice to hear your voice, too, bitch," Kristy chuckled. "I just wanted to see how things went last night at the gala, and how things are going with Alden."

"Umm," I said, biting my lip. I looked at Alden, who was looking at me. "Kris, let me call you back in a few minutes."

She made a sound of exasperation. "I've spoken to you *once* since you left here."

"I'll call you right back," I promised and ended the call amidst more objections. "I'm going for a walk so I can talk to Kristy," I said to Alden.

He raised an eyebrow. "You can't talk to Kristy in here?"

"I would like some *privacy* speaking to Kristy," I explained impatiently.

"I can give you privacy," he said.

Right. Doubtful.

I handed him my wine, turned away from him, and headed toward the door. "I'll be back soon."

"You would rather go all the way downstairs and all the way outside than just lock yourself in the bedroom?" Alden asked incredulously as he followed close behind me.

"Yep." I grabbed my coat out of the closet by the door.

"Fine, fine," he relented with a sourpuss face and helped me pull on my coat. "I'll give you fifteen minutes, and then I'm coming after you."

"It's going to take me at least five minutes just to get out of the building," I objected.

"Fine. Twenty minutes," he said firmly as I opened the door. "Twenty minutes, Little Noa, and then I'm coming for you."

"Sounds kinky," I said and laughed at the surprised look that came over his face. Then I regretted saying it because it just opened more doors for Alden, of course.

"If you want me to come for you, sweetheart, all you have to do is ask," he said in a tone of voice that implied wickedly delicious and dirty things.

Oh my freakin' goodness.

"I'll be back," I murmured and scurried to the elevator.

"So, what's happening?" Kristy asked when I called her back.

"You tell me," I snapped. "You seem to have enough confabs with Alden."

"First of all, who says 'confabs'? Don't lure your significant vocabulary over me!" Kristy flashed. "Unlike you, Alden has been taking the time to call me once in a while, but he mostly just asks questions."

"Why are you discussing my personal life with him?" I asked angrily as I crossed the street to get to Central Park. "Just because he's your favorite musician doesn't mean that you can tell him all of *my* secrets."

"I don't tell him *every*thing! But for the record, I think he really likes you – and you're vagina, apparently."

I stopped short, making angry New Yorkers crash into me, but I ignored them as I stomped my foot and let out an angry, growly scream. Kristy seemed undeterred by my little tantrum.

"I'm kind of upset that I had to hear it from him and not you," she muttered, but then continued in an excited tone. "Noa, you had some of the most skilled fingers in the music industry *inside your vagina*! If I didn't just get married, I totally would have tried to get those masterful fingers to slide inside me."

I wanted to throw my phone down on the sidewalk and jump on it. A lot. Or toss it into the street and let a cab run it over. Or hand it to the leering weirdo next to me.

"Why does he feel the need to let the world know that he can make me squirt!" I yelled, gaining very few looks from the people around me. It was New York, after all. They didn't really care if I could squirt.

"Wait, he made you squirt? For real?" Kristy shouted it. "Hon, Alden made Noa *squirt*!"

Okay. Now I wanted to lay *myself* on the ground and have someone jump up and down on me.

Shit. That's how I got into this situation in the first place.

"Am I no longer allotted any privacy?" I snarled to my closest friend.

"It's just Trent," Kristy said dismissively. "I can't believe you're dating Alden Breck. This is something we used to dream about as young girls and it's actually happening to you!"

Kristy's jubilant attitude was making me want to puke.

"Let's get a few things straight," I said icily, "I am *not* dating Alden. I barely even *like* Alden! He's a fucking peacock, always strutting around and thinking he's so damn desirable! But he's not! I don't desire him, okay? So get that shit out of your head and *stop* talking to him about *me*!"

"You think I'm a peacock?" Alden's voice startled me.

I spun around. He had popped on some sunglasses – even though it was dusk – but otherwise didn't bother to try to hide who he was. And he was standing there with his hands on his hips, grinning.

Fucking peacock.

I let out an exasperated sigh and moved away from him.

"Kristy, I meant what I said," I warned.

"Calm down," she said in a bored tone. "You're overreacting. Listen, I gotta go. I'm on my honeymoon after all."

"Yeah, okay," I said bitterly. I mean, hadn't I mentioned that to her when she first called me?

"I'll call you when I get home. Have fun, Noa. Millions of other girls across the globe would give their lives to be in your shoes. Appreciate what you've got going for you right now."

"Any one of those millions of girls can have my shoes without forfeiting a life," I snapped and ended the call.

I turned around to find Alden. A few women were standing around him – where the hell they had come from, I didn't know. Maybe they sprouted out of the ground. They were grinning, giggling, and giving him "come fuck me" eyes as they touched him and allowed him to touch them. I was a little satisfied that I was right about him being a peacock. As I approached, one of the women completely lost her damn mind and *launched* herself into Alden's arms. With impressive quickness, she wrapped her legs around his waist and pulled at his head in an attempt to kiss him. To my surprise, Alden resisted as he tried to peel the girl off him. She was undeterred as she clung to him and begged him to kiss her. Finally, Alden was able to push her off. Without a second look at her, he moved toward me, leaving the poor woman pouting with her friends.

"Looks like you just plucked away a definite lay," I said as we made a wide berth around the women.

"I know I can be an asshole, but even I am not *that* big of an asshole. I will never try to pick up another woman when you're with me, I promise."

I glanced up at his face when I heard the sincerity in his voice.

"You really don't have to keep that promise. You don't owe me anything and you're not my boyfriend."

"It's disrespectful to you. I may be crass and do things to piss you off, but *that* is over the top, even for me. I want you to enjoy your time with me, not worry about what skank I will pick up next."

I was quiet for a long time. I didn't think I had ever heard Alden sound so sincere before. It almost seemed that he was even a bit disgusted with himself. When he said "skank," it sounded very bitter.

In the elevator, I again glanced up at him. His eyebrows were lowered, his mouth was clamped shut – for a change – and he looked straight ahead with a distant look in his eyes. I actually felt bad for him, despite my irritation with him and Kristy. I felt the ice melt a little. After all, I really was being a bit of a hypocrite. Before Tucker rescued me, there were things I did that I will never be proud of.

"Dinner came while you were in the park," he said in a low, lifeless tone as the doors slid open on his floor.

"Great," I said, trying to sound light. "I could eat a whole moose, I'm so hungry."

His face changed. Just like that. I was surprised by how much better I felt when it did. He looked down at me with amusement, a smile playing on his lips.

"A moose?" he asked, unlocking the door.

I stepped in ahead of him and said, "Yes, a moose."

"Do you eat moose often?" he teased.

"Only when I'm very hungry," I answered with a giggle.

He grinned and shook his head before kissing my forehead. It was the chastest thing he had ever done with those lips on my body, yet my insides hummed with deep satisfaction.

After dinner, I changed into a sweatshirt and a pair of shorts and pushed my feet into my fuzzy slippers. I sat down at the dining room table with my laptop, ready to get some work done. Alden sat on the couch in the living room, softly strumming on a guitar and humming every now and then. I watched him surreptitiously, watching his skilled fingers move over the strings and the look of peace on his face. Despite the small bite of the winter night in the apartment, he was shirtless with a pair of flannel lounge pants that hung low on his hips. His hair was a little messy and he had a bit of scruff on his jaw and chin. I couldn't deny how beautiful he looked. He really was breathtaking like this.

Doh! I just called Alden breathtaking.

Just pay attention to your work! Ignore the peacock on the couch!

Except, he's totally not looking like a peacock right now. He really is breathtaking.

"Can you teach me how to play a guitar?" someone asked Alden. It took a moment to realize that person was me. *Ah well. May as well learn something while I'm with him.*

Alden looked at me skeptically. "Wouldn't you rather someone from a band you actually like teach you?"

"Don't be a girl about it," I teased. "I don't like you much but I've never denied your musical talent."

“Fair enough,” he said and then waved me over. “Come over here.”

I really should have impressed upon him the fact that I didn't mean he needed to teach me right then, only that I wanted to learn sometime in the future, but his eyes were bright and eager. I almost batted him down for fun.

Except, I wasn't that mean. So I got up and went across the room to sit beside him, but he flipped the guitar up, leaned back, and gestured for me to sit between his legs on the couch. I eyed him suspiciously.

"This is my lesson, Little One," he said with a smile. "Take it or leave it."

"Fine," I sighed.

I settled down between Alden's strong legs. He scooted forward until the front of his body was pressed against the back of mine. He took my left hand gently into his and put it on the neck of the guitar. His fingers lingered on mine for a moment before he took my right hand and put it on the body of the guitar.

"Okay, ready?" he asked. His breath was warm and silky on the side of my face.

"Yes," I whispered.

Over the next half hour, Alden gave me a very simplified guitar lesson. He made fun of me when I messed up, which was often, making me laugh and giggle. He praised me when I did well, which was not very often, and he followed up those praises with a quick kiss to my cheek. His hands only stopped touching me when he was playing. Gentle, humble, sweet touches that made my skin burst with goose bumps. His fingers trailed over my arms as I struggled to play a few notes, or he would put his hands over mine, trying to guide me.

"I give up," I sighed, dropping my hands to my lap. "I'm not coordinated enough to play an instrument."

"You're not going to get it in one night, Little One," Alden said and landed a kiss on my neck. "I mean, I did, but no one is as awesome as me."

I gently elbowed him in the ribs, making him chuckle.

"Okay, Little Noa, pick a song for me to serenade you with."

I hesitated. I really needed to get back to work, but Alden was being so...human, and I was enjoying his company. It was possible that he was slipping drugs into my food and drink all day so that I would think he was actually a decent person and not an obnoxious, slutty, dickhead.

But if this was what Alden was like with me on drugs, I was okay with becoming an addict. I actually more than kind of liked him and his sedated, yet playful manner, and I would be such a lying bitch if I told you that sitting tucked between his legs and in his arms wasn't the most comfortable seat in the city, and I had no real desire to move. That alone was amazing, considering he was the first man that I allowed to touch me since leaving Larson, and I was no longer afraid. Alden had a way of making me forget about my fear, my anxiety, and my unhappy past.

Oh, screw it. The writing can wait.

"How about…'Crash Into Me,'" I suggested. I angled myself so that I could look at his face.

"By Dave Matthews Band?" he asked with a questioning expression that I regretfully found adorable. His brow was pulled down between his hazel eyes. He looked like a little boy wondering if the moon really had cheese on it.

"Yes." I smiled softly. "Unless you don't think you're uh…skillful enough for that."

With his brow still pulled down, he narrowed his eyes at me. "One day your mouth is going to get you spanked."

"You wouldn't dare put me over your knee while I'm injured," I said innocently. I fluttered my lashes for effect.

Something like surprise passed over his face, making his mouth drop open a bit as his eyes widened, sending his brow up. Then his eyes suddenly looked like they were barely containing a fire from within. It made me squirm a bit, but I saw something else in those eyes, too, though I wasn't able to put my finger on it just yet.

"You're such a fucking tease," he growled and then looked down at his guitar.

I watched as his fingers began to strum the opening notes of the song. Alden's fingers moved gracefully over the strings as he began to sing the sensuous song. His voice was soft, sensual, and downright arousing. When he started the chorus, he pressed his body into mine, in essence, crashing into me. I pressed back without a thought, my body moving on its own. As he played, I felt the muscles in his chest flex against my back, and then the muscles in his arms flexed against my arms. His hands looked strong and confident as they found every chord exactly right. I felt the soft rumbling of his chest as he sang the song just as easily as if he had been the one to create it himself.

Amazed, and a little fucked up in the head, I watched as Alden became one with the guitar and the music. As close as we were, I felt like I was one with Alden. I felt like he *was* the music, surrounding me, swathing me…cocooning me. I felt it on my skin, under my skin, in my flesh, through my bones, into my organs, and into my soul. I tilted my head back onto his shoulder, rested my hands on his rock hard thighs, and allowed myself to float away in his capable hands and voice. I felt caressed, through and through.

When the last chord was struck, Alden carefully put the guitar down on the side of the couch, but moved purposely and quickly when he tilted my head to the side. He started to kiss my neck while he simultaneously pulled my shirt up to my belly and pushed his hand under the cotton of my shorts and panties. My body felt extra sensitive to his touch. Even his other hand running up and down my arm was sending little shockwaves of pleasure through my body and to my core.

As his fingers circled my clit, he cupped my chin possessively in his other hand.

"Hearing me sing to you made you all hot for me, Little Noa," he rasped into my ear before pulling the lobe between his teeth for a quick bite. "Tell me what it did to you."

I couldn't answer with words, only with moans and groans as I pushed my hips up against his fingers.

"Tell me what it did to you," he commanded more harshly. "Or I'll stop."

"Umm…" I moaned.

"Did it make your nipples hard?" he asked and released my chin to savagely squeeze a breast.

I yelped and nodded arduously.

"Say it," he growled, gripping my chin again. "Say it now."

"It made my nipples hard," I murmured and licked my lips.

"What else did it to you, Little One?"

I cried out as he lightly plucked my clit.

"Say it or you don't get to come," he warned.

Oh my motherfuggin' word.

"You made me wet," I said breathlessly as I writhed between his legs.

"*What* made you wet, baby?" Alden whispered. "Is it just the song? Hmm? Or was it *me* singing the song?"

"You singing the song," I managed between moans.

"Good girl," he murmured and kissed my neck. "I'll let you come now."

Without hesitation, Alden pushed his two middle fingers into my heat and released my face. He put his hand under my shirt and twirled my nipples between his fingers.

"Ride my fingers, Noa," he demanded.

Holy shiz!

I eased up until I felt only the tips of his fingers before slamming down on his hand.

"Yeah," he groaned in my ear. "Ride em' baby."

I rose and fell on Alden's hand as his mouth assailed my neck and his other hand tugged and squeezed my nipples. As I screwed his fingers, I felt his erection sliding over my ass. I felt powerful knowing how hard I made him, but my power was without control. Alden had complete control over me, and if he pulled that monster out of his pants and told me to ride it, I was afraid that I wouldn't have been able to say no. I wouldn't have been able to speak at all because I would be too busy trying to find a way to make that thing fit inside of me. It was that image in my head that threw me over the edge.

"Alden!" I cried out as I grinded my orgasm out.

"Noa," he growled in my ear as his skilled fingers helped me coast through my climax.

I settled again between Alden's legs and rested my head on his shoulder as my body began to recover. He slowly pulled his hand out of my shorts; his other hand caressed my belly as his kisses on my neck became gentle and sweet. When Alden's hand accidentally slipped over my ribcage, I gasped.

"Shit, I'm sorry," he said, immediately removing his hand. "I keep forgetting you're hurt."

"It's fine," I said and slowly started to stand up on wobbly knees.

"Where are you going?" he asked, gently tugging me back down. He planted his palms on my thighs to keep me in place.

"To take something for the pain that won't knock me out, and then I have to actually work."

The truth was that I needed to get away from Alden, because that whole scene did something to me. When he was trying to teach me to play, it was cute and comfortable, and there was nothing awkward between us. While he serenaded me, I felt such powerful emotions emanating off him and I didn't want it to end. I could live with feeling his body wrapped around mine as he strummed his guitar and sang in his silky voice for a very, very long time.

I needed to get away from him because I did not trust myself with him. That music was doing stupid things with my brain.

And my heart.

Alden was quiet for a few moments after I gave him my false reasons for getting up, and then I heard and felt him sigh against me as he lifted his hands.

"Carry on," he said, but I thought I detected a hint of bitterness in his tone.

I craned my neck to look at his face, but he conveniently looked away and gave me a tiny push, indicating that I should get up. Slowly, I stood up. I looked down at him for a moment, but he still would not look at me. His gaze was fixed on something across the room, but the muscle in his jaw was tense.

I kind of felt like a jerk. In essence, I was using him for my own pleasures and I gave him nothing in return but a hard time, but I couldn't afford to invest myself any further. Not with Alden, Mr. Sex God of the Universe, hell bent on bedding anything with a va-jay-jay. I had to keep myself emotionally distant, for my protection as well as his.

But I didn't have to be a bitch about it.

I put my fingers in his hair and ruffled it up a bit, trying to come off as playful. I bent over and kissed his forehead, and then walked away humming "Crash Into Me" as if I totally didn't feel like Alden had just crashed into me on so many levels.

I went into the guest room to dig out something for the ache in my ribs. When I walked out of the room a few moments later, I found the couch empty. I sensed movement in Alden's room behind me. I glanced over my shoulder as I walked toward the kitchen. He was in there, moving around and pulling a shirt on, though I didn't know for sure what he was doing. I went into the kitchen and got a glass of water to swallow my pills. I was just washing the glass when Alden came out of his room fully dressed and wearing a leather jacket.

"I'm going out," he said, not looking at me.

"Where?" I asked, feeling a gnawing in the pit of my stomach.

"Just out," he said, swiping his keys off the table by the door. "If you need to leave for anything, there is an extra key in the drawer in the kitchen."

Then he was gone. He left me staring at the closed door, knowing damn well that he went out to fuck.

thirteen

Oh, wow.

My pillow was heavenly. It felt like…like a flesh pillow. I didn't know they made such things. Whoever created a pillow that simulated being held in a pair of strong arms and pressed against a firm body was a fucking genius. I snuggled up closer to the pillow, and the pillow held me tighter.

What?

My eyes flew open as my mind really woke up and comprehended the truth behind my flesh pillow.

I was securely wrapped up in Alden. My arms were wrapped around him and his arms were wrapped around me. My legs were comfortably trapped between his.

When did this happen? How did I not notice a man climbing into my bed and shrouding my body with his? Fuck, I must sleep like the dead.

I looked up into Alden's sleeping face, wondering when the hell he had come back. I went to bed a couple of hours after he left, after failing to write more than a whole paragraph because I kept checking my phone or looking at the door. It's not like I cared, because I didn't. If he wanted to go fuck around, he was entirely within his rights to do so. I had chased Vicodin with a shot of Patrón because I really didn't care. I just didn't want to lay awake in the bed the whole night thinking about how much I didn't care.

I still didn't care. Despite my little smile that I bit off by biting my bottom lip, I didn't give a flying fuck that he had come home sometime during the night and felt the need to be this close to me.

Right after he probably fucked some other woman stupid, my brain screamed.

Oh...

I pushed hard against his chest to get out of his grip. Alden's eyes fluttered open. He loosened his hold on me, but he didn't let me go.

"What the hell is your problem, Little Noa?" he asked groggily, holding his head up to look down at me.

"You can't come in here like this and...and...and put your arms around me like this after you...you fucked some groupie!"

Oh my goodness. I wanted to punch myself in the mouth for not being able to say that without some control.

He looked at me with his brow pulled between his eyes for a moment, like he was unable to comprehend what I had just said. Then his brow smoothed out and his head fell back on the pillow.

"Noa, I didn't fuck anyone last night," he said through a yawn. "I went out, had a few drinks with Greg, and I came back. I promise."

I eyed him with suspicion. He looked at me and let out an exasperated sigh.

"I was definitely fucking sexually frustrated enough to fuck, trust me on that," he said bitterly. "But the few girls that tried to slide into my lap last night didn't appeal to me. I didn't want any of them. I was hard as a rock, but I didn't want them, okay?"

"I don't care if you fucked someone else," I lied. "I would just care if you fucked someone else and then thought it would be okay to come in here and be all cuddly with me." That part was true.

He stared at me for a moment. I couldn't read what was going on behind his eyes. Finally, he said, "Do you really think I'm that much of a scumbag?"

I rolled my eyes. "Puh-lease. You've done it before! How can you not remember banging your three women and then the very next morning giving me an orgasm?"

"I remember giving you that hot, wet, liquid orgasm," he grinned, but then his smile faded. "But I only just now remembered those women."

He frowned deeply and stroked his knuckles along my jaw. I didn't care for the touching. That's why I trembled under his touch. I trembled with apathy. Yup.

"I really am a scumbag," he whispered. "Shit. I'm sorry."

"You're just being yourself," I bit out. "Using women and throwing them away without a second thought."

"And they're not using me?" he asked incredulously.

"Oh, come on," I rolled my eyes.

"Seriously," he argued. "They want to be able to tell their friends they screwed the Great Alden Breck, Superstar Rock God."

Pea. Friggin. Cock.

"Well, that's not really something I'm looking forward to bragging about," I said. "Now let me go."

"But I'm so damn comfortable," he groaned, pulling me closer.

"Why are you in here anyway? Don't you have your own bed?"

"Yeah, but you weren't in it. So, here I am."

"Isn't that the point in putting me in the guest bedroom? That I'm not in your bed and you're not in mine?"

"As I recall, I dropped your bags in my room," he said with a grin. "Once you realized you were in my room, you picked your shit up and hauled ass into the guest room."

"That should have been a clue," I snapped.

"I like sleeping with you," he said, stroking my arm. "You're so soft and warm, and you smell really good."

"Buy a puppy. They're warm and soft."

"Why have a puppy when I have you?" He sighed with contentment.

Oh for the love of...

"Let me up, Alden," I commanded.

"No way."

The one-eyed monster in his lounge pants was stirring, right against my...

Oh!

"Hey, let me up," I said with urgency. "I have to pee really badly."

"You're lying," he murmured, closing his eyes.

I reached under his arm, grabbing the skin there, and twisted.

"Shit!" he said and reflexively pulled away.

I took the opportunity to untangle myself from his body and rolled out of the bed.

"You play dirty, Little One," he growled and got up to come after me.

I shrieked and scurried into the bathroom, locking myself in just as he reached the door.

"You will have to come out sometime," he said through the door.

"Why don't you make yourself useful and make me some breakfast?" I said as I indeed sat down on the toilet to pee. "You *are* The Great Alden Breck after all. Surely you could manage some eggs."

"Very funny," he said. "But because I really, really like you, I will make you breakfast. You little brat."

I heard him move away from the door, his bare feet gently slapping the hardwood floor.

"Flesh pillow," I muttered to myself. "How stupid."

***

Alden went to the studio to "get some thoughts out of my head and into music" later that morning while I went to visit my friend Sahara. I had met her when I was with Larson. She was the ex-girlfriend of Larson's friend Ian, but Sahara and Ian continued to have a close relationship after their breakup. She was the only friend I bothered to keep that had any connection to him.

"Well, well, well," she said when she came out of her office building where we were meeting. "If it isn't the beauty that has Alden Breck by the balls."

"Oh, no," I sighed. "Not you, too."

"Not me, too what, honey?" she asked, looping her arm through mine. "Let's get out of here. I only have an hour for lunch that I plan on stretching into an hour and ten minutes." She winked at me with her long, thick eyelashes.

I felt so insignificant walking beside Sahara. She was probably the most beautiful woman that I personally knew. Her mother was Indian and her father was of Italian descent. Her skin was bronze in color, even in the winter months. During the summer when she got darker, it only made her big grey eyes that much more prominent. She was tall – well, everyone was taller than me – and athletic, but with soft, enviable curves. She was a very confident woman and it showed in the way she dressed, the way she spoke, and the way she walked.

"So, tell me all about him," she said in a voice that was naturally deep and raspy in a phone-sex operator kind of way.

"Do we have to talk about Alden?" I whined. "Everyone always wants to talk about Alden. My pharmacist wanted to talk about Alden. My doctor wanted to talk about Alden. The homeless guy that sleeps on the corner on my street wanted to talk about Alden. Please, Sahara, please don't make me talk about that peacock."

Her rich laughter made me smile. "You can't blame us all. He's one of the most intriguing men in the world."

"There isn't anything intriguing about him," I said, disgusted. "He's rich, talented, slutty, and arrogant."

"And *hot*, sweetheart. Don't forget hot."

We walked to a restaurant around the corner from her office. The first twenty minutes after we sat down was spent talking about her recently failed dates. As beautiful as Sahara was, she was completely single and had the hardest time finding a steady man, but she had very high standards for herself and refused to lower them for anyone.

"Okay, enough about me," she said slyly after making me laugh at her disastrous dates. "Spill the beans. How is he in bed?"

"I don't know," I said, stabbing my salad. "You tell me. I haven't slept with him."

Okay. Technically, that was a lie. We've shared a bed more times than not since we've met.

"I don't believe that for a second," she said dubiously. "He is *known* for his sexual prowess and *you* are one hot little piece of cake."

"He *is* known and he practices said prowess on other women – women that aren't *me*."

Sahara's looked at me with skepticism. I didn't blame her. If I were in her position, I'd look at me skeptically, too. What woman spends this much time with Alden and doesn't have sex with him?

"He promised that he wouldn't try to have sex with me," I added.

"Really?"

"Yes, really. It's the only reason I've agreed to be friends with him."

"Then I was right when I said you have Alden Breck by the balls, sweetheart." She grinned.

"I most certainly do not. I told you, he screws other women. He hasn't stopped being a slut," I pointed out.

"No, but he doesn't really make friends with other women, does he? Except for that actress, or so I've heard."

"Well, he's made friends with me," I said, ignoring the comment about Trisha.

"Okay, so he's promised not have sex with you, but is he *sexing* you?" she asked slyly.

"Sahara, you really are a much nosier bitch than I ever could have imagined."

That rich laughter again made me smile.

"Come now," she said. "Is he getting you off? I have a feeling he isn't the type of man to keep his hands to himself."

I eyed her as I thought about what to share and what not to share. Oh hell, at least two of my friends, plus a spouse, and a few pedestrians were already aware that the man had made me squirt.

"He doesn't keep his hands to himself," I murmured so low I wasn't sure she heard me.

"Holy shit," Sahara said, and Sahara rarely cursed. She didn't think it was lady-like or the way to catch a good man. "When did it first happen? Tell me the details, sweetheart."

So, I told her about that first night in front of my mirror and the subsequent squirting. She asked me very personal questions regarding the dirty things he had said, and how many times I had come. I told her about the limo and how I felt afterward, which helped me transition into the serenade and how I felt after that. Thankfully, she was very quiet during the second half of my experiences.

"Wow," she said when I finished. "You have feelings for him."

"I do not!" I exclaimed, making a few people around us glance at us.

"Noa," she said almost sympathetically as she softly shook her head.

"I hardly know him," I argued. "I've known him for less than three weeks!"

"My parents met in Central Park and were married a month later," she reminded me. "They have been together for forty-two years."

"That's different," I said as I pouted.

"How is it different?"

"One of them wasn't an arrogant rock star."

"Listen to me," Sahara said, reaching across the table for my hand. "I understand why you may feel the need to deny it to me and yourself. You are right; he is a slut, and who knows if he will ever settle down. And I know after Larson, you are afraid, but maybe it wouldn't hurt for you to have a stormy, short love affair. I'm actually amazed that you're going on tour – that's a big adventure for you."

"You make it seem like I'm some kind of hermit that rarely sees the light of the day," I said, frowning.

"Practically." She smiled softly. "Since Larson, you have been. I mean, when I first met you, you weren't way out there or anything, but you were more…you were just *more*."

She pulled back her hand. I tugged on my ponytail, frustrated.

"You're right, I'm different," I said. "And honestly, Sahara, the old me – the one from before Larson – would have already fucked Alden, but then we wouldn't be in this situation. I think he likes me so much because I'm not that easy."

"Okay, so don't make it easy." She grinned. "Make him work for it every time, but give it to him and give it to him good."

"I don't know if I want to," I said with an exasperated sigh.

"Of course, you do. You just don't want to get hurt. Look at it from a different angle and do it."

My lips twisted to the side as I considered what she was saying. This whole conversation just shook up a whole bunch of feelings I wasn't even sure were real.

"Oh, before I forget," I said, digging into my bag. "Alden invited you to the gala." I handed her two tickets.

"Oh, how lovely!" She beamed at the tickets. "I have a date Saturday, but I will reschedule."

"Why not bring him with you?"

"Sweetheart, I would never go on a first date with a man I do not know to a function like this. I have no idea if he knows how to behave in such company."

I snorted. "Have you seen my date? It's *his* party and I'm not sure that *he* knows how to behave in such company."

Laughter was our constant companion for the rest of our meal, and not once did we talk about Larson. When Sahara and I parted ways on the sidewalk in front of her building later, I was in high spirits. I was in the best city in the world, with all of its unfriendly, bustling people, crazy taxi drivers, and insane traffic. I had another opportunity to spend time with my good friend at the gala on Saturday, and then there was Alden.

The thought of him made something flutter in my belly. I was going to meet him for dinner in a few hours, but I suddenly had the desire to see him sooner. I wondered if I could meet him at the studio and watch him work. I pulled my phone out of my jeans pocket to give him a call.

My head was down, focused on the pictures Kristy sent to me of her and Trent on their honeymoon. New York was probably one of the worst places to walk with your head down. The city was teeming with people at that time of day, and probably most of them would have been pretty disgruntled if I ran into them. And then I did. Run into someone. I just barely kept my phone from flying out of my hand as I uttered apologies to the body that had not moved.

Pushing my phone back into my jeans, I said, "I'm so sorry. I should watch where…" I looked up into *that* face, that angelically beautiful, masculine *face*.

My eyes were so wide that it hurt the skin that pulled taut around them. My mouth fell open in a silent cry, but my feet, my damn feet didn't move fast enough. His fingers bunched the material of my coat at my chest as he drew me closer, closer, and closer still until our bodies touched.

"How many times have I told you to pay attention when you are walking? When will you learn?" Larson Wright asked me.

***

My insides froze and became as heavy as rocks as I stared up into those devastatingly blue eyes. My body shook violently. The only reason I remained standing was because Larson was holding me up by my coat. His smiling mouth was so close to mine that onlookers most likely thought we looked like a couple caught up in the moment, about to kiss.

"I see that you are still friends with Sahara," he said conversationally. "How was lunch?"

I couldn't answer him. I couldn't speak at all. I'm not even sure I was breathing. I could only stand there, like a coward, shaking.

He looked me over carefully, his eyes assessing the knit cap on my head, my hair, my eyebrows and eyes, my nose, my mouth.

"I like your hair down like this, but then again, I really liked the ponytail you had it in the day you came to the city to shop for your gala dresses. You looked…adorable."

I didn't even remember what my hair looked like that day until he mentioned it. How did he know? How could he have known? Did a few pictures spring up online?

"Did you enjoy riding in Breck's Gran Turismo? Did you tell him about the Bugatti you have waiting for you at home?"

Home… Where ever he was would never be home to me again. I would never go *home* to him. He could take that car and shove it up his –

"It is a shame that you have chosen that Camaro over such a fine car like the Bugatti, but then again…" He chuckled softly. To anyone else's ears, it probably sounded jovial and warm, but it was menacing to me. "Then again, you are still eating in the car. Your crumbs are scattered across the seat and floor and even in the gearshift. There are coffee stains on the console and in the cup holders. Noa," he said, shaking his head disapprovingly, "you do know how I feel about that. You know I do not approve. It is so…déclassé."

Somehow, my hands found his. Absently, I attempted to free myself from his grasp. I felt like prey gripped in the jaws of my vicious attacker. My breaths were coming so fast, I was beginning to hyperventilate.

"Ssshhh," Larson hushed me, leaning impossibly closer. "It is okay, my love. I will forgive you when you are ready to return. When you are finished playing with Breck, I will be at our home waiting for you."

He sighed heavily before running his nose along my cheek. A choking, squeaky sound left my mouth.

"Noa, my love," he sighed again before speaking near my ear. "Why do you run around with that trash? Do you really believe he can love you when he so enjoys copulating with all of those harlots? Or are you simply having fun?" He stood upright again, but still too close to me. "I will allow you your fun for now; I am not here to collect you. You will come back on your own when you are ready, but please do not try my patience and wait too long, Noa."

His lips pressed against mine and my gut clenched with revulsion. I was prepared to bite him if his tongue slipped into my mouth, but he was already pulling away and releasing me. One large hand covered one side of my face.

"Come home soon, love."

He stared at me for a second longer before stepping away from me and then disappearing into the busy crowds of the city.

I slid in the booth across from Alden nearly twenty minutes later than our agreed upon time.

"It's about time, pokey," he teased as I pulled off my coat.

"Sorry," I said, immediately looking at the menu and not looking up at him. "I took a nap and overslept."

"It's cool. How was your lunch with your girlfriend?"

"Great. She's happy about the tickets and she would like to reimburse you."

"It's taken care of," he said quickly. "Why won't you look at me?"

Ignoring his question and avoiding his eyes, I asked, "How was your music making…thing?"

"It was good. Why won't you look at me?" he asked again, but with less patience.

"How am I supposed to decide what to eat if I'm not looking at the damn menu?" I snapped.

I was only mildly surprised when the menu was yanked out of my hands. Slowly, I raised my head to look at Alden.

"What the fuck?" he said, staring at me with discerning eyes.

"What the fuck what?" I asked innocently as my hands twisted in my lap.

"You look like you've been crying," he said with enormous eyes, like he couldn't believe what he was seeing. Like I wasn't freakin' human and couldn't possibly cry from time to time.

Biting back my irritation, I said, "I told you, I was sleeping." I reached for my menu, but Alden withheld it from me.

"Alden," I sighed.

"What happened? You were fine this morning – and don't tell me any bullshit about sleeping, Noa. Your eyes weren't even this red after you had two hundred screaming skanks stomping on your back."

"I feel like I'm getting sick," I said and rubbed my eyes. "Maybe that's it."

"We're not ordering until you tell me the truth," Alden deadpanned.

I looked at him carefully and realized that he was going to hold his ground. We would sit in that booth all night if necessary, or until I gave him the truth or something that sounded true enough. I couldn't tell him I literally ran into Larson. He would go ballistic, and I didn't want him to be worried about it. I needed to handle it on my own.

So I lied.

"Okay," I blew out a long breath. "I was upset about some news I heard today. I don't want to talk about it. Now give me my menu."

Alden stared at me with his mouth set in a firm line as he tried to figure out whether or not I was telling the truth.

"What was the news?" he asked.

"Damn it, Alden," I tried not to yell. "I just told you I don't want to talk about it."

"Well, if it is making you cry, I want to talk about it," he snapped.

I grabbed my purse and coat off the seat, and then slid out of the booth without another word. I had no problems eating somewhere else, alone.

I walked outside, right into a freakin' asshole with a camera. There were two more assholes nearby. When they started calling Alden's name, I didn't have to turn around to know that he had followed me outside. With his hand on my back, he guided me to the ever-waiting limo and ushered me inside.

"Take us back to the apartment," Alden told Al and then closed the privacy window.

He turned in the seat and glared at me. I was sitting on the other side, as far away from him as I could get.

"Get over here. Now," he commanded, pointing to the space right next to him.

"Stop telling me what to do!"

I was just irritated that he wouldn't let it go, but not irritated that he was being his typical bossy self. His commands were different from Larson's. Larson didn't yell; he didn't get dramatic. But that was worse than if he lost his temper, because I never knew when he would strike. I didn't think for even a second that Alden was going to hit me if I didn't obey him.

"Noa, if I have to move you over here, I may hurt you in the process. If you don't move over here, I *will* move you myself."

With a loud sound of exasperation, I moved over to the space right beside him, but for Alden, that wasn't close enough. He put his hands under my thighs and ass and lifted me into his lap. He still wasn't satisfied, however. Even as I tried to fight him away, he forced me to straddle him and then held me securely around my waist.

I sighed in defeat.

He softened as he peered into my face, frowning. "Do you want to tell me what's going on with you?"

"No," I said softly, choosing to look at my hand on his shoulder rather than look him in the face.

"You look so sad, Little One," he said and tugged on my ponytail.

"A little bit."

"Did something happen at lunch?" Alden asked and wrapped his big, warm hand around the back of my neck. His touch sent shivers down my spine.

"I told you. I heard some news that upset me," I lied again.

"Are we going to keep going in fucking circles with this or are you going to tell me what the hell is wrong?"

I picked at some invisible string on his shoulder.

"Damn it, Noa, look at me."

My eyes shifted away from his shoulder to meet his hazel eyes.

"Please, don't make me talk about it," I whispered as I felt tears building in my eyes again. I had spent the entire afternoon in the penthouse crying and staring out the window, wondering if Larson was somewhere nearby watching for me.

Alden looked at me with alarm. His other hand reached up and cupped my face. After a moment, he gently pulled my head forward, resting my forehead on his.

"Okay," he said softly. "I'll let it go. For now."

I breathed a sigh of relief. "Thanks."

I felt his light breathing on my lips as he slowly moved his hands over my shoulders and down my back. They slid under my jacket and under my sweater, and then smoothed over the bare skin at the small of my back. I shuddered slightly and involuntarily rocked my hips forward, surprised when I felt him hard and rigid against me. I surprised both of us when I purposely rocked forward again. Alden's breath hitched with my own. I interlaced my hands behind him and rocked forward again. I moaned lightly as his hardness went over my clit through our jeans.

He put one hand on my hip to pull me forward again, making both of us moan. With his other hand, he pressed lightly on the back of my head, and it was at that moment that I realized I had not really kissed Alden yet. Somehow, it felt as if things would turn a corner if we kissed, that our physical relationship would go from casual to serious. Kissing was something I took for granted in the past. It never really did anything for me. It didn't turn me on, it didn't strike any emotional chords. It was a cursory act, but when I wrote about it, I wrote how I imagined a kiss *should* feel – the physical need to become one with the other person, the arousal, and the emotions that could make the hardest of hearts stumble…

I knew that if I kissed Alden, it would feel right; it would feel the way I'd always written in my books, but never experienced for myself. If I kissed Alden, he would infiltrate me in ways I wasn't sure I was prepared for, but the 'ifs' didn't matter, because it was about to happen.

His lips lightly brushed mine at first, tentative, testing. When I didn't rear back or slap him, he did it again, but a little harder, with more confidence. Then his tongue tasted my bottom lip, seeking permission to enter. As I rocked over his erection again, my lips fell apart to allow a moan to escape, and Alden's tongue slipped into my mouth. He groaned loudly when his tongue made contact with mine, and he pushed his hips up as I moved on him. My moans were lost into his sensual mouth. If I had any doubts about Alden's kissing skills before, they were lost. His tongue stroked over mine in a way that made my sex clench in want and my nipples pucker with anticipation.

I tightened my hold around his neck. I needed this distraction. I needed to be closer to him, but damn the coats and sweaters we wore to keep warm on a winter's day. To hell with the layers of clothing when we had each other to keep us warm.

Alden pressed on the back of my head a little harder, deepening our kiss. He raised his hips up again and I grinded over him harder. Groaning, his fingers curled in my hair. When I felt his hips beginning to rise again, I moved forward. The kiss broke when we both gasped as his cock slid over the opening to my core.

"Alden," I whimpered his name as I slid over him again.

In response, he planted his lips on mine and swirled that magical tongue around in my mouth. I felt his hand between us, close to my belly, but not until I heard his zipper did I understand what he was doing. Alden was so…*big* his jeans couldn't possibly contain the monster for what we were doing. A moment later, when I felt the wide tip of his cock pressed against my lower belly, I groaned so loudly, I would be surprised if Al didn't hear.

His hands gripped my hips where he lifted me and repositioned me so that my jean-clad heat was directly over his partially clad cock. Holding my hips in a killer grip, Alden began to move me as he pumped his hips up. The friction in all of the right places was driving me crazy. The roughness of my jeans pressed against my sex by the hard cock beneath me was undoing me. Knowing that even part of his bare cock was touching me was going to kill me.

I broke away from his lips so I could try to breathe as I called out his name again. He stared into my eyes as he simulated fucking me. I was so close. The pressure building inside of me couldn't be pushed back down.

"I like watching your face when you come," Alden whispered and nipped at my bottom lip. "I like having that power over you."

Yes, power! This…this is the kind of power a man should have over me. This perfect, sweet, hot power.

I was right there. His hard shaft, his words, his face, everything about him was going to make me come. My hips began to jerk against him and I started to whimper with pleasure, and then…

"Mr. Breck, we've arrived at the apartment," Al said over a speaker I didn't know existed, and just like that, my orgasm fell away from me.

Just like that, I went from blind pleasure to feeling horror. If this scene had happened in a bed, Alden would have already been inside of me, but the bigger issue was that damn kiss. I still felt it on my lips even as I scrambled off his lap and he zipped his dick back into his pants. The inside of my mouth and my tongue still felt totally possessed by Alden. My whole body felt possessed by Alden after that damn kiss. My *heart* felt so heavy after that damn kiss with Alden, and if I had let him, he would have begun to possess that, too.

I felt his gaze on me as he started to open the door. I couldn't look at him. I busied myself with my purse and waited for him to get out ahead of me. I heard his heavy sigh just before he stepped out, and as usual, he waited for me with his hand extended. I took it and climbed out of the limo. He led me into his building and onto an elevator. The ride to his floor was oppressively silent, but he did not release my hand until we were inside his apartment.

I was dreading the conversation that we needed to have, but a beautiful, blonde surprise waited for us inside. I simultaneously felt relief and outrageous jealousy when I saw Trisha Livingston lounging on Alden's couch as if she owned the place.

I felt his body tense next to mine.

"Hey, there you are!" The starlet called brightly to Alden. "I tried texting you and calling you but you didn't answer."

"I didn't answer your texts and calls because I was busy," Alden said tightly. "Why are you here, Trisha?"

I took this opportunity to pull away from Alden and retreat to the guest room.

"Noa," Alden said, reaching for me, but I moved faster across the spacious room. "Noa, you don't have to go anywhere."

"Oh, no, it's fine." I forced a bright smile. "Don't let me interfere with your usual activities when you're at home. I'm tired, anyway." I smiled at Trisha, who was watching me with a bland look on her face.

"Noa," I heard Alden at my back, moving toward me. I ignored him as I closed and locked the bedroom door just as he reached it. I heard his sigh before I heard him snap at Trish. "You can't just show up here whenever the fuck you feel like it."

The rest of the conversation became muffled as I moved away from the door. I kicked off my sneakers as I pulled off my coat. I stripped down to my camisole and panties. I rooted through one of my bags until

I found my Xanax. I took two instead of the recommended one and crawled into bed.

To say that I was overly anxious would have been an understatement. I could still feel Alden's tongue sweeping leisurely through my mouth. I could still feel the hard length of him rubbing against me. But I could also still feel Larson's breath on my face, the sensation of being pinned to his body as he spoke in that low, deadly voice. I felt *his* lips on my lips and the revulsion that had coiled in my stomach.

I covered my mouth when a wretched, tearless sob tore through my throat. I was suddenly breathless, struggling to take in air and push it back out of my lungs. I kept my hand to my mouth to try to mute any sounds I made as I had a mini breakdown. I dropped down in a chair in the corner, put my head between my legs, and urged myself to calm down.

You're safe. You're safe. He's not here. He can't get in here.

But he had been in my car. He had seen my hair the day I came to New York with Alden to get my gowns. He had known I had lunch with Sahara. What else did he know and how did he know it?

In a panic, I got up and threw the curtains aside to peer outside. I was too far up to see if there was a blond-haired, blue-eyed man on the street watching me.

Which means he can't see you, either, I told myself.

With shaking hands, I closed the curtain, dropped back into the chair, and put my head between my knees.

I wished Alden was there rubbing my back, caressing my hair, and making me feel safe.

But I couldn't tell him. I had to handle this on my own. Larson was *my* problem.

I am not here to collect you. You will come back on your own when you are ready, he had said.

Did that mean that he was going to leave me alone? Or did it just mean that he wouldn't *make* me leave?

What happens if I never go back on my own?

When sleep finally took me that night, I dreamt that Larson stalked back and forth in Alden's living room in front of the windows as he glowered at me. He wanted to reach for me, he wanted to get his hands on me and do awful things, but he couldn't. I was in Alden's arms on the couch as he strummed his guitar, and not even Larson could touch me.

***

The scent of Alden's skin woke me from my slumber. I didn't even wonder at his ability to get into my locked room. He probably had a spare key somewhere, or even knew how to pick locks. I forced my eyes to open and looked right into his face. He was lying on his side facing me, watching me carefully.

"Hey," he said softly.

"Hi," I replied groggily. "What time is it?"

"Like four in the morning. You've been asleep since at least seven."

I stretched my arms above my head and winced slightly. My ribs were still pretty sore. "Guess I was tired."

"Or it was the Xanax you took," Alden said, frowning.

How the hell did he know that I took Xanax?

"You left the bottle on the bed," he said, answering my silent question. "Why didn't you talk to me instead of taking those damn pills, Noa?"

"What was there to talk about?" I asked innocently.

"Don't try to pull that bullshit with me," Alden snapped. "I want to know what happened when you had lunch with your friend, and I want to know why you ran away from me last night."

"I didn't run away from you," I said dryly. "You had company and I didn't feel like being sociable."

"*Or* you *ran away* because you regret what happened in the car," he said.

Thinking about what happened in the car made my whole body heat up. I loved what happened in the car, and that's what worried me most. For a brief time, Alden's hands on my body, the friction that was between our bodies, and his mouth on mine had made forget all about Larson. It made me forget about *everything*. I was lost, *so lost* in him.

I couldn't afford to get lost. In anyone.

"Okay," I said, pulling myself into a sitting position. Alden followed suit. "I do regret it. In fact, I regret all of it. We shouldn't be doing anything…physical. I don't even like you like that," I lied. "If you can't keep everything platonic, I can't continue from here."

Alden stared at me as if I had just told him that the earth was about to collide with the sun. His eyes were the widest I had ever seen them, and his mouth hung open in genuine shock.

"You're full of shit," he said, his tone incredulous. "You are so full of shit."

"Don't tell me I'm full of shit," I snapped. "I'm telling you how it is, Alden."

"You don't fucking mean what you're saying, Noa," he said, getting to his feet. "You know it and I know it. When I played that song for you, you felt something – don't fucking deny it. When I kissed you, you kissed me back and I *felt* what you felt, so don't fucking deny that shit, either."

"The only thing I felt was horny," I shrugged it off. "But I'm perfectly capable of getting myself off."

"Bullshit!" Alden yelled, pointing at me. "If you didn't feel anything then you wouldn't have felt the need to take fucking Xanax." He picked up the bottle off the table next to the bed and threw it across the room.

"Maybe the way I was feeling had nothing to do with you," I said, getting off the bed.

"Right," he said dryly. "That had something to do with your lunch with your friend."

"Right," I agreed, walking toward the bathroom.

"Well, then," he said, following me into the bathroom. "If the kiss and everything else meant nothing to you, then it won't hurt to repeat."

I turned around to tell him how stupid he was being, but I yelped when he put his hands on my waist and hoisted me up onto the vanity. Before I could get down, he had pressed himself between my legs.

"What the hell, Alden!" I yelled, slapping at his hard chest.

He grabbed my wrists and painfully yanked my arms down to my sides. He tried to kiss me, but I turned my head away, cursing him. He pulled my arms behind my back and gripped my wrists in one hand. He put his other hand on my chin to force my head where he wanted it.

"Stop it, you asshole!" I yelled, flailing against him. "You're hurting me!"

Immediately, he released my wrists, but before I could push him away, his lips were on mine, kissing me with vehemence. My goodness, it was hot. My womanly parts were heating up and moistening, clenching with need. I wanted to lace my fingers in his hair and kiss him harder, but the kissing would lead to touching. The touching would lead to his fingers sliding inside of me, priming me for what would come next: his entirely too big erection. I wasn't one to fall in love just because I had sex with a man, but Alden…Alden would be different. Maybe I wouldn't fall head over heels in love, but surely, I would be all kinds of fucked up from it, and the fact still remained that he was Alden Breck. He was incapable of being monogamous, therefore, he was unable to be properly claimed. And the more he kissed me, the more I wanted to claim him. So, I did what I had to do.

I bit him. Hard.

"Fuck!" Alden cried out, pulling away from me. A small trail of blood oozed out of his mouth and I felt sick for hurting him like that, but it was necessary.

"I told you to stop," I said, breathing heavily. My voice quaked as I continued. "I don't want you, Alden."

He stared at me as he used the back of his hand to wipe away the blood. He didn't speak; he only stared. I stared back, though my chest was heaving and my eyes were burning with unshed tears.

"You're a liar," he finally said. His voice was soft, but it cut through me with ease. "You're a fucking liar, but fine. We'll play your way."

He left me alone in the bathroom without another word. I sat on the vanity trembling as I listened to the sounds of things crashing in his room a moment later. It quieted for a minute or so, and then I heard his footsteps pounding across the hardwood floor. Seconds later, I heard the door slam as he made his exit from the apartment.

A few days later, in the back of the limo on the way to the gala, I kept nervously smoothing my dress and rearranging the way my hair fell over my coat. I was more nervous about the New York gala than I was about Philly. More A-listers were supposed to appear at the NY function, a lot more.

I stole a glance at my number one A-lister. He was already looking at me, and he didn't bother to look away when I caught him staring. I turned away, but I continued to feel his eyes on me.

After Alden had come back the afternoon after our fight, he was still visibly angry and hurt, but he tried to be nice. We went to a couple of museums together the following day and had dinner at one of the big steakhouses. We chatted, argued, and teased each other, but it was all lacking in its usual gusto.

Afterward, I went to work on my laptop and he disappeared until late into the night. The following morning, I went with him to a couple of the news stations where he talked about the upcoming gala, and then we spent the afternoon watching movies as it begun to snow outside. We sat on opposite ends of the couch, with a big empty space between us.

Alden still held my hand when we went out, he still gave me little pecks on the cheek or the head, and he was still full of himself and poked fun at me, but there was no mistaking the rift that was between us. I knew that he was going out at night to do nasty things to other women and he knew I had secrets, but we said nothing more on either front. Sometimes I would hear him in his room or in his office or studio, murmuring in conversation on the phone. I wondered whom he was talking to, wondered if it was Trisha. I never asked, and he never told.

The unspoken things were like water trickling down into our new foundation and freezing, slowly pushing us apart though no one could tell from the surface.

Thursday morning, Alden did the radio shows and visited a couple of the group foster homes in the city, something he had also done in Philly one afternoon. I went with him to the foster homes and I couldn't help but feel warm as I watched him interact with the kids. Often, he would slip up and start to curse but immediately replaced the offensive word with some other ridiculous word. I covered my lips to keep from laughing every time. At one point when he caught me, he gave me a wink and a smile that I probably didn't deserve.

He was remarkably good with children. He played and roughhoused, but seemed to be ever mindful of their smaller, more delicate bodies and egos. He had brought the same acoustic guitar he had played for me Sunday night. He let the kids play with it, and when a couple of strings broke, he didn't seem to care.

"You're a natural with kids," I told him on the way back to the apartment.

He smiled and shrugged a shoulder. "I treat them as I wished I was treated as a kid," he said, running his hands over the guitar. "I'm going to have my own kid to take care of. I'll treat him the same way, try to give him a good, happy life."

I looked at him with surprise. "You want to have children?"

It was the wrong thing to say.

"Don't look so surprised, Noa," he said, his smile fading. Bitterness laced his tone. "I know I don't seem like the type of person who can settle down and have a family, but it is something I want. You still don't see who I am under the women, the drinking, and the partying and bad language. You still see what you want to see."

I stopped talking then, because nothing I could possibly say seemed like it would be the right thing.

"Al, pull over so I can get out. Take Miss Eddington wherever she wants."

I had watched on with something like shock as Alden threw his guitar on the seat between us and got out of the car without another word. I had not been out by myself since I saw Larson. I told myself it wasn't because I was petrified, but just because I had nowhere to go on my own.

"Take me back to the apartment," I told Al, hoping he didn't hear the hysteria in my voice.

I didn't see Alden again until Saturday morning…after the kind men at the NYC police department released him from a holding cell for assault and disorderly conduct. Alden's lawyers were very quick and efficient about getting the matter swept under the rug with a happy sum of money thrown at the man whom Alden had slugged, but the arrest still made the gossip news shows and blogs. It was an otherwise normal day in Alden Breck's life.

"What was the fight about this time?" I had asked Alden after the lawyers left the apartment.

"Apparently, the girl I was hooking up with in the bathroom had a boyfriend. He didn't like the fact that I was screwing his girl, but if he would have asked me nicely to stop, I would have and moved on to the next one." He had grinned while he told me, grinned proudly. It was like he was trying to rub it in my face.

Dick wipe.

I brewed up the sweetest smile I had. "Hooking up with a stranger in a public bathroom and beating up her boyfriend while you were probably drunk out of your mind are all very exemplary parenting traits.

His smug face fell just before I closed my door. I felt a little bad for it, but he deserved it. If he thought he was going to be able to adopt a kid with fame and fortune alone, he was wrong. It didn't matter if the kid was his brother or not.

I didn't talk to him again until we were leaving for the gala and he told me I looked nice in my red gown. I had thanked him, but we said nothing more until the limo ride to the party. The more we crept along in traffic, the more anxious and fidgety I got.

"Do you want…?"

"No," I said, cutting him off. I assumed he was going to offer to finger me into relaxing again. Of course, I *wanted* him to finger me, but things were so awkward between us and I wasn't sure that all of the sexual things going on were even a good idea.

"I was going to ask you if you want a couple of shots before we get there," he said patiently, and then gestured to the minibar in front of me.

"Oh," I said, feeling a little stupid. "Sure."

He slid over close to me and reached over to the bar. He opened a little door and pulled out a bottle of *Rey Sol Extra Añejo* tequila. He poured two shot glasses and handed one to me. I wasn't much of a drinker. I looked down at the glass with leeriness.

"Don't be a girl," he teased and then swallowed his shot.

"Last I checked, I was a girl," I mumbled.

"I agree," he said, already pouring another glass. "Last *I* checked, you *were* a girl."

"Very funny," I muttered and then took the shot.

While the liquid burned my throat, Alden poured me another shot as he spoke.

"Actually, it isn't very funny at all," he said with a frown.

I ignored his remark and took my second shot. I was already feeling the effects warming through my body.

Oh yeah.

I could get used to that tequila, but not for two hundred plus a bottle.

"Feeling better now?" Alden asked, looking down at me a few minutes later.

"Yes, I think so," I said. "Maybe one more shot?"

"Nah," he said putting the bottle away. "You'll feel it when you stand up. I don't want you to feel it *too* much and fall on your face on the red carpet."

"Okay," I conceded and folded my hands in my lap to keep from fidgeting.

"I can do it for you, you know," Alden said quietly.

"Do what?" I asked without looking up at him.

"I can make you relax like I did before." It was a whisper that barely reached my ears.

My hands twisted in my lap.

"No, that's okay," I said.

"You need it, Little One," he said, slowly running his hand down my leg. "I want you to feel better."

His hand was under my dress now, moving slowly back up my leg.

"No, you don't have to," I whispered as I felt his hand waiting for entry between my clenched thighs.

"I *want* to," he whispered in my ear. "Open your legs and I'll help you relax."

"I'll just regret it later like I did before," I said, trying to sound mean, but it came out unsure instead.

"Yes, maybe so," he said with his lips against the skin on my neck. "But at least you won't be nervous *now*."

He nudged my thighs apart with his hand and quickly assailed my sex, running his fingers along the lace crotch of the panties I was wearing. I shuddered slightly as his thumb grazed over my clit.

"Your panties are already wet, Little Noa," he whispered in my ear as he nibbled on my earlobe. "Why is that? If everything we ever did in the past was a mistake, you wouldn't be so fucking hot and wet for me right now. Tell me why you're wet."

His thumb pressed down hard on my clit and started to massage it in small circles. I gently lifted my hips off the seat and licked my lips as I moaned.

"Tell me why you're wet or I'll make you squirt all over your pretty red dress," he demanded.

My mother effin goodness.

I almost didn't want to answer so that he would make me squirt again, but I really didn't want to do it in the backseat of a car, nor in my beautiful gown.

"You," I managed the one word as thumb continued to push me higher.

"Me what?" he demanded and pressed harder.

"Unnhhh," I moaned instead of giving him the answer he required.

"I guess you're going to ruin your pretty dress, Little One," he said.

Alden quickly spun me so that my legs were in his lap. He was careful not let my head hit the glass behind me. As he was busy shoving my dress up over my thighs, I tried to stop him.

"Alden, no," I said, trying to push away his hands. "Don't."

"You wouldn't answer me," he said in a no-nonsense tone. "I told you what would happen."

"I'm sorry," I said, shoving at his hands even as he started to *tear* my panties away. "I'll answer now."

"Too late," he said and tossed the black scrap to the floor. He pulled me closer so that my ass was in his lap.

"You're going to make me go to the gala without panties on?" I asked incredulously as he began to run a finger through my swollen lips.

"You only have yourself to blame," he said, and without any further delay, he pushed two fingers inside of me.

I cried out as my hips shot up off his lap. He put an arm across me to hold me in place.

"Alden, don't…mmmm…don't make me do it. I don't want to ruin this dress and uhhhh…oh damn…Alden…"

"Okay, I won't make you squirt – *this* time," he said with a little growl at the end as he pushed his fingers in knuckle deep. "I'll just make you come."

He looked down at his fingers moving in and out of me and groaned. "Noa, you're so fucking beautiful. Even your cunt is beautiful. It's so fucking perfect."

He pulled his two fingers out and replaced them with three, stretching me and sending me closer to my impending orgasm.

"Alden," I whimpered as I felt the pressure in my pussy building.

"You're so *wet*, Noa. I made you this wet, didn't I?" he asked, looking into my face again. "It's always me, isn't it, baby?"

I bit my bottom lip and nodded quickly as he pushed his fingers deep. I tried to circle my hips and grind onto those fingers, but his arm was still holding me down.

"Please," I begged, spreading my legs as wide as I could. "Please, Alden."

In answer, Alden's thumb again found my clit. Moments later I was crying out his name and bucking my hips, and didn't give a shit if Al could hear me up front or not. As I came, Alden moaned as he watched my face. He reached up and stroked my cheek until my body began to settle. He pulled his fingers out of my aching core and I could only watch, mesmerized, as he kept his eyes on me while he licked and sucked each finger that had been glistening with my excitement.

"We're arriving at the ball," Al announced over the speakers.

"Park, but don't let us out yet," Alden answered after pushing a button above us.

"No problem, sir," Al said.

Alden helped me sit up and fix my dress. I ran my fingers quickly through my hair as he picked my panties up off the floor and stuffed them in his pocket.

"Beautiful," Alden said before applying a soft kiss to my lips.

I couldn't help the stupid smile that appeared on my face.

"We'll let ourselves out, Al," Alden said to the driver. "Are you finished resisting me?" he asked me as he threw the door open.

"No," I said stubbornly. "Never."

He grinned. "Good. I like fighting for you."

For me...not with me...

He got out of the car and held out his hand. I scooted out carefully, but when I stood up, the alcohol had indeed hit me.

"Oh, my god," I said, grasping his arm. "I think I'm a little tipsy."

He chuckled and wrapped an arm tightly around my waist. "Don't worry, baby. I got you."

"Don't let me fall," I giggled, clutching onto him.

"I'll never let you fall, Little One," he said and caressed my cheek even under the flashing bulbs of the press.

There was so much implied in that sentence, but I had no time to think about it. I got my wits about me and allowed Alden to escort me onto the red carpet.

***

Sahara was enviable. Her long dark hair hung down her back in waves. Her large chocolate eyes were bright, her skin flawless. She wore a gold and red saree that left her bare at her waist, showing off her fit abdomen. A thick band of gold wrapped around her right upper arm and she wore gold bangle bracelets on both wrists. Large gold earrings hung like teardrops from her ears and she even wore her gold nose ring.

I was delighted that she had come. With her superior beauty and shining personality, she fit right in. She walked through the clusters of stars as if she was one of them, and they in turn took note of her. She even knew a few already, thanks to the men she had dated in the past.

"I had no idea that she would be so fucking hot," Alden had whispered in my ear in awe as we watched her work the room with one arm looped through Greg's arm. He had taken an instant interest in her after they were introduced.

I nodded, unfazed by the fact that he was checking out my friend. *I* was checking out my friend. "She is the most beautiful person I know," I admitted to Alden.

"She comes in a close second," he said instantly and looked away from her to kiss my jaw tenderly.

I smiled instead of pushing him away or chastising him. I was determined to enjoy my night and to forget about Larson. I didn't want him to have that power over me. I didn't want the ghost of him following me around.

"Come on, baby," Alden said, taking my hand into his. He kissed my knuckles and said, "Let's go meet some celebrities."

Alden and I joined Sahara and Greg where they stood in a group of celebrities and politicians, chatting. I was no longer nervous; Alden had taken care of that for me. I met the actress that starred in my favorite political drama, and the older British actor who was old enough to be my grandfather, but whom I was secretly in love with.

Alden kept a possessive, but gentle hand on me at all times, my neck, my lower back, my hand. I didn't shrug him off. I even reached for his hand on more than one occasion.

Something was swiftly changing between us, or it had been changing all along and I just didn't accept it. I don't know if what I was doing was acceptance or not, but all I did know for sure was that I didn't want another stretch of days like what we just had to pass between us again.

"Noa, you seem to be getting used to your company as of late," Sahara commented later at dinner. "You used to fidget at the idea of even meeting senators and diplomats. Now you're rubbing elbows with world-class movie stars and not batting an eye. I must say, I am proud of you."

"It's all superficial, Sahara," I admitted with a giggle. "I had a couple of shots in the car and I've been drinking ever since."

"What?" Alden whispered in my ear. "You don't want to tell her I made you come?"

My thighs clenched together at the thought. His hand was on my thigh, so he felt it. He laughed lightly as he pulled away.

"I can't imagine my Little Noa being so shy," he said to Sahara.

"There's been nothing shy about that girl since the second she started giving Alden the evil eye in California," Hash commented from across the table.

"Yeah, I'm only shy around *important* people and *talented* people," I teased.

"Do you really not like Friction?" James asked seriously. I realized that I might have offended him and instantly offered him a warm, apologetic smile. I hadn't spent much time with James or Hash, so they didn't understand that I met no harm. They didn't understand that I, in fact, had a lot of respect for all that they had accomplished as a band.

"I do," I said. "I just don't like Alden."

There was some chuckling from around the table at Alden's expense. He rolled his eyes at me but smiled anyway.

"Honestly, I didn't listen to much of your music before the concert, but I didn't really have anything against you as a group or musically, I just *couldn't stand* Alden. He's so…*arrogant* and self-important – I hated the way he strutted across the stage as if every girl in the audience wanted to screw him." His own band members and Greg nodded in agreement with me as they chuckled.

"Sweetheart," Sahara cut in. "Every girl in the audience probably *did* want to screw him."

"Thank you, Sahara," Alden grinned at her.

"Don't make his head any bigger," I said to her.

"Well, look at him," she gestured with her fork.

"No," I said, looking at her as if she was crazy. "He gets looked at enough. Almost every woman is already looking at him. I don't need to look at him, too."

"You do realize I can hear you, right?" Alden said from my left, but I refused to turn to look at him.

Sahara laughed warmly and I followed her suit. She easily changed the conversation, focusing on Greg instead of Alden. I was happy that Alden was okay with taking the spotlight off himself for a change. Conversation always seemed to revolve around Alden or the band as a whole, but people tended to forget about Greg always being there to keep them going. Sahara really seemed to enjoy listening to Greg's stories, and he really seemed to enjoy talking to her. Soon, the rest of us were nudged out of the conversation until the pair was only focused on each other. I smiled to myself. Greg would definitely not be a disastrous date for Sahara.

A little while later, Alden pulled me out to the dance floor for a slow dance. He held me much closer than necessary, but I didn't try to pull away from him as we slowly glided across the floor.

"I have your panties in my pocket," he said in my ear.

"I am well aware, sir," I answered.

"Sir?" he looked down at me with a raised eyebrow. "I think I kind of like that."

"So, what are you going to do with my ruined panties?" I faked a disinterested tone. "Why haven't you already thrown them away?"

"Well," he started softly. "After I get you off again tonight and knock your ass out, I'm going to pull those panties out and put the crotch up to my nose and inhale your fucking intoxicating scent."

Ohmygoodnessgracioius.

Shamefully, I heard myself gasp and my pussy responded with throbbing.

"Then I'm going to run my tongue along the seam," he continued, pressing me impossibly closer as we continued to dance. "And then I'm going to wrap them around my dick and jerk off until I'm close to coming, and then I'll shoot my load into that scrap of cloth that was pressed against your beautiful cunt."

How the hell I managed to stay on my feet was beyond me.

"Sounds like a lot of work when you can just go out and get something real," I said, trying to hide how hot he had just made me.

"The only thing real that I want is you, Noa," Alden said fiercely. "I'm tired of fucking other women and pretending they're you when they're so fucking not. I want *you*."

"You…you promised," I said in a burst of air.

"You can relinquish me from that promise, Little One," he said, smoothing his hand down my back and openly cupping my ass. "You can stop the bullshit and I can make you not want another man ever again."

I kind of wanted to throw him down on the ground and screw him right there, but fortunately, I had more sense than that.

"I have to think about it, Alden," I said, my voice quavering.

"Why do you have to think about it?" He pulled away to look down at my face.

"I…I don't want to be hurt, Alden," I admitted and looked away from him.

Oh my god! I all but just admitted to him that I had feelings for him! Stupid, stupid, stupid.

I decided at that moment to blame it on the alcohol. I wasn't knocked down drunk, but I wasn't very sober, either.

Alden's hand slid up and away from my ass and returned to my back where it belonged. The song ended and he led me off the dance floor. Since it was technically his party, people had been coming up to him all night to shake his hand and to chat. We didn't get too far before an infamous couple approached us. He was himself, no sign of the seriousness that just took place on the floor moments before. By the time we made it back to the table, Alden had been stopped too many times to remember. He didn't even have time to sit back down because Friction was up next. Before Hash rushed him away, he managed to lean down and whisper in my ear.

"We'll talk later," he promised and then he was gone.

When Friction came on stage, I made sure that I was up front, right against the stage, right where Alden would be. He looked at me with surprise at first, and then his whole face lit up. My recovering body was jostled around a bit by the energetic crowd, but I didn't care. I stayed there throughout their set, and when it was over, Alden rewarded me with a brief, but deep kiss.

***

"When I invited that chick to my party, I didn't mean for her to steal the heart of Dr. Greg," Alden whined as we walked through the door of the apartment.

"Yeah, well, he's a good guy if he's had to put up with you for all of these years, and Sahara is a beautiful person, inside and out. She has very high standards and if Greg is meeting them, then great, but we're getting way ahead of ourselves. They only left together to go out for coffee."

I threw my coat on the back of a chair and leaned against the back of the couch to pull my heels off. Alden walked into the kitchen as he undid his bowtie and came out with two beers. He handed one to me, even though I really didn't need anything else to drink.

"What if they fall in love?" he asked with his brow down. "Would she be willing to come on the road with us when we're away?"

I made a face that answered his question before I could speak. "Sahara worked her ass off to get where she is in her company. I honestly don't see her throwing that away."

"Well, Greg is the kind of guy that would leave the band for a really good woman," Alden complained. "She might steal my doctor!"

I rolled my eyes. "Maybe you'll need to get someone else to kiss your boo-boos."

"I don't want anyone else to kiss my damn boo-boos," he growled.

"Then maybe you should stay out of trouble," I suggested. "Stop screwing other peoples' property in public toilets."

"Low blow." He frowned.

"But a good one." I shrugged.

"No, that's the thing. She wasn't a good blow at all."

I rolled my eyes again and walked to the guest room.

"I guess I shouldn't have said that," Alden said behind me.

"Probably not, but you seem to have a knack for saying and doing stupid shit." I put my beer down and pulled my hair aside, looking over my shoulder expectantly until Alden pulled the zipper down on my dress.

"I've been thinking about what you said," he said softly as he ran a knuckle over my bare back.

"I've said a lot," I said. "What are you talking about?"

"Don't play stupid," he said in a tone that told me he wasn't joking around. "You tried to push me away a few days ago. You lied and said you didn't want me."

"Who said I was lying?" I whispered.

"Don't fucking play with me, Noa. I know I'm an asshole, but I've always been a very honest asshole. You can't deny that."

I couldn't. So, I said nothing.

"I wanted to hurt you," he admitted in a low voice. "I wanted to fuck everything and hope that it hurt you, but in the end, I realized I was only hurting myself. I know it's only been a very short period of time, but I have very strong feelings for you, Noa. I've tried to shut them down by burying my dick in other women, but the feelings don't go away. They only get stronger."

"Umm…" I said and then looked up at him over my shoulder. "Was that supposed to be romantic?"

He dragged his fingers over his face in frustration. "I don't know how to do this romance shit."

"It *was* supposed to be romantic?" I asked incredulously.

"Can you give me a fucking break, Little One?" he growled. "I just said I don't know how to do this shit."

"Well, what are you trying to say?" I turned around to face him. I had to hold my dress up to keep it from falling.

"I thought I said what I was trying to say!"

"No," I said, shaking my head. "You said you stuck your dick in other women to try to hurt me and erase feelings you had for me. You've accomplished one of the two."

His eyes pinched. "I hurt you?"

"A little bit," I said, looking at the floor. "But go on with what you were saying – or trying to say."

Alden groaned as he ran a hand through his hair. "I guess what I'm saying is that I won't push you to have sex with me, but I also won't stick my dick in anyone else, either. I'm willing to wait until you're comfortable. I don't want to hurt you – again – and fuck knows very well that I'm capable of fucking up. I feel like I need to prove myself to you that I can be a good guy."

"You *are* a good guy, Alden," I said, putting a hand on his chest. "But you're a good guy that is also a major slut."

He closed his eyes for a moment. "I will try to be much, much less of a slut," he said.

"That's not exactly the same as not sticking your dick in anyone," I said dubiously.

Alden growled and stripped out of his tux jacket. Muttering under his breath, he walked out of the room. I could hear him talking to himself in the next room. I couldn't help but giggle a little. The great Alden Breck was having a hard time telling me something romantic, and I was enjoying it. It was a big change from a few days ago, I realized.

He returned a couple of minutes later, wearing only a pair of boxers, even though the apartment was nippy. I didn't mind too much. I got to admire the ink on his muscular body. I had changed into a pair of shorts and a T-shirt. I was already in bed when he came in. He turned off the light and got into bed with me.

"I don't remember inviting you to sleep in my bed," I said, even as I snuggled up to him.

"Yeah, I'm a bastard, always inviting myself in. You know I came in here while you were sleeping?"

"When?" I demanded.

"Every fucking morning before the sun came up. You know, when we were talking but not talking. I would come in here and just lay here until you started to stir. Then I'd haul ass out of here because I didn't want you to know I gave a shit."

"Creepy," I murmured, closing my eyes.

He was quiet for a few minutes. I had thought that maybe he was asleep until his voice stirred me from my near-sleep state.

"You know there is something between us, right?" he whispered. "You can't deny it now. No matter how much you tell me you dislike me, you still let me do the most intimate things to you. A few days ago, you were biting me to make me get the hell out of your face, but now you're wrapping your body around mine. You can't deny that there is some kind of force pulling us together, Little One."

I swallowed hard as his hand laced with mine on his chest.

"Alden, I agree, but…it feels too fast too soon," I said.

"Who the hell said that there had to be a certain amount of time before two people could claim one another?" he demanded.

"Society as a rule, but that's not really what I'm worried about. I'm worried about you hurting me or me hurting you. We hardly know each other."

"I'll tell you any damn thing you want to know about me," he said.

"Well," I sighed. "I wouldn't even know what to ask – it's not a twenty questions kind of deal, Alden. Some things you just learn about people along the way."

"So…what do we do? I don't want you dating any other douche bag and I'm sure you don't want me fucking around. What does that make us?"

"We don't have to put a label on anything yet," I said cautiously.

"You're still afraid I'll hurt you," he said and I couldn't miss the sadness in his voice.

"I am," I admitted. "But I could very well hurt you, too."

"Impossible."

"You don't know me that well, Alden."

He sighed. "So, when are you going to let me in and so that I *can* get to know you?"

"It's just going to take some time," I said. "Hell, maybe I should put everything up front now. You'll probably run the other way."

"There isn't anything about you that will ever make me run the other way," he said.

"You don't know that," I whispered.

"Listen to me closely," Alden said and tilted my chin up to his face, illuminated only by the soft glow coming from the cable box across the room. "You would've had to have done horrific things to make me run away from you, Little One – like burn a Friction album, or hooked up with the lead singer of Thirty Seconds to Mars."

I gasped. "Jared Leto is hot sex personified!"

"Arch. Enemy," Alden bit out.

"What did Sexy Hotness with the Fuck Me eyes ever do to you?" I asked.

Alden growled at me and I giggled.

"He's hot, what can I say?" I laughed. "What did Jared Leto ever do to you?"

"Don't call him hot, and I don't want to talk about it. Wait. You didn't sleep with him did you?" His question, sadly, was serious.

"No, but if he was the one lying in my bed, there wouldn't be *any* talking going on right now." I sighed.

"I'll solve the not talking thing," Alden said, rolling to his side. "But you have to promise me to never ever hook up with that guy."

"Does he have some kind of disease?"

"Not that I am aware of."

"Does he have a little, little penis?" I asked.

"Why would I care to even know that information, Noa?" Alden asked, sounding disgusted.

"Then I can't promise never to hook up with Jared Leto."

"You would have sex with Jared Leto before you'd have sex with me?" Alden asked incredulously.

Without any hesitation, I said, "Yes. No offense."

"I'm so offended I can't see straight."

"You can't see straight because it's dark in here," I giggled.

"Noa?"

"Alden?"

"Shut up."

He kissed me, and I happily complied. Again, I was lost, and all was forgotten, *especially* Larson.

"What the fuck?" Alden cried out when I took off my cover-up.

"What?" I asked, throwing my hands up.

"Where's the rest of your damn bathing suit?" he demanded, throwing a towel over me.

"Stop it," I said, pushing the towel off. "I mean it!"

"Put some clothes on!"

"We're on the beach in Miami," I pointed out. "I'm wearing just enough clothes."

"The hell you are," Alden grumbled, standing there with his arms crossed.

"It's just a bikini," I said and settled down in the lounge chair.

"That's the problem," he growled. "It's *just* a bikini."

"Alden, sit down or go somewhere," I sighed as I slipped on my sunglasses. "You're blocking the sun."

Grudgingly, he sat down in the chair beside me. I didn't know why he was freaking out. We were on a private beach and there weren't too many people around.

There were almost two weeks between the New York and Miami galas. We spent a couple of days hanging out with the band, having lunch with Sahara and Greg (much to Alden's chagrin), and lounging about Alden's place.

My new favorite thing was to be serenaded by Alden Breck, the very man who I couldn't even stand to watch on stage at one time. Sometimes, I sat between his legs like I did the night he played "Crash Into Me" and I would sometimes try to learn. Other times, while lying in bed, he would rest his head on my belly and play that way. But my favorite way to be serenaded by Alden was curled up in his lap, with my head resting on his shoulder and my arms around his neck. It was an awkward position for him to play, but he never missed a note, and apparently, it was his favorite position, too.

We spent Valentine's Day in front of the fire in Alden's apartment, eating and drinking, talking, and laughing. And kissing. And touching.

Before going to Florida, I headed back to Philly to prepare properly for the weeks I'd be gone. Alden had to fly to Minnesota to work on some legal matters regarding Peyton, but when he returned, we spent a day in Philly before flying to Miami on a private jet owned by Frictitious.

I was so glad to be in warm weather that I had decided to be bold and buy a bikini. I never thought I had the body for a bikini, but one of the sexiest men in the world couldn't keep his hands off me. It was a total boost in self-confidence. I was being bold, but not stupid. It wasn't a string bikini, and the bottoms were like boy shorts.

I was also eager to put a thousand plus miles between Larson and myself. I had no idea how he had kept track of me like that, but I imagined I put a damper on his stalking by being so far away. That helped me to relax in a way I wasn't able to do even in New York with Alden. I was going to pretend the whole affair hadn't happened and that my ex wasn't a psycho and just enjoy myself.

"I'm telling you," Alden grumbled as he picked up one of my books, "if any guy even looks at you for more than two seconds, I'm breaking his jaw."

"There are better bodies to look at in Miami than mine." I sighed. "Trust me."

"I thought we went over this," Alden said with a sigh. "You're fucking beautiful and anyone with eyes can see that. Do we need another lesson in front of the mirror?"

"No, we don't need another lesson on how delusional you are," I said dryly. "Read your book and be quiet."

"Hey, listen here, bossy bikini bottom," he started, making me snicker. "Don't make me smack your ass."

"Whose ass is getting smacked?" Hash asked, taking the seat on the other side of me.

"Mine," I said.

"I'd join in on that ass smacking party." He grinned.

"I'm not above putting my fist in your jaw, Hash," Alden warned. "Stop ogling my girl."

"Then your girl should put some damn clothes on." Hash laughed. "At least the bruising is mostly gone."

"Yeah, it's looking better every day," I said, gently running a hand over my ribcage.

"Hey, Face Plant, can you trail that hand over your tit, because that would be fucking hot," Hash said and barely had time to get up before Alden was after him.

"Boys," I sighed and settled back in my seat and closed my eyes.

"Miss Eddington?" a male voice asked gently.

I thought maybe it was one of the guys that worked for the resort we were staying at, but when I opened my eyes and lowered my sunglasses, I immediately knew he was not from the resort. The staff at the resort dressed in light green and white. This guy was just wearing a pair of black swimming trunks and a tank.

"Can I help you?" I asked, on my guard.

He looked around quickly, probably looking for Alden before sitting down, facing me in Hash's vacated chair.

"I'm not going bullshit you, Miss Eddington," he started quickly. "My name is Nathan Velacross. I'm with the *Inquisitor* magazine and I have a few questions for you."

The press had been approaching me since we were in Philly, but I usually blew them off, unless they asked me something in which I could respond to with humor, or when they asked me what I thought about Alden. I would tell them the truth, that I thought he was a peacock.

"Look, if you want to ask me questions about Alden, you're not getting any answers out of me. You need to go."

"Then you don't care to comment on the allegations regarding Trisha Livingston and your boyfriend caught in a compromising position last week in the alley of a New York club?"

Well. That caught my attention, but then again, that's what he wanted. Velacross wanted me to react. That's how the paps are.

"That's all you got?" I asked blandly. "That's boring. Why don't you spice it up a little, Velcro?"

"Velacross," he said nervously and then looked around for Alden. "So, you aren't going to comment, Miss Eddington?"

I slipped my glasses back into place, laid back down on the lounger, and closed my eyes. "There is nothing to comment on, Velcro," I said nonchalantly and waved him away. "I wouldn't still be here when Alden returns if I were you."

I heard him sigh heavily. "I'll leave this with you along with my card, Miss Eddington. If you would like to comment on this story or share anything else with me, I'll listen."

Something was laid carefully on my bare belly. I cringed and opened my eyes, ready to snap at him for coming so close to touching me, but he was already walking away. Muttering to myself, I plucked a business card and a flat piece of paper off my stomach. I was ready to crush the picture, but I froze for a moment, taking in the dark figures in the dark background. I pushed my sunglasses up again and peered closely at the photograph.

My heart sped up. And then it stopped.

There was a timestamp in the bottom right corner of the picture: 1:57a.m. 2/16/2014.

I had left for Philly the previous morning. I was in bed at 1:57a.m., staring blankly at the Kiera Knightley version of Pride and Prejudice. I was too terrified to fall asleep. Every sound I heard coming from the hallway, every footstep that passed by, I seized up. I was afraid that I would go to sleep and wake up to *him* in my room.

Alden, however, at 1:57a.m., two days after Valentine's Day, was in a back alley, scarcely lit. He was leaning up against a brick wall. Kneeling at his feet with his belt in her hands was Trisha Livingston. It appeared that Alden was about to get a blowjob.

"Who the hell was that?" Alden demanded as he walked toward me. Hash followed not too far behind, shaking sand out of his short, spiky pink hair.

I stood up on shaky legs as I crushed the card and picture inside of my hand. "No one," I said. "Listen, I'm suddenly not feeling that great. I'm going to go inside and lay down."

"What?" Alden asked, staring at me. Even under his sunglasses, I knew he was studying me. "Who the hell was that, Noa? I'm not stupid. You were fine when I left and when I come back, some asshole is scurrying away, and you're 'suddenly not feeling that great.' What the hell is going on?"

My head felt like it was about to explode with all of his yammering.

"Alden, just shut up!" I snapped as I picked up the bag I had carried out with me. "I'm going inside to lay the hell down."

"Fine," he growled, grabbing his towel off the chair. "I'll come with you."

"I don't want you to come with me," I said patiently and turned away from him.

"See, man?" Hash started. "If you would have just let me smack her ass with you, none of this would be happening."

"Shut up, Hash," I snapped over my shoulder.

"Hey." Alden grabbed my arm just as I reached our room.

"Alden," I growled in warning as I yanked my arm free.

"Don't fucking 'Alden' me," he snapped. It was all the warning I had before he swept me into his arms.

"I *hate* when a guy picks a woman up to make her comply!"

"I hate when my woman doesn't comply and makes me have to pick her up!"

He tossed me onto the bed, and before I could even think about scrambling away, his body was on mine. He straddled my legs and pinned my arms above my head. My hand was forced open and Nathan's crumpled card and the crumpled picture fell onto the bed. Alden's eyes narrowed at them, but he didn't release me to reach for them.

"What's that?" he asked, nodding his chin at the incriminating evidence.

"A picture," I answered snippily.

"Of what?"

"Of you being your typical slutty self. Look at the picture."

Slowly, reluctantly, Alden eased off me, sat on the edge of the bed, and picked up the crumpled picture. Several silent seconds ticked by before he made any movement or sound. He sighed, but then several more seconds ticked by without anything further.

Why was he so still? Why was he looking at it for so long? Was it because it was real? It wasn't a doctored photograph? Had he really done it?

He made no real commitment to you, I had to remind myself. With that, I got up and retrieved the sundress I had taken out to wear later. I slipped it over my head and pushed my feet into a pair of flip-flops.

"What are you doing?" Alden's asked with alarm as he jumped up off the bed.

"I'm going to the front desk to get my own room," I said calmly as I looked around for my bag. I realized I must have left it in the living room and headed out the door.

Alden was right on my heels.

"Why the fuck are you doing that?" he demanded. "Noa, look at me," he said pleadingly when I didn't respond. "It's not what it looks like, I promise you."

"It looks like a blowjob," I said, walking toward the door.

Strong arms circled around my waist and my back was pressed to his chest.

"I know what the fuck it looks like, but it's not that. I didn't get head from her that night. Look at the picture, Noa." He held it up with one hand while still holding me securely in his other arm. "*Look at it*," he commanded.

With a sigh, I looked.

"My hand is on her fucking forehead, pushing her away. And look closely at my body language. I'm turned slightly away from her because I was about to walk away. I know it's hard to see, but look at my face, Noa. Do I look like I'm getting ready to get a blowjob?"

I looked carefully at all of his points. His hand *was* on her forehead, not in her hair as I had originally thought. He was also turned at an angle, like he was trying to wriggle away from her, and his handsome face was one of anger and…disgust.

But…

"How did she get your buckle undone then?" I asked him quietly. "If she wasn't about to give you head and you weren't at one point ready to receive it, why is your belt undone?"

"Al was picking me up at the other end of the alley," he explained. "I went out the back way so I would avoid the crowds. I had to take a piss. My jeans were too tight for me to simply just pull the zipper down and pull my dick out, so I had to unbuckle my belt. I was still pissing against the wall when Trish came out looking for me. I barely had time to shake it and stuff it back in my jeans before she reached me. I turned around without thinking to talk to her as I buckled back up, but she looked down, saw an opportunity, and embarrassed herself by taking it. I pushed her away, Noa. I was so pissed because she knows how I feel about you, I told her that night when she was last in the apartment."

I was silent for a minute as I took it all in. I hadn't heard their conversation that night because I was having a meltdown, but he *had* yelled at her for just popping in.

"You can't just show up here whenever the fuck you feel like it."

"Why were you out with her?" I had not meant to ask that out loud and sound like a jealous girlfriend.

"I wasn't out with her," Alden said softly as he balled the picture up in his hand. He tossed it aside onto the floor. "I was there to check up on Hash, because he was hanging with a couple of guys that are no good for him while he's in recovery. I hung around until he found himself a couple of girls and left out the front door, and then I called Al and slipped out the back. She showed up a little while after I got there. Maybe she caught wind that I was there and that's why she went. I don't know for sure."

"Why did it take you so long to say something when you first saw it?" I asked, with a trace of doubt.

"I was trying to figure out who the fuck took the picture."

"Did you figure it out?"

I felt him shrug. "I thought I saw someone as I was heading to the limo, but I was a little drunk. I could have been seeing shit."

"What do you think you saw? That just sounds creepy," I said, leaning back into him. I was beginning to relax. I believed his explanation about Trisha. James had told me that she was willing to be hurt ten times over just for the off chance that Alden would give her what she sought. It did leave a bit of a sour taste in my mouth, though. If my relationship with Alden continued to grow, how many times was she going to try?

"I thought I saw a guy with blond hair," Alden said casually. "But like I said, I could have been seeing things."

My heart stuttered.

No. No way, Noa. Now you're just being paranoid. There's no way that Alden's phantom was really Larson.

Alden's cell phone rang. If the ringtone had been anyone else's, he probably would have ignored it, but it was Peyton's ringtone. His conversations with his brother were few and far between. He looked really torn about walking away from me to answer the call, but the truth is that I wasn't quite ready to hear him finish that sentence.

"Are you and I good?" he asked close to my ear.

"Yeah." I nodded and patted his arm. "We're good. I'm sorry I overreacted."

"At least I know that you won't put up with anyone trying to take your man," Alden said teasingly and kissed the top of my head.

He released me and hurried into the bedroom to answer Peyton's call.

I picked the picture up off the floor and threw it in the trashcan. I stood in front of the sliding glass doors for a couple of minutes, trying to shake the unease that was creeping into my bones. It couldn't have been Larson. There was no way it was Larson. Larson wouldn't creep around the city's back alleys, following Alden around. Hell, in the very least, he'd hire someone to do that dirty work.

Yet, I couldn't calm my worried nerves.

I went to find my own phone. While Alden was talking to his brother, I could take my mind off Larson and give Kristy a call, or Sahara. Greg had not come with us to Florida because he was still in New York. I was curious about that. Maybe I could call Tucker and find out what was up with him and the mystery woman that he wanted to make squirt. I hadn't spoken to him for more than a few minutes since lunch that day. Once I got talking to one of my friends, I would again forget all about Larson.

I found my phone tucked in my beach bag in the bedroom. Alden slapped my ass as I walked by without faltering once in his conversation to Peyton. Grinning as I walked away, I unlocked my phone and tapped the icon for my messages. My brother and my agent both sent me text messages that I decided I'd answer later. I clicked on a message that had a number but no contact name attached. Seconds later the phone fell from my fingers onto the hardwood floor. The screen shattered.

"I told you to put a cover on that damn thing," Alden said walking toward me.

Quickly, I bent over and scooped it up off the floor.

"It's okay," I said as I continued out of the room.

I was glad that Alden hung back to continue talking to Peyton. I was glad he didn't try to take the phone from me to assess the extent of the damage, because if he had, he would have seen the same picture that I had just thrown away. He would have seen the text under it that read: Soon you will get tired of this and come home.

“Where are we going?”

“You will see when we get there,” Alden said with a wink.

I turned my attention back to my window and watched the Dallas scenery whiz by. We had arrived the previous morning after spending over a week in Miami. That gala had the potential to be my favorite. It was held outside at an oceanfront venue, under strands of thousands of soft lights and the moon and stars above that. Alden had been extra affectionate that night and only left my side to perform. He could have been that way because the scene was romantically inspiring, or maybe it was in response to the pictures of him and Trisha that had hit the media a few days prior. Maybe he sensed that something was wrong, no matter how hard I tried to hide it, and maybe he was trying to make me feel good and safe. And I did feel safe with him.

“You’re really quiet, Little One,” Alden said in a soft, worried tone.

“I’m always quiet, at least in comparison to you.”

“Noa,” he said my name so softly I almost didn’t hear it. He was dividing his attention between me and the road, and at the speed he was going, I didn’t feel comfortable with that at all. I didn’t want to become a chunk of Noa-Alden metal.

“Hey, I’m fine, okay?” I said, taking his hand and holding it with both of mine. I really loved how his hand felt in mine. I loved his long musically talented fingers – his orgasmically talented fingers. I appreciated the ruggedness of his hands. They weren't the soft hands of a spoiled man who did nothing for himself, but they were the hands of a man unafraid to get dirty and work hard. I especially relished the way those hands touched me, gentle and firm at the same time, sensual yet commanding, but never hurtful.

I shook myself from my thoughts about his hands. That line of thinking gave the impression that I was falling for Alden, like, in love. I was surprised by how much that excited me, and how much it scared me. The fear ran very deep.

"Pay attention to the road, Danica," I said at last and released his hand. I folded my hands together to keep myself from reaching for him.

"Out of all of the people you could have called me, you call me Danica? Seriously?"

"Hey, hot chicks that drive fast cars are cool. Take it as a compliment."

Alden grinned at me. "So, are you into chicks?"

I rolled my eyes and ignored him, and he focused on the road ahead.

A little while later, we pulled into the parking lot of a marina. I looked at Alden with apprehension. I had never been on a boat before and I was not in a hurry to do so. I watched enough of *The Poseidon Adventure, A Night to Remember,* and *Gilligan's Island* not to bother with the risk of going out on the water. I wasn't too keen on pirates either, unless it was Johnny Depp pretending to be a pirate, and I didn't think Johnny was going to be anywhere near this Texan inland body of water.

I didn't ask questions though. After parking, I waited for Alden to walk around and open my door. I put my hand in his, expecting to walk toward the area where there had to be dozens of boats tied up, but he lead me in the opposite direction. I looked up at him questioningly and he winked at me. We followed a path through a small patch of trees and when we emerged, I immediately saw where he was taking me. A few yards away on what looked like a private dock, there was a very large boat waiting for us. I didn't know anything about boats, but I later learned that it was a yacht. It looked like a small cruise ship.

"I've never been on a boat," I said as we walked toward it.

"Are you nervous?"

"A little bit," I admitted.

"Don't worry," Alden said, squeezing my hand. "I'll take care of you."

It was such a simple sentence, you know, about not letting me drown or get lost on a desert isle, but it felt loaded with an unsaid meaning.

I glanced over my shoulder as I boarded. There were only the trees and the parking lot beyond that behind us. I had been glancing over my shoulder a lot since that first message from Larson in Miami. Two more passive-aggressive messages had followed that one throughout the week. One was just a picture of me…me in Miami. I was standing outside of a café with Hash, but he had been cropped out of the picture or the person taking the picture didn't include him. He was my buddy when Alden couldn't be around. We liked to share funny cocaine stories, which shouldn't be funny at all, but we'd done stupid things on coke in the past. Hindsight isn't always 20/20, but hell if it isn't funny sometimes.

The second message was a link to an online article about the top ten political sex scandals of the twenty-first century. It was a veiled threat, albeit an empty one. It didn't make it any less daunting.

I had been glancing over my shoulder a lot since getting that last message from Larson in Miami. I was afraid one day I would look over my shoulder and he would be there, smiling beatifically, holding dozens of daffodils, and beckoning me to come to him. That's how he used to lure me to him after an incident. All smiles, pleasantries, and flowers and candy. Things would be fine for a time and then I would somehow mess up, or maybe I wouldn't mess up at all and he would just be in a foul mood over something that had nothing to do with me. Then the flowers would end up on the floor, pedals torn and crushed, stems broken, water splashed across the floor, and sometimes glass shattered. Then I would end up on the floor with the flowers, struggling to pick up the pieces, to clean up the mess so that it wouldn't further infuriate him even as I was being punched, kicked, slapped, tugged, and yanked.

"You're gone again," Alden said, jarring me from my thoughts. There was a man dressed in khakis and a white polo standing behind him holding a tray with two flutes of champagne, but Alden ignored him and blocked him from my view.

"What?" I asked dumbly.

"You got super quiet again and you were gone. Where are you going?" he whispered, putting a hand on my cheek.

“I was right here,” I said. “I was just thinking about every shipwreck movie I’ve ever seen.”

“I told you I’ll take care of you,” he said with a smile and then “You know that, right? You know I’ll take care of you?”

We weren’t just talking about physically drowning anymore. Now we were talking figuratively. Alden had to go and say something that every girl would love to hear, say something that I myself would have written into one of my novels.

I put my hand on his chest and playfully pushed him away. I gave him a smile and a rueful shake of my head and moved past him to grab a much-needed glass of champagne.

“Are you going to tell me what we’re doing on this luxury liner or what?” I asked and carefully took a sip of the champagne. I really wanted to down the whole glass and take Alden’s glass, too, but then he would know something was wrong. I didn’t want him to know something was wrong. Larson was *my* problem.

“I just wanted to have some time alone with you away from a stuffy hotel room without having to worry about our privacy,” Alden said, taking his glass of champagne.

The khaki guy walked away without a word. The engine came to life and when I looked back on the pier, I saw another guy in khakis climbing aboard just as the boat began to move.

“Come on,” Alden said and took my hand.

He led me to the bow of the boat. I was pleasantly surprised to find a comfortable looking seating area for two set up for dining. In the middle of the table, a vase held long stem roses of various colors. Instead of using the bright lights from the boat, the area was lit by lanterns and a few candles.

“It’s reminiscent of Miami,” I said, smiling.

His arm slipped around my waist and he kissed my temple.

“I know. You really liked the setup and I thought you would like it even more without all of the people.”

“Alden Breck, you *are* romantic under all of that braggadocio attitude.”

He shrugged and smiled. “Only for you, Little One. Only for you would I spend hours setting something like this up.”

I blinked.

"You mean you had someone set it up."

"No, I mean I came out here before I went back to the hotel after my interviews this morning and set this up with my own hands. I had someone light the candles and lanterns when we were on our way, but that's all."

It was the most romantic scene I had ever laid my eyes on and Alden had done it. For me. I swallowed hard and then forced another playful smile.

"You're getting soft, Breck."

I gasped when he took my hand and pressed it against the hard outline in his jeans. He smiled devilishly and said "There's nothing soft here, baby."

Just to be a bitch, I gave his cock a firm squeeze, making him groan and thrust gently against my hand. I removed my hand with a smirk and stepped away from him.

After dinner, we pulled on our jackets and stepped outside onto the deck. Spring was around the corner, but not close enough. It was still cold, especially out on the water. Alden stood behind me with his arms wrapped around me as I stood against the railing.

"Sometimes," Alden started. "I wonder how the fuck we got here, and I wonder what would have happened if that barrier never gave."

I laughed. "You would have tried to kiss me and I would have punched you in the face. And your feelings would have been hurt because for once, someone wasn't interested in your cooties."

"You *did* hurt my feelings! You were so fucking mean. I mean, I saved your damn life, you ingrate."

"Again, it was your fault that I almost died in the first place, you fustian windbag."

"Fuck, I love your grandiloquent mouth," he said amorously.

"Grandiloquent, huh? Did you have to look that one up?"

"Fuck may be my most favorite word ever for many fucking reasons – like its versatility for example – but I am capable of using big, fancy words."

"Okay," I said with a shrug.

A few short moments of silence passed between us.

"I looked it up like two weeks ago and I've been waiting for a chance to use it," Alden said quietly.

I smiled and held back my giggles. “Well, if it’s any consolation, I am impressed. It’s a good, impressive word.”

His voice dropped to a softer timbre when he spoke again. His breath fanned my face when he said, “I have another good, impressive word for you.

“What’s that?”

“Trust.”

My smile faded. Probably fearful that I would try to pull away, Alden’s hold on me tightened.

“I think that I have proven that you can trust me,” he continued. “Do you trust me, Noa?”

Did I trust him? I had to trust him enough for me to go on the road with him for over two months.

“Yes, I trust you,” I answered.

“Then I think it is time that you tell me what has been going on with you,” he said gravely.

I hoped that he didn’t feel my heart rate picking up pace, but even if he didn’t, my too-high voice was a dead giveaway.

“What do you mean?” I asked.

“You know what I mean. In New York, you gave me some bullshit story about hearing some bad news, but I *know* something else happened.”

He grew more intense as he spoke, all signs of our earlier banter gone. “You were skittish for days. You think I didn’t notice the way your eyes darted everywhere when we went out? It was like you were looking for someone you didn’t want to see. Then you seemed to be getting better until that day that asshole pap showed up and gave you the picture of me and Trish. You’re looking over your shoulder all of the time, wincing before you check your text messages, and you hang on to me at night as if the fucking boogeyman is going to come in and steal you away.”

He sighed deeply, and when he spoke again, he tried to speak more calmly. “I know you are a strong woman, Noa. I know you want to be able to take care of shit yourself because you’ve been doing that since you were a kid, but you don’t fucking have to.” The last four words came out harsh and angry. “We’re not getting the fuck off of this boat until you tell me what the fuck is going on.”

I realized that I was gripping the railing fiercely when Alden gently began to peel my hands away, finger by finger. My breaths were ragged.

"Tell me," Alden whispered as he held my hands in his. His thumbs traced random patterns on my palms.

Larson was my problem. In a few weeks, Alden would be going his way and I would be going mine, and Larson would *still* be my problem. What would I accomplish by telling Alden anything? I would feel better for a few minutes, maybe even for a few days, but then what? What was he going to do? Go start a fight with Larson and then I would be the one to pay the consequences once Alden returned to his life in L.A.?

"How can we move forward if you don't trust me, Noa?" he asked admonishingly.

"Move forward?" I questioned between my broken breaths. "What do you mean by that?"

"What the fuck do you mean what do I mean by that?"

Alden stepped back and turned me around. His eyes narrowed furiously on mine. I tried to take a step back, but I was already against the railing.

"Did you think that after your obligatory nine weeks were over that I was just going to put you back on a plane to Philly?" he demanded, gripping my shoulders. "Did you think I was just going to go back to my fucking life as if I never knew you?"

Exasperated, anxious, and scared, I shouted at him. "Yes! Yes! That's exactly what I think!"

And that was true. I always had that nagging thought in the back of my mind, even during my happiest moments with Alden. I didn't doubt that he cared about me, but I didn't think that we wanted the same things. We were too different. I would do nothing but hold him back from being the person that he loved to be, the same person that the world was wild about. Then he would resent me for it.

"You're out of your fucking mind!" Alden shouted at me.

"And you're in denial! I'm not 'crazy rock star' girlfriend material, Alden. These past weeks should have proven that to you. Do you know what the *Inquisitor* said about you a few days ago? They called you Boring Breck because you haven't been seen out with the rest of the band drinking and partying and fucking around."

"So?" he said, but he looked unsure of himself.

"It was trending on Twitter!" I shouted. "Hashtag boring Breck! I'm the one that made you boring and you're not a boring person. When is that going to become a problem for you?"

"So, let me get this straight," he said, putting his hands behind me on the bar. He leaned over so that we were nearly nose-to-nose. "You're upset that I am giving up being a slut and partying and getting into trouble so that I can be with you?"

I nodded after a second of reluctance.

"You're upset that I am giving up the loneliness and emptiness that comes from banging random skanks so that I can be with the one person that makes me feel like a dying man that has stumbled upon the elixir of life?"

After a little more reluctance, I nodded my head again.

Alden moved until his body was flush with mine. He brought his hands up to hold my face. "Do you know what I think, Little One?" he asked in a barely audible voice.

"What?" I breathed.

"I think that you're in love with me and you're terrified that I really will put you on a plane back to Philly. To protect yourself, you don't tell me anything that makes you vulnerable. You won't tell me what is frightening you and who or what is hurting you. You take my affection, but you're afraid to give it because you think it will be rejected. You're so sure that I don't really want you that you wouldn't even put up a fight for me when you thought I was getting blowjobs from Trisha in a fucking alley. It would have been an easy out for you because it was something you would expect me to do, to fuck around on you when I told you I wouldn't." He leaned down and kissed me with passion, but it was so quick that I was barely beginning to respond to his warm mouth before he pulled back.

His thumbs skimmed over my cheeks as he stared into my eyes. "I love you, Noa. You fucking wreck me. You have been wrecking me since I first saw your scowling, beautiful…" He kissed my lips. My nose. My cheeks. "…stunning face. And then you opened your little big mouth. I think you had me at 'obnoxious' and 'cocky.'"

"You're still obnoxious and cocky," I whispered around the lump in my throat. I swallowed and swallowed, trying to force it down, but it stayed lodged there. My hands were on his chest, trembling. My whole body was trembling, but I couldn't feel the cold, night air.

"I know I'm an asshole," he laughed softly. His face quickly grew serious, though. A crease appeared in his brow. "I know I have done some seedy shit. It wasn't that long ago that I was getting head in the back of a Philly pub. I don't even remember the chick's name or what she looked like – well, she had red hair. I remember her hair, you know, the top of her fucking head."

I tilted my head a little, wondering if he was trying to make me feel better because he was failing. Then again, he was being so typical Alden that I just barely resisted rolling my eyes.

"Anyway," he said and then scrubbed a hand over his face. "What I'm trying to say is that I want to help you. I don't want you to hide anything from me, Noa."

He put a hand on his neck and looked at me with…what? Was Alden…embarrassed? Even with the partial moonlight peeking through the clouds, I could see that his cheeks had a slight rosy tint to them.

Oh Em Gee! Some brethren to the Loch Ness Monster is going to come up out of the lake and devour the entire yacht in one swallow!

The lake monster was just as mythological as I once believed the chance of Alden Breck ever getting embarrassed. If Alden was capable of humility, the monster could very well be real, lurking just out of our sights, waiting to attack.

I held my breath, waiting for Alden to speak whatever it was that made him blush. I just couldn't imagine…

"I want to be your hero," he said softly. "I want to take care of whatever demons that are chasing you, Noa. You are…magical. You've changed me, forever, and I will never resent you for it. You've made me a better man, a man worthy of someone as extraordinary as you."

His hands cupped my face again. "Baby, let me take care of you. Let me make it all better. Tell me where it hurts and I'll fix it." One hand dropped to my chest over my heart. "I'll fix *you*."

Tears. I hate tears, but they came anyway, flowing out of my eyes so quickly that I hardly had time to prepare myself. Alden wiped them away as he spoke softly to me.

"Talk to me, Little One. We're not getting off this boat until you do."

I wanted to talk to him, I wanted to tell him everything, but the desire to kiss him was much stronger. I put my hands on his shoulders, stood on my toes, and smashed my mouth against his. He didn't hesitate to part his lips and allow my tongue to press into his mouth. Alden moaned but then pulled away until our lips were barely touching. I felt the smile on his lips.

"That's not talking, Little One," he murmured.

"I don't want to talk," I said and pressed my mouth to his again. He indulged in me again and let me control the kiss for a few moments before he pulled away once more. I growled with frustration. Alden laughed lightly.

"You're not getting out of this," he said and kissed my lips gently. "You have to talk to me." His fingers wiped at my tears. They had slowed, but still fell sporadically.

"We'll talk later," I said huskily as I touched his mouth with mine. "Kiss me, Alden."

I didn't give him a chance to respond. I kissed him hard, making him moan again. He wrapped my ponytail around one fist and gently tilted my head back to get better access to my mouth. His tongue battled with mine as we fought for control over the kiss, but when he nipped hard at my tongue, I conceded and submitted.

His free hand traced over my cheek and down my neck before dropping into the tight space between our bodies. When I felt his hand cup me through my jeans, I groaned loudly into his mouth. His fingers expertly found the sensitive bud through my jeans and pressed hard. I put my arms on the railing behind me and began to grind against his hand.

"You're so fucking warm," Alden breathed against my mouth. "How does that feel, sweetheart? Hmm?"

He rubbed the rough seam of my jeans against my clit, finding a rhythm with the rocking of my hips. The heat radiated from my pussy and spread up over my belly and up to my nipples, making them harden in my lace bra. Alden kissed me again, deeper, harder, and without mercy, stealing my breath entirely.

"Your jeans are getting wet," he groaned as he continued to rub me. He used his other hand to pull the zipper down on my jacket. When my coat fell open, his fingertips trailed down my neck and down to the swell of my breasts. I hissed when they feathered over my hard nipples, and then groaned in frustration when he began to tease me by drawing circles around the puckered peaks.

"Please," I begged and bit my lip.

"Please what?" he asked teasingly.

"Touch me," I panted.

"I am touching you." He grinned. Suddenly, he squeezed my nipple and I bucked against his hand with a low, long cry. "You want to come, Noa?" He asked in a husky voice.

I nodded fervently, unable to form actual words as he squeezed and released my nipple repeatedly through my T-shirt and continued to rub my aching pussy through my jeans. Suddenly, his hand began to move faster and harder, making it impossible for me to continue grinding against him, but it didn't matter. I was so close, so, so close.

"Alden!" I screamed his name as my orgasm hit me suddenly, making me reflexively squeeze my thighs over his hand and trapping it against my sex.

He laughed softly before flicking his tongue over my bottom lip. Slowly, he wriggled his hand free from between my legs and wrapped his arms around me. He pulled me close, pressing his erection against my belly as his nose grazed over mine.

"Alden?" I whispered his name as my heart pounded ridiculously fast in my chest.

"Hmm?"

I swallowed twice before speaking again. "Take me to bed."

He froze for a few seconds before pulling back slightly to look me in the eyes. "What?"

I pressed a gentle kiss against his lips and repeated myself, slowly. And so that he could not misunderstand, I reached between us and grasped his cock through his jeans, making him hiss through his teeth.

"Take. Me. To. Bed."

"Are you sure?" he whispered back to me, though he pressed his erection into my hand.

"I'm sorry, I thought I was talking to Alden Breck. Since when does the great Breck second guess going to bed with a woman?"

He smiled, but it was a small smile, not with his usual gusto. "Guess I'm losing my touch a little, huh?"

“I just think you’re out of practice,” I said huskily as I nipped at his jaw.

He groaned and pressed against me again. He opened his mouth to question me, I could see the doubt in his eyes, but I kissed him again, thrusting my tongue into his mouth almost violently.

“Shit,” he said, staring down at me with wonder after we pulled apart. “I should have told you I fucking loved you a long time ago. I could have tapped that ass weeks ago.”

I rolled my eyes. My Alden was back, saying ridiculous shit.

My lips were throbbing, sore, and plumped from Alden's kisses and tiny bites, but I couldn't pull away from him. My lips repeatedly crashed into his and I made him moan every time I sucked his lip or tongue into my mouth and between my teeth.

My hair, wild from Alden's hands constantly finding their way in it, clung to my cheeks, his cheeks, our lips. He'd pull away long enough to push it off of my face, but one of us always moved again to reconnect.

Our clothes were strewn across the room – a pair of jeans on the floor, a shirt on the bedside table, my bra hanging haphazardly off the foot of the bed, and my panties lay on a chair where Alden had thrown them after he had wickedly put them to his nose and inhaled deeply.

I sat on his lap, straddling his thighs as he leaned against the headboard. My bare breasts were smashed against his broad chest, and resting against my lower belly was his long and thick erection. It was warm and moist with the constant flow of pre-come seeping out of the tip, and every now and then, it would twitch and react to my kisses and my touches.

His hands eased down my back and to my ass. He pulled me closer until the shaft of his cock was nestled against my wet slit. I groaned and rocked against him, sliding along his cock and coating it with my arousal.

Finally able to break away from my mouth, Alden's lips painted a picture down my throat, over my collarbone, and across my shoulder.

At first, I wasn't sure how to do it, how to make love. I had never made love with a man. Sure, a couple of them had been gentle and sweet, but it wasn't love, it wasn't this all-consuming burn inside of me that I felt with Alden, this intense need to become one with him. I was worried that I wouldn't know what to do or how to do it, but then his lips connected with mine and I was engulfed and naked in his arms. I knew how silly I was being. There was no wrong or right way, no plan to follow; there was only him and me and the love that blazed between us.

"Are you ready for me, Noa?" Alden whispered against my neck as one of his hands slipped into the tight space between us. Two fingers dipped inside of me. He groaned and it vibrated against my skin. "You're ready for me."

He attempted to roll me over onto my back, but I grabbed onto the headboard to stay upright.

"I want to do it like this," I said when I saw the confusion on his face.

"Fuck no! I'll tear you apart like this," he objected.

"We'll go slowly until I get used to you."

He shook his head and frowned as he whispered, "I don't want to hurt you with my abnormally large, but superb and delicious cock."

I tilted my head. "How do you know your cock is delicious?"

"Everything else about it is so great, I'm just assuming…"

I kissed his lips. "Shut up, Alden and make love to me. *This* way."

He looked at me with doubt even as he grabbed a hold of his cock and rubbed it against my pussy. "When your ass is literally in a sling tomorrow, I am going to just wear a shirt that says 'I told you so' so that I don't have to keep saying it all day."

I raised myself up and when I felt the tip of him slide over my entrance, I sucked in a soft breath. I nodded my response and braced myself by placing my hands on his shoulders. His hands firmly gripped my hips for control as he carefully lowered me onto his erection. Inch by lovely inch, he eased into me. I felt myself stretching to accommodate his girth, and I bit my lip to keep myself from cursing, though I moaned and my fingers dug into his shoulders. Alden grimaced as if it were taking every bit of his control not to take me in one hard thrust. When he hit the resistance of the opening to my womb, I was sure that he had to be all the way inside of me because I felt filled to capacity with his throbbing flesh.

"Can you take more?" he asked through gritted teeth.

My eyes widened. "More?" I squeaked.

His brow crinkled. "We should change positions."

"No, no," I said hurriedly. "Please, keep going."

Without any further argument, his fingers pressed into my flesh and he continued to lower me onto his cock. I wanted to look down and see this impossible disappearing act as I took him deeper. Alden was right, he was tearing me apart, straight down the middle. My body protested at the invasion and even though I whimpered and moaned softly, I was holding myself back from screaming and shouting for him to stop. As much as it hurt to be spread so widely and penetrated so deeply, I wanted it. I wanted to feel him all the way inside of me until his balls were pressed against the curve of my ass. Until I was impaled on him and we were hooked together like two pieces of the same puzzle. Maybe it was cruel for me to finally give him this – to finally give *myself* this – only to walk away in the near future and probably break his heart, and mine, too. Maybe it was cruel, but I needed this, Alden needed this. For once in my life, I wanted to make love, to be joined with someone who truly loved me and wanted me for who I was inside and out, because it would never happen again. I would never allow myself to love someone again.

Alden cursed as the soft walls of me swallowed the last inch of him. I could hear my breaths, loud and ragged as I stared into his hazel eyes, afraid to move, but then I did. A small movement of my hips and my fingers were digging in to his skin again as a low moan left my mouth. We couldn't sit like this forever, and I could tell by the look of concern mixed with lust on his face that he was afraid to move, too – afraid to hurt me. So, I moved and began to rotate my hips.

"Oh, god," I gasped. It was painful. It was also pleasurable. It was unlike anything I'd ever felt before.

"Noa," Alden breathed my name as his hands closed over my ass.

As I began to grow acclimated to his size, I started to move in faster and wider circles. One of Alden's hands palmed my breast, flicking the nipple with his thumb and pinching it between his fingers. My hips moved on their own, grinding on him a little bit harder as the pleasurable sensations from my nipple shot straight to my sex. His hand slipped down between our bodies and his fingers discovered my swollen, sensitive clit. He rubbed it firmly, making me whimper and make wordless sounds, or speak words that didn't exist.

Alden growled softly before kissing me. I moaned into his mouth and then against his lips when he retracted his skilled tongue.

"That's it, baby," he murmured against my mouth, his voice husky and breathless. "Come on my cock, Noa. I love you so much. I want you more than anything in this world. Come on my cock."

I shrieked as my body suddenly tightened with tension and then uncoiled. I rocked on his hard cock, scratching at his shoulders and back and trying unsuccessfully to call out his name as my orgasm ravaged me. Alden's hands gripped my waist and he thrust into me, making me shriek once more.

"Let me love you, Noa," he whispered against my mouth. I could hear the restraint in his voice. He wanted control and he wanted to move at his own tempo.

"M-make love t-to m-me, Alden," I stuttered, wrapping my arms tightly around his neck.

With another growl, this one louder, deeper, and more animalistic, he began moving inside of me with long strokes. With every upward thrust, he brought my body down to meet his. My nipples rubbed against his hard chest and grew harder and more sensitive by the second. There was a sweet fragrance enveloping us – Alden's light, but masculine cologne fused with his body chemistry, mixed with the scent of my shampoo and body wash and the heady smell of sex.

Our mouths mashed together, tongues seeking and then colliding. Every moan and grunt vibrated in each other's mouths, and then against my skin when he pulled away to kiss my neck and shoulders. As if he couldn't stand to stay away from my mouth, he abandoned the trail he had been kissing across my chest and slipped his tongue into my mouth again.

Deeper. Harder. Faster.

Alden was losing control, and I wanted him to. My pussy ached with his intrusion, but I wanted more. More aching, more blinding hot pleasure. I wanted him to take me completely, to own me, and to ruin me for life for any other man.

My fingers wove into his hair and pulled his head back, exposing his throat. My teeth had grazed over his chin before my lips left hot kisses along his skin. When I reached his lower neck, I opened my mouth, licked away the slightly salty perspiration that had gathered there, and then sunk my teeth into his flesh and sucked. Alden cursed and groaned as his tempo increased.

"Fuck, Noa," he growled. "Fuck!"

When I pulled away, there was a fresh red mark on his neck. I loved the way it looked against his creamy skin, standing out in stark contrast, announcing to the world that he was mine. A strong, gut clenching possessiveness came over me, banishing any thoughts of ever leaving this man. He was mine, *mine*, and I was his. I wasn't going to let anyone break us apart, especially *me*.

My finger traced over the mark, and I growled, "Mine."

All of Alden's control vanished.

Suddenly, I was rolling onto my back, Alden rolling with me. He braced himself, planting a hand on either side of my head and straightening his arms. Before I could object, he slammed into me, making me cry out so loudly that it hurt my own ears. Again and again, he pounded into me, taking me apart thread by thread. My nails drew blood as they penetrated the flesh on his back. He groaned so loudly that his voice competed with mine in an erotic song that glanced off the walls of the room.

"Wrap your legs around me," he demanded.

I complied and nearly cried when I felt him deeper inside of me. I chanted his name and unintelligible words as his cock destroyed me in the most sensational ways. A pressure in my core built quickly and then burst suddenly as the head of his glorious cock slid over the bundle of nerves hidden inside of me. I screamed as my orgasm hit an all-time high and liquid passion erupted from my pussy, showering both my lover and me. My legs trembled with violence, my body shook with spasms, and my eyes rolled to the back of my head.

Incensed by my eruptive orgasm and having no mercy on my poor, over-sensitized body, Alden crushed my body with his when he dropped onto me and wrapped his arms around my back. With shaking limbs, I put my arms around him, needing and wanting to feel him as close as humanly possible. His movements became more turbulent, his hips painfully slamming into my hips. Tears stung at my eyes, not because it hurt, but because it was nearly too much for my over-stimulated body, but at the same time, I didn't want him to stop. I'd never felt so close to another human in my life, so full and so complete, but all good things must come to an end, or so they say.

Alden kissed me brutally before pulling away with my bottom lip between his teeth. Groaning loudly while sucking and licking my lip, I felt his cock pulsate inside of me and felt the first burst of warmth as he began to climax. His teeth released me and he dropped his head to the space between my neck and shoulder as he continued to come inside of me, moaning my name and thrusting jerkily. His body gave a hard shudder and then he became boneless atop of me, breathless and chest heaving.

I rubbed his back, kissed his shoulder, and ran my fingers through his hair as we lay there, still joined and recovering. Alden lifted his head and his eyes roamed over my face with concern.

"Are you okay? Did I hurt you?"

My fingers stroked over his face as I spoke in a raspy voice. "You made me feel perfect."

He smiled and left a gentle kiss on my lips. "You were already perfect."

***

I couldn't put it off anymore. I had to tell Alden about Larson. He wouldn't *let* me put it off. He had been serious when he said he wouldn't let me off the damn boat unless I told him what was going on.

We settled in the salon with mugs of hot chocolate spiked with marshmallow-flavored vodka, topped with mini marshmallows and whipped cream. We were both only half dressed. Alden was shirtless but had on his jeans. I wore Alden's FML T-shirt and a pair of panties. Yes, FML is the acronym for Fuck My Life, but it is also the acronym for Fictitious Music Label. Alden loved it, because either way, someone would get the shirt.

A fire crackled from a gas fireplace and we sat side-by-side under a blanket we had swiped from the cabin we were in.

"Tell me about New York," Alden said as his free hand caressed my hair.

I sighed softly and stared at the melting whip cream in my mug.

"I had lunch with Sahara and everything was fine. I was in a really good mood. I was going to call you and ask if I could come visit you at the studio. I really wanted to see you, just to be with you regardless of what you were doing. I was looking down at my phone and not really paying attention, which is really stupid in the city, but I was being careless. I bumped into someone, and I was apologizing before I even looked to see who it was."

I felt Alden stiffen slightly. "Who was it?"

"Larson."

Alden's hand stilled on my hair as he stared at me. "What happened?" he demanded.

"He…he held on to my coat so I couldn't really go anywhere, and…Alden, he's stalking me. He knew about my lunch with Sahara, he knew about the day I was in New York shopping for the gowns for the galas. He even knew about my first ride in the Gran Turismo with you. And he's been in my car! I don't know how, but he knew about things that weren't out in the open."

Alden got up so fast that hot chocolate splashed out of his mug and onto the floor. He slammed the mug down on a table, making more of the brown liquid slosh out.

"What else?" he bit out through gritted teeth. "What else did he say to you?"

He began to pace like an angry lion, never taking his eyes off me.

"Um," I swallowed hard. I had a feeling I was in a bit of trouble. "He said he wasn't going to chase me, that I would go back to him on my own, but he implied that he would only wait so long."

"What happens when his patience runs out?" Alden fired the question at me, his voice hard.

I shrugged helplessly. "I don't know."

"And Miami? What happened in Miami? Did that motherfucker show up in Miami?"

I shook my head as I reached forward and put my mug down on the table next to Alden's. My hands were shaking too badly to hold it. I didn't want Alden to see them shaking, so I pulled the blanket up to my chin and folded my hands in my lap.

"I didn't see him in Miami, but…" I trailed off.

"But what, Noa?" he barked, making me jump.

"It's easier if I show you," I said softly as I started to get up. "I have to get my phone."

"Sit," he commanded. "I'll get it."

He stalked out of the room but returned a minute later and thrust my phone at me. I took it quickly to hide the tremble of my hand. I punched in my password on the shattered screen as Alden watched on with angry and questioning eyes. I went to my text messages and then handed it over to him. He took it and his confusion deepened as he looked at the picture of him and Trish.

"I don't understand," he said. "Who sent this?" He looked closer and his eyes widened slightly. "It was sent the same day we got the picture, but it didn't get published until a couple of days later."

"Larson sent it to me," I answered quietly. "And I think he's the one that took the picture. I think he was the blond head you saw in the alley that night."

Alden cursed under his breath as his one hand at his side balled into a fist. He went through the next two messages with his brow drawn down in fury and puzzlement.

"I don't fucking understand what he's trying to do," he growled.

"I do," I responded in even quieter than before. Alden's eyes met mine and he waited for the explanation. "Larson Wright is probably the only person I know who has a bigger ego than you do. He thinks he is above chasing me down and trying to woo me to come back to him. He said that he won't come after me. He even told me that on the day I left him. I don't know if my relationship with you was the trigger for his latest behavior, or if it was only a matter of time, but he's trying to corral me back without physically coming for me."

Alden's fury intensified as his face grew red. He squeezed my phone so hard I thought he would crush it in his hand.

"What was the point in sending you the link?"

Ah. Right. The sex scandal.

I had hoped he would overlook that, but he rarely overlooked anything.

"I don't know." That was half-true. I didn't know what Larson thought he knew besides the little bit I had shared with him, but I knew who it was about. I did not want to have that discussion with Alden just yet.

He searched for the lie in my face, but I guess I had been convincing, because he finally stopped searching. He didn't look away, though.

"Why the fuck didn't you tell me this shit sooner, Noa? Why did you keep this from me?"

I swallowed. "It was – it *is* my problem."

He looked incredulous. "You really thought you could handle this on your own?"

I was getting a little irritated myself. "Alden, I've been handling shit on my own since I was like twelve."

"What the fuck is wrong with you?" he bellowed. "Don't you understand that he could have hurt you? He can still hurt you! Have you thought at all about your fucking safety? Have you thought at all about the other people around you that may be affected by this dildo's obsession with you? You don't have to do shit on your own, Noa. There's bravery and strength, and then there's pride and stupidity."

I flinched. Alden took in a deep, long breath.

"Noa, you can't keep shit from me like this," he said in a calmer voice as he held a hand to his forehead and squeezed his eyes shut. "It scares the fuck out of me to know that you were dealing with this by yourself." He opened his eyes and looked at me. "You need to rely on me, okay? You aren't alone anymore. This isn't *your* problem, it's *our* problem."

He bent over and kissed my forehead. "I love you."

"I love you, too," I said and realized that was my first time saying it out loud.

Alden's thumb had caressed my cheek for a moment before he stood up again.

"I have to make some phone calls," he said. "I have to make sure you'll be safe." He handed me my phone and then disappeared down the corridor.

Alden wanted me to meet Peyton as soon as possible after that night on the yacht. That hot, sexy, lovely, and then conflicting night…

"I want the two people who matter most in my life to become acquainted," Alden had said.

So immediately after the Dallas gala, we used the private jet to fly to Minneapolis to visit with Peyton. Fortunately, the foster family and the caseworkers involved didn't give him a hard time when he gave them a couple of days' notice.

I had never seen any childhood photographs of Alden, but if I had to imagine what he looked like at eleven years old, Peyton would be the face that would come to mind. He looked like a miniature version of Alden; it was so damn amazing. He had the same sandy blond hair, the same hazel eyes, and even moved like him.

I watched as Alden lifted the kid in an embrace and shamelessly kissed his face. Peyton laughed and shouted that Alden was going to squeeze him to death, but made no effort to unwrap his thin arms from around Alden's neck. A middle-aged woman with a badge hanging around her neck stood off to the side beside a middle-aged couple. Peyton's foster mother shook her head disapprovingly, but the corner of her mouth was pulled up in a slight smile as she watched the brothers with kind eyes.

"Alden, he is entirely too big for you to pick him up like that," she admonished.

Her husband stood beside her, holding what I assumed was Peyton's guitar.

"I want you to meet someone," Alden said to Peyton as he put the boy down on his feet. He held his hand and led him across the room where I stood, nervously fidgeting with the hem of my shirt.

Peyton looked up at me with a childish curiosity that I rather missed. I'm not sure if I ever had that kind of innocent quality.

"Hello, Peyton," I said quietly, holding my hand out to him.

"Peyton, this is my beautiful girl, Noa," Alden said proudly.

Peyton's eyes widened as he put his small hand into mine. He looked up at Alden and said "Like *girlfriend*? I thought you said that you would be single for life; that no piece of pussy would tie you down?"

My mouth fell open and my hand dropped to my side as I stared disbelievingly at Alden.

"That is entirely inappropriate, Peyton," the woman I assumed was a caseworker said, just as she pulled out a clipboard, probably to document what Peyton just said.

Alden grinned down at the boy. "Noa's not *just* a pussy, kid. She's a fucking diamond."

"Mr. Breck!"

"Listen, lady, he hears worse than that on Nickelodeon, I'm sure," Alden argued. "That Spongebob character says some fucked up shit."

"Stop. Talking," I said to Alden, shaking my head.

He didn't seem to need any help from *me* losing his chances of getting Peyton. He seemed perfectly capable of screwing that up by himself.

I refocused on the little boy in front of me. "Peyton, I've heard a lot about you. I am happy to finally meet you."

"It's nice to meet you, too," he said before glancing back up at Alden. He whispered his next sentence, as if I wasn't standing a foot away from him and couldn't hear everything he said. "She's really pretty."

Alden looked at me with a gentle smile and whispered back "I know. She *is* really pretty."

We sat down for lunch a little while later – all six of us. Peyton's foster parents, Jim and Mary, were kind and gave the boys as much space as they possibly could under the circumstances. They sat at the opposite end of the table and didn't interfere in any way. They spoke when necessary but seemed to do their best not to take any time away from the brothers. The caseworker, Lynn, watched Alden and Peyton carefully and didn't hide the fact that she was studying every move Alden made and every word he said. Sometimes, I got the impression that she had already made up her mind about my rock star, and I didn't particularly like it.

Peyton spoke animatedly about everything – school, friends, food, television, and music. He talked so much that he hardly ate any of his lunch. Alden hung onto every word as if the kid was about to reveal the deepest secrets of the universe. I was amazed that the brothers had only just met less than a year ago. They were so much alike and so familiar with each other that it made me realize how lacking my relationship with my one sibling was. I had known Warren my entire life and we weren't as close as Alden and Peyton were after only a few months. There was such an open exchange of love and adoration on both sides. Peyton clearly revered Alden, and not just because he was one of the most illustrious men on the planet, but because he was his big brother, and Alden was absolutely luminous in his brother's presence.

After lunch, they sat down on the couch with their guitars. Peyton played one of Friction's songs as a surprise for Alden.

"I practiced for hours and hours and hours every day for *weeks*," Peyton said after he had strummed the last note.

"I can tell," Alden said proudly as he ruffled his hair. "That was fucking amazing, Peyton."

He looked at him with such pride, and even I was mauled over by the kid's skills. He obviously inherited Alden's talent.

"Have you been practicing the other song?" he asked the younger, budding musician.

Peyton frowned slightly. "Yeah, but it's a hard one."

"It's okay," Alden assured him. "You'll keep practicing and get better, but I want to hear what you got, little man, and..." He leaned over and whispered conspiringly into the child's ear. Peyton's eyes lit up as they flickered over to me, betraying his brother without realizing it. Whatever it was Alden was whispering was about me.

I glanced at the other three adults in the room, and they looked curiously from me back to the boys.

"Ready?" Alden asked Peyton aloud.

"Let's rock it," Peyton said excitedly.

Just before strumming the first note, Alden gave me a wink that made me shiver with delight.

As soon as Alden cleared his throat, I knew what the song was. I didn't know it was possible to play Jet's "Are You Going To Be My Girl" acoustically, but Alden's fingers gracefully and easily found the notes as Peyton tried to keep up. I became a total fan girl, clapping, singing, and squealing when Alden looked at me as he sang the chorus. He got up from the couch with his guitar and walked over to where I stood, serenading me with the repetitive question of the song. I grinned and my heart fluttered about in my chest.

"I'm already your girl," I told him when the song came to a smooth end.

Ignoring the instrument between us, I stood on my toes and pulled his head down to meet mine. The kiss I bestowed upon him was at least PG-13, which was already too much for the eleven-year-old a few feet away from us and definitely too much for the crotchety caseworker. When I pulled away from him, his mouth hungrily followed after mine.

"French kissing has to be the grossest thing ever!" Peyton exclaimed, halting Alden's pursuit. "Who wants to share each other's saliva?"

He sounded so disgusted that I covered my mouth with four fingers to hide my giggle. Alden gave me a grin that promised naughty things before turning to face his brother.

"Bro," he said as he walked back to him. "One day you're going to want to share saliva with some hot chick. Trust me."

***

"How did you meet my brother?" Peyton asked me an hour later.

We were sitting side by side on the couch, playing the Xbox that was set up in the room. It was some first shooter game that I was sucking gloriously at. Alden was sitting at a table on the other side of the room, talking quietly with Lynn, Jim, and Mary. Anxiety had me glancing across the room constantly, looking for trouble. More than once, I looked over to find Lynn looking at me speculatively.

"He nearly killed me at a concert," I said absently to Peyton.

He looked up at me as if I had just said the most ridiculous thing ever. I couldn't help it. I laughed lightly.

"It's true," I said. "Your brother's enormous ego nearly killed me. I didn't really listen to Friction, but I went to the concert with my best friend because she's a manipulative little monster, and would have cried if I refused. Of course, Kristy got pit tickets, and *of course,* we ended up right against the guardrail. As soon as the band came out, the crowd surged forward and I was smooshed up against it. I wasn't happy about that and I wasn't happy about watching Alden strut around the stage as if he were God's gift to the entire female gender."

"Girls dig my brother," Peyton said with an air of authority.

I snickered. "Yeah, they do, but I wasn't one of those girls. Your brother got on my last nerve. I hated everything about him, and he knew it. He stood up there on stage, trying to make me smile and swoon and all I did was scowl. I was so glad when I thought the concert was over, but they came back out for *three* encore songs. Toward the end of the third song, Alden jumped off the stage so all of the crazy, idiot girls could touch him. They went *nuts*. I was pushed up against the railing so hard that I couldn't breathe. The closer he got to where I was, the worse it got. Then the absolute worst thing that could happen in that situation happened."

"What?" Peyton had paused the game to listen to me tell the story. He stared up at me with wide eyes, totally enthralled by the tale.

"The railing *broke* and I fell on the floor. All of those girls were so *insane* about getting to Alden that a lot of them stomped right on me like I was part of the ground."

"What happened next?" Peyton asked eagerly.

I looked down at him with a small smile. "Your brother saved me."

"Get out! He was your hero?"

I looked across the room and just happen to catch Alden's eye this time. Despite the clear tension in his jaw and neck, he winked at me and offered me a sweet smile.

"He's still my hero."

"He's my hero, too," Peyton said softly. I turned my attention back to him. "Someday soon he is going to come get me, adopt me, and let me live with him. I like Jim and Mary, but Alden is my *real* family, and he seems like he really, really loves you. So, I guess that makes you my family, too, since he really, really loves me, too. I can't wait until we're all together."

My heart squeezed in my chest and I had to blink rapidly to keep my tears at bay. I'd only known this kid for a couple of hours and I was head over heels in love.

"Alden will be a very, very happy man when the adoption is finalized," I promised in a slightly quavering voice. "And no matter what, he will always be there for you, and he will always love you, because even though he is a complete idiot, Alden Breck has the biggest heart I've ever known."

Peyton's brow furrowed. "Are you about to cry?"

"No, I think it's just allergies." I smiled and got to my feet, putting the controller on the couch. "I'm going to go find something to take. I'll be back in a few minutes."

I hurried away from the kid before the dam broke. I mistakenly glanced over at Alden again. He watched me with his brow furrowed just like Peyton's. When he ignored Lynn and started to stand up, I gave a small shake and jerked my head at the caseworker, and then looked away before she could see my stricken face.

Inside the en-suite bathroom, I stood in front of the sink with the palms of my hands pressing into my lower back as I stared down at the floor. Big, fat tears hung on the ends of my eyelashes before dropping to the tile.

I hated that Alden had to go through so much shit to get Peyton. He was his brother for heaven's sake! It shouldn't have to be so hard. Peyton's life had been hard enough already. With Alden, I knew he could be happy, healthy, and above all else, *loved.* Alden had a bit of a Peter Pan complex, but I knew he was really trying to be a better person for Peyton's sake. I knew that he would do whatever he had to do for his little brother, the only flesh and blood he had in the world to love.

Love.

I loved Alden, despite the fact that I had tried so hard to hate him before. I never knew it was possible for me to love someone in the way that I love this untamed man. I thought for sure that my teen years and my years with Larson had sucked my soul and heart dry, leaving me incapable of ever trusting another man, let alone loving him. I wasn't sure that I even knew *how* to love someone. I thought I was utterly, thoroughly broken, as the ink on my chest claimed, but Alden Breck snuck up on me. He claimed me, fixed me, cared for me, and loved me, and he demanded nothing in return. This was a man who never allowed himself to feel more than passing lust for a woman, who swore never to fall in love. It's not like he needed a permanent girl on his arm, he had millions of horny women across the globe willing to step in as needed. He had been happy living his life just like that until I literally fell at his feet.

Someone rapped on the bathroom door, but I knew without asking who it was. I wiped at my eyes with the hem of my shirt before pulling the door open. Alden stood with both arms up on the doorframe, making his T-shirt pull up over his taut abdomen. His jeans were hung low on his hips, belted with a leather strap studded with small silver spikes and an obnoxious silver buckle that spelled out "Friction." His black shirt was a Friction brand, too, featuring a visual of all of the guys in the band. With Alden at the center, the band fanned out on either side of him and the band name was written out in white scripted letters across the top. Wearing his own band's T-shirt was audacious, and when I had told him so earlier that day before Peyton's arrival, he had reminded me that he was a "conceited fuck and a brilliant musician," so why shouldn't he strut around in his own band gear.

"And I look damn good." He had grinned at me. I was in no position to dispute that because my hands had been sneaking under the hem of his shirt to touch his bare skin.

I used to find his pompous jackass-ness annoying and off-putting, and it used to strike a desire for violence inside of me, but not anymore. I began to find it endearing, one of the many pieces of Alden that made me smile as much as it made me want to punch him.

Blocking my exit from the bathroom, he studied my face for a moment. I knew he wanted to dig around in my head, but he bit the inside of his cheek and I knew he was going to refrain for the time being. I couldn't tell him what I was thinking anyway. I couldn't tell him of the plan formulating in my head.

"Peyton is about to leave," he quietly informed me.

"Right." I turned away to dry my hands on a hand towel. "How do you think it's going with Lynn?" I asked in a low voice that didn't carry past the bathroom threshold.

"She thinks that my manners are lacking and that I am teaching Peyton some very bad habits, but she admitted that she can't argue against me in court for that."

I turned back to face him. He dropped one arm and gently put a hand on my cheek. His thumb caressed my skin as he continued to speak.

"I have to take a drug test, attend a court approved parenting class, and let someone take a walk around my house in L.A."

"And stay out of trouble," I added, hooking my thumbs in his jean's pockets.

"And stay out of trouble," he agreed with a small smile as he pushed hair off my face. "She wants to check out a few more things, but said if everything is okay, that they she can *try* to get things moving a little faster."

He didn't say it, but I knew that I was one of the "few more things" that needed to be checked out. Why wouldn't I be? My biggest sins weren't documented anywhere – not anymore, but it still made me uneasy. Larson knew a lot about my past and could talk if he wanted to, but I didn't think anyone would listen. He would just look like the jealous ex-boyfriend.

"You've been crying," Alden said, breaking a short lapse of silence. His eyes locked intently with mine.

"It's hard to look that kid in the face and see how hopeful he is," I said, sniffing.

Alden frowned. "Are you having doubts? Do you think I can't do this?"

"Yes, of course I think you can do it, Alden," I said soothingly, rubbing his arm. "It's just that they are making it a lot harder than it has to be. I know he's a child and they need to be sure he'll be safe, but I think they're being unfair because of what they read in the papers."

He sighed. "Yeah, but what can I do? I'm doing every fucking thing they want me to do. Jumping through every fucking hoop. I don't know what else to do." He pushed a hand through his hair. "I think I want to hang around here for another week. This week, he'll be on spring break and Mary and Jim said it was okay with them if we hung out."

"Does every visit have to be supervised by a caseworker?"

"Fuck no, thank god."

"What about all of the work you have to do?"

Alden shrugged. "I'll do what I can remotely and just make sure we're back in L.A. next Monday for the meeting."

"Alden!" Peyton shouted from the living room.

"Be right there!" Alden called over his shoulder. When he turned back to me, he pulled me in close for a kiss. "I love you."

I didn't think I'd ever get used to hearing him say that to me. I just hoped that he would still feel the same way in a couple of weeks.

I moaned and bit down on my bottom lip as Alden's teeth lightly grazed my neck. One strong hand slipped beneath the waistband of my shorts and under the scrap of lace. His index finger trailed lightly over my swollen clit, but when my hips automatically began to shoot up off his lap, his other hand restrained me, resting heavily on my abdomen. Two fingers pressed on the sensitive knot and I moaned again.

"We're supposed…ahhh…to be talking," I managed breathlessly.

"I want you to come on my hand first," he said huskily, his lips against my neck. "Then I want you to come on my face." He abandoned my stomach and pinched a hard nipple through my tank top. His hips rose as he grinded his cock into my ass, making him groan with want. "Then I want you to come on my cock. When we're all finished, we'll talk."

I feebly attempted to remove his hand from my pants. "But this is important!"

His two fingers slipped inside of me. I gasped and my legs slammed shut around his hand automatically.

"This is important, too," he insisted and pushed his fingers deeper inside of me.

"Alden," I whimpered his name as his other hand pulled on my leg until my thighs were wide open again.

"Mmm, Noa," he growled in my ear. My head fell back on his shoulder and my eyes closed as my mouth fell open in a moan.

When I had sat down on the couch beside him ten minutes earlier, it was to tell him I was leaving. Not forever, but there was something I needed to do back on the east coast. Considering the circumstances with Larson, I knew I'd have a fight on my hands, but what I had on my hands was a hot rock star that wanted to pleasure me. Just before my thought process got all garbled, however, I realized that talking to Alden in an after-sex haze may work out better. I decided to take it all in, to store away every touch, lick, and nick of teeth, every moan and every groan, and every breath.

Later, I would remember in sharp detail how he held me, kissed me, and felt inside of me.

"Look at that," he commanded in a whisper. "Open your eyes and look at my hand moving in your shorts. Open your eyes, baby."

I opened my eyes and tilted my head to look. I watched the outline of his hand as he slowly fingered me and palmed my clit.

"It looks so fucking dirty," Alden purred. "There is something so very obscene about my hidden hand making you come in your panties and in your shorts."

I cursed as my legs began to tremble. My nipples pressed against my T-shirt, aching for his touch again.

"Ride my hand, sweetheart. That's it, ride my fucking fingers, Noa."

I rocked against his hand, taking his fingers deep. I put my hands over his hand and pressed hard as I grinded against him.

"Yeah, baby," Alden encouraged. "You're getting so close. You're about to come all over my hand, aren't you, sexy?"

He pinched a nipple between his thumb and forefinger and squeezed. I screamed as my orgasm rolled through me, my hips bucking wildly against our hands. He whispered declarations of love and adoration in my ear as I recovered, shaking helplessly. My head had fallen back again and my eyes were closed.

"I love you, Noa. You're so fucking beautiful. You look like a fucking angel when you come, baby."

He slowly removed his hand from my shorts. A second later, I felt his fingertips probing at my mouth and I immediately parted my lips.

He pressed his wet fingers into my mouth, making me clean my essence off them.

"Good girl," he murmured.

I let out a small yelp as he suddenly lifted me to my feet. My legs were a little shaky, but I managed to remain standing as he pulled my shorts and panties down. I stepped out of them, noting how wet they were even though I hadn't ejaculated. His hands palmed my ass as he groaned with appreciation. I bit back another yelp when his teeth sank into the flesh. I looked back at him just as he released me and stretched out on the couch.

"Bring that sweet pussy over here," he said with a hungry look in his eyes. I mean, *hungry*, famished, desperate for something to eat. That something being *me*.

I turned to face him and looked at him skeptically. He waved a finger, beckoning me.

"Sit," he commanded with a wicked smile. He pointed to his mouth. "Here."

Oh!

Hesitantly, I moved toward him. I could honestly say that in all of my years of various types of sex, I had never straddled a guy's face, and I was feeling a little uneasy about it.

When I didn't move fast enough, Alden sat up, reached for me, and yanked me over. Awkwardly, I swung one leg over him and came down on my knee, but my other leg remained on the floor.

"What are you afraid of, Little One?" he asked in a husky whisper.

"Smothering you with my fat thighs?" I squeaked.

He chuckled and lightly slapped my ass. In a voice dripping with sex and desire, he said, "Come here and let me taste you."

Carefully, I placed my other knee on the couch by his head, but I was still nervous about covering his face with my vagina. Alden, however, was eager. He lifted his head and licked my clit, and I shuddered. With a groan, he grabbed my hips and forced me down to meet his hungry mouth. I gasped and then moaned loudly when he vigorously began to suck on my clit.

His eyes bored into mine as he feasted on me. His hands smoothed up my stomach and cupped my breasts. When his fingers squeezed my puckered nipples, my hips instinctively rocked, making me grind my vulva on his face and making Alden groan deeply.

Panicked, I immediately froze and said, "I'm sorry! Did I hurt you? Are you okay?"

I felt very inadequate, clumsy, and stupid. Being with Alden always made me feel inexperienced when I was far from it, but he was so good with his hands, his mouth, and his cock, and always worked me over with such care, that he seemed to wipe out everyone before him. Though I had never been in this cunnilingus position before, I wasn't new to sex, but I felt almost virginal during any sexual act with Alden.

His hands fell away from my tits and once again gripped my waist. He began to move me, making me grind on him again. He growled his approval, and wordless sounds fell from my mouth as erotic pleasure and heat seared through me. His tongue was inside of me, probing deep at the fleshy walls, moaning and tasting me with delectation, and his hands returned to my breasts as I continued to move against him.

Alden's eyes never left mine, even when they became hooded with satisfaction. I knew he could sense the emotions that I had temporarily tucked away. I knew he could see deeper into me than anyone I'd ever known or ever will know, but he couldn't see everything. Not yet anyway, and I needed that advantage for a little while.

I came, shuddering and shaking as my hips jerked wildly. Alden groaned as he lapped at my pussy and caressed my body as my orgasm died down. After I eased off him and stood on shaking legs in front of the couch, Alden sat up, spun me around, and then pulled me backward onto his lap. With a couple of small readjustments, a few seconds later, I was poised over his erection, the tip poking at my entrance.

"If this hurts, we'll change positions," he said softly and kissed my shoulder.

Slowly, I eased down on him, taking him little by little until I was firmly seated on him and he was deep inside of me. It was almost uncomfortable, to have something that barely fit lodged inside of me. I moved slowly on him, making him hiss in my ear.

"You feel so good, Noa," he groaned.

In response, I turned my head at an awkward angle and shoved my tongue into his mouth. I kissed him with a brutality, hard and unyielding, and bit his tongue and lips nearly hard enough to draw blood. He groaned, even as he tried to pull away from me with surprise, but I pressed a hand at the back of his head, refusing to let him go. When I finally broke the kiss, we were both breathless and he had begun to move slowly inside of me.

“Please, fuck me hard,” I whispered on his lips.

He was reluctant. He didn’t want to hurt me, but sometimes, pain is fucking awesome.

With some effort, I dislodged one of his hands from my hips and brought it up to my tit. Alden growled as his hand kneaded the flesh and his fingers plucked at the hard bud. My lips were still lightly pressed to his as I removed his other hand and slid it down to my clit.

“You fucked me hard the other night,” I reminded him softly. “And I loved it.”

“Different position,” he murmured, and then his tongue darted out and licked my lips.

“If it becomes unbearable, I’ll ask you to stop,” I promised. “I want you deep and hard.”

He groaned again when I reached down and squeezed his balls. On a reflex, his hips jerked hard a couple of times. I pushed myself up slowly until only his bulbous head remained inside of me. He froze as he waited to see what I would do, ceased moving and breathing. When I dropped down on him hard, he let out a pitiful groan as I held back a scream. He really wanted to take me hard, but he didn’t want to admit it. Again, I rose, slowly easing up his shaft, and again I fell hard, impaling myself on him.

“Fuck, Noa,” he groaned as he thrust into me. “Why the fuck do you always fucking undo me!”

He abandoned my breasts and clit and tightly held onto my hips again. Without any further hesitation, he lifted me and slammed me down onto his thrusting cock. He began to fuck me like this, always moving my body to meet his with brutal force. His tongue dashed into my mouth and he swallowed my moans and screams as he rammed his engorged appendage into my pussy again and again. With each thrust, I felt him deeper and deeper, slamming into the opening of my womb ruthlessly.

The pain was indescribable. His cock was like a battering ram inside of me, made to break down walls and cause destruction. I knew I would be bruised and swollen for days afterward, but I didn’t want him to stop. I cried out for him to fuck me harder, begged him to give me his hardest. He was reluctant at first, but assuming that my cries were strictly cries of pleasure, he relented. He returned one hand back to my pussy, rubbing my clit in hard, fast circles. I was shocked and aghast when I felt that familiar uncoiling inside of me, that hot pressure building and then begging for a release.

"I love you, Noa," Alden panted in my ear. "You're mine, you'll always be mine. This pussy, this body…" His other hand flattened over my heart. "This heart…it's all mine."

I screamed as my orgasm exploded from me, soaking Alden's hand, our legs, the couch, the floor. I couldn't seem to stop coming and practically sobbing, a fucked-up combination of emotions and sensations. Alden roared as he began to spurt his seed inside of me, still pumping his cock hard against my sore cervix. My body convulsed as we rode the waves of our orgasms.

I wanted to curl up in his lap and sleep, but I had to talk to him while his brain was still a bit muddled.

"Alden?" I whispered his name.

"Hmm?" I didn't have to turn my head to know that his eyes were closed. One hand was clasped with mine and the other lazily caressed my thigh.

"I was thinking that maybe while you're here with Peyton this week I can go back to Philly to take care of some things."

I felt his body stiffen against my back. "To take care of what?"

"Well, I don't know how long I will be in L.A. after the gala. I should probably get a few more things."

"I will buy you whatever you need. Clothes, shoes, personal care shit, whatever you need."

"I also need to see my doctor," I hastily added.

"Are you sick? Because I can pay for a doctor, too, since Sahara stole mine," he said grumpily.

"No, but I'm on the pill. Before, if I missed a dose or two, I didn't have a reason to panic. I think I should get a shot or something."

"Did you miss a pill?" he asked worriedly.

"No," I said carefully. "But I don't want to take any chances."

He sighed. "Well, same thing, Noa. I can pay for you to see someone here or in L.A."

"And I want to see my brother and Tucker."

"If I told you I'd fly Tucker and Warren here or wherever you want, you're just going to find another excuse to use, aren't you?" he asked with a hint of bitterness. "What's up, Noa? Why do you really want to go? Is it me? Is it Peyton? Are you not cut out for parenting a pre-teen boy?"

I turned my head to look at his face. I was surprised that he would think that. I'd known about Peyton since very early in our relationship and never once gave any indication that I had a problem with it. Furthermore, why would he think it was him?

"You self-centered cretin," I snapped at him. "Not everything is about you. Maybe it's about me. Maybe I've never been away from home for more than a week and I just need to be among my own things for a few days. I know that you're used to this life, living out of hotels and tour buses and not seeing your home for weeks and sometimes months, but I'm not used to it. I want to sleep in my own bed for a little while, see my own old-lady neighbor, and drive my Camaro around the streets I'm familiar with. It's only for a week or so. God knows when I'll be back since we haven't really spoken about how we plan on making our relationship work with you being a west coast guy and me, an east coast girl."

We looked at each other for a long moment before he seemed to deflate a little.

"I am not comfortable with you going back where Larson will have easy access to you," he admitted.

"Well, it's my home. I'll have to go back eventually, but besides that, he seemed to have no problems accessing me when I was a thousand miles away, either."

"I know." He nodded slowly. "But the distance still makes me feel better. What if he surprises you on the street again? What if he shows up at your apartment? Hides in your car?"

"I don't know, Alden," I admitted, and then remembered something he had said to me what seemed like ages ago. "I can't not live my life because I fear something, or in this case, someone."

"Who was the asshole that said that?" Alden growled.

"You," I said with a small smile. "You were that asshole."

He groaned and let his head fall back against the couch. "Noa, I am fucking terrified that something will happen to you. It would fucking kill me if I let you go back and he hurt you."

"I'll call you every day," I promised.

"Ten times a day and maybe a few times in between," he amended.

"And I'll text you several times a day."

"Every hour on the hour."

"How about four hours?" I suggested.

"Every two hours and that's final."

"Okay," I said. I wasn't going to text him every two hours, but I wanted to appease him.

"And your ass better be in L.A. by next Monday morning."

"I will do my best."

"When are you leaving?" he asked, sounding very unhappy.

"I think I'll go tomorrow morning."

He dropped his head and looked at me again, and then put a hand possessively on my neck.

"I don't want you to go," he whispered.

"I know," I whispered back.

"Promise me you will be vigilant of your surroundings at all times, and promise me you will get the locks done on your car *immediately*."

"I promise and I promise."

"And you won't go anywhere alone after dark. You'll call your brother or Tucker."

"I promise," I said.

"Fuck, Noa," he pressed his lips to mine. "As much as I want to lock you up and never let you go, I know I can't. Just promise me you'll stay safe."

"I promise," I whispered.

I kept that promise. I stayed safe. But I would lose something else during our separation.

His trust.

Todd F. Canyon was born into a blue-blooded family in North Carolina. He attended school at Princeton, where he met his wife Giordina. After grad school, the couple decided to settle in New Jersey, but after twenty-two years, Todd moved his family back to the state of North Carolina where he ran for and won a seat on the U.S. Senate. Now, he and his wife and their four children and dog and cat live in D.C. in a beautiful home in the neighborhood of Berkley-Foxhall. Although Senator Canyon got a new phone and a new number when he obtained his position, he was a bit of a nostalgic man and still retained his old number as well on a separate phone. It wasn't a secret phone, like a Hoe-phone or Mistress-phone, but it was the phone that was strictly non-work related. The line would never be tied up with business calls when his family and close friends, like say, his very close friend, the governor of Minnesota, wanted to reach him. The American people loved that about Canyon, that he still put his family first, even before the state of North Carolina or our great nation. Add in his dark hair, bright green eyes, his athletic physique and his fighting spirit for the poor and middle-class, single parents, and women's rights, and you had the formula for the makings of a future president of the free world.

So, it must have sucked for him to receive a phone call from me that Sunday afternoon while he was enjoying a luncheon in his home with his wife, kids, and a few of his politician buddies.

"This is Todd Canyon," he said jovially when he answered his phone. In the background, there were many voices, young and old, laughter, and the tinkling of silverware on plates.

I was silent at first, choked up on my wrecked nerves. Other than on the television, I hadn't heard his voice in years, and it immediately stirred up all sorts of memories and emotions.

"Hello?" Todd said when I didn't answer.

"Hi, Todd," I said in a rush of breath.

He didn't speak right away. For a few seconds, I heard only the dinner party in the background and his light breathing. He couldn't even pretend that I was someone from his office because this number was just for family and friends, and me. I knew he was startled to hear my voice all of these years later, and I couldn't even imagine what was going through his mind.

"It's me, it's—"

"I know," he said in a hushed tone. "I can never forget the sound of your voice."

I felt color rush into my cheeks, but I ignored it.

"I'm sorry to call you like this, but…" I took a breath. "Can I see you?"

"Yes," he said the word before I could even finish my sentence. "Yes, of course."

I noted that the party sounds were muted. He must have walked into another room.

"When and where?" Todd asked. "Are you in New Jersey?"

"No, I'm in D.C. So, as soon as you can. Just name the place."

"Tonight," he said with readily. "I want to see you tonight. Do you have a pen and paper?"

"Yes, go ahead," I said in a slightly shaky voice.

He gave me an address and combination number for the key lock box on the door.

"I'll try to be there by ten-thirty," Todd said just before we hung up. "You can go in anytime. No one is there."

"Okay. Thank you."

"See you tonight, Noa," he whispered and ended the call.

With a shaking hand, I dropped my phone onto the seat of the rental car beside me. Todd Canyon wasn't just a U.S. senator, but at one time, he was my Ethics Professor. He was also, ironically enough, the man I was caught having sex with in his wife's car the day of my arrest.

My. Heart. Pounded.

Where have you been
Where did you go
Who did you see
While I was wondering about you
"Back Again"
Friction

Alden

You ever get a feeling like shit just isn't right? Like you can feel it in your chest, squeezing the fuck out of your lungs and your heart, and it makes you all jumpy and shit? That's exactly how I felt when I let Noa get out of the car at the airport a few days ago, and the feeling just intensified every day that she was gone.

I shouldn't have let her go, or maybe I should have gone with her. She didn't think that her ex-asshole Larson would do anything drastic, but obviously, my Little One never saw *Sleeping With the Enemy*.

As much as I wanted to keep her with me, I couldn't. I often had the illusion that I was the one in charge in our relationship, but it was just that, an illusion. Noa did what she wanted to do, and sometimes, it just happened to be what I wanted her to do, too.

I started to fall in love with the little beauty when she defiantly refused to smile or acknowledge my fucking awesomeness and the awesomeness of my band while in the front row of *my* concert weeks ago in San Francisco. I was having all kinds of fantasies of putting my tongue in her sweet little scowling mouth at the end of my third encore, and maybe pulling her backstage to get to know her a little better and find out why someone who hates my band so much was at a Friction concert.

I had *no* intentions of taking her backstage unconscious and with both of us just escaping with our lives. Fucking horny skanks stomped all over my little scowling beauty! I'm pretty sure she had put her claws in my heart after she regained consciousness, saw me, and unleashed her wicked little tongue. I was so tempted to just lay down on top of her and shut her up, but then I wouldn't have heard the funny little shit she had to say about me in her sweet, melodic voice.

When I ran into her at the airport, it was purely by accident. As I was adding my contact information and getting hers, a reminder flashed on her phone. That had nothing to do with me switching from the private jet I was going to take with the guys to a commercial flight that left way earlier in the morning than I'd liked. When Kristina mentioned that Noa was a writer, I really had no intentions of using her books as props. Maybe I wanted to catch up on some reading and read my first ever romance novel, though I seriously never expected to get that drawn in that quickly, and certainly never expected that some parts of the book were so pornographic that maybe *my* cheeks may have turned a soft shade of pink. When I convinced her to go to dinner, I especially never thought I'd hang on to every damn word that came out of her mouth.

This woman who was comfortable in jeans and a T-shirt, didn't do anything fancy to her hair, had no funky designs on her nails, and who seemed to be offended by the idea of wearing makeup on a daily basis was the complete opposite of any woman that I ever even considered spending time with, and she was *fucking perfect*. Her beauty was in her brain, but it was also in her simplicity. I was a goner long before I saw her in her gown the night of that first gala. I just couldn't admit it to myself, and sometimes, I'm pissed off that I lost all of those days with her, pretending that my heart was unaffected by her.

Sliding into her for the first time was unlike anything I've ever had before. Like I said, I have been with a lot of women – young, old, skinny, curvy, big, and beautiful, and even a few ugly ones because they had nice tits or a nice ass. I have had actresses, other musicians, and even a couple of porn stars, but not one of them could come close to what Noa's snug, warm pussy did to my cock. None of the beautiful faces I've seen at the height of climax looked anything like the heavenly, perfectly resplendent face of one N.H. Eddington in the throes of passion. I have always appreciated the delicate curves of a woman's body, but not as minutely as I enjoyed hers; the slender column of her neck, her shoulders, her chest, her full, rounded breasts, and even the depth of her sexy navel. I loved the way her smooth thighs felt pressed against my legs, the way she inhaled whenever my fingers caressed the backs of her pretty little knees, and the little giggles she couldn't help but to release when I stroked her dainty little toes. I loved the sighs she made and the adoration in her eyes when I reverently kissed each finger and the soft flesh where her arms bent at the elbow. I loved running my hands down her smooth back, down to the tiny dip just above her lush ass, and I loved the soft moans she made when I pulled her cute little earlobes between my teeth and flicked them with my tongue. There was not another woman in the universe that had a body like my Little One.

Even if she had never let me touch her, make her moan and writhe and come so explosively, I would have fallen in love with Noa. She was everything I didn't know I ever wanted or needed. In a matter of weeks, she had become a part of me, sewn into the very fabric of my soul.

And now she was gone, not for good, but for too damn long. Gone off into enemy territory. Her brother and her friend Tucker promised to keep an eye on her, but my confidence in them was shaken on her first day back in Philly when they lost her. Seriously fucking lost her. Tucker had gone to pick her up at the airport, but he said either she walked past him out the door or she was never on the plane. That was bullshit. I bought her ticket. I put it in her hands. I dropped her off at the correct terminal and watched her walk inside.

Later, when she was supposed to be home, Warren didn't find her there. Noa said she must have just missed the guys both times. When Warren went over there the following morning before he went to work, he found her sleeping soundly in her bed, but I wasn't able to shake the uneasiness that was knocking around in my chest. Especially since I had fucking lost her, too.

We had agreed upon a reasonable schedule for phone calls and text messages. I wasn't trying to be a controlling bastard like Larson had been to her. I was trying to be sure she was safe from *him*. Yeah, I am possessive, but I didn't want her to feel like she was on a leash, but on that first day, I wished I *had* put her on a leash, so that I could have given it a good yank to get her back. She was in the wind for hours, and when I did get a hold of her, she blamed it on poor reception and just being busy. I made myself believe her, even though my gut told me she was lying.

***

I spent the first couple of days after Noa left with Peyton. We played video games, watched movies, and even built a snowman in his foster parents' backyard (because there's a *shitload* of snow in Minnesota in the month of March). Of course, we made some incredible music, too. Even though he was still learning, Peyton definitely had talent. I wasn't too surprised; he *is* my brother.

Sometimes we just sat back and chilled, and talked about everything and nothing. He was such a cool kid. He had a good head on his shoulders, was smart as hell, and stayed out of trouble. He was the exact opposite of what I was at his age. It was hard to believe we came from the same womb, and very similar backgrounds.

When I first realized I had a brother, another kid that Tammy threw away into the foster care system, I was mad as hell, but I was also so damn scared. I went through terrible things at her hands, shit that had scarred me for life, shit I'll never talk about. I was so scared that she messed the kid up, or let someone else mess him up, and I was worried about what kind of foster families he was stuck with. I guess most mean well, but there are always those fuckers that slide under the radar, the ones that use the state's money to buy drugs and other shit and do nothing for the kids; or the fuckers that beat the shit out of the kids, or worse. Fortunately, Peyton has only moved around twice, and the latest family was very good to him. Plus, they weren't star struck, babbling idiots when I was around.

I had to make sure that Peyton continued to be treated right, and he would be treated the best if he were with me. The kid would never have to live the way I lived when I was with Tammy. He would never have to live in a flea and roach infested filthy apartment, he'd never be hungry, he would always have clean, nice clothes and shoes, and I would never beat the piss out of him or let anyone else hurt him.

It wasn't fair that the people at child services used whatever they read about me in the gossip magazines, or saw about me on TV against me. Half the shit wasn't true, and what was true, certainly wasn't bad enough to warrant me not having the rights to my little brother. There were kids out there being abused and neglected by parents that did far worse things than I did, but their lives weren't broadcasted for all to see. They often got a free pass while I had to fight my ass off just to get a few minutes with him at first. Things had gotten better, but not enough. It had been months and I was still fighting for him. I would fight for him forever if necessary, but as it turned out, I didn't have to…

Thursday morning, four days after Noa left, I got a phone call from my attorney, Rick the Dick, aptly named because the man was ruthless with legal matters. He couldn't directly represent me in Minnesota since he was out of California, but he worked very closely with the law firm in Minneapolis that was handling my case.

"What's up, Rick?"

"I don't know whose prostate you massaged, Breck, but I got some incredifuckable news for you."

"I'm not getting any younger, so maybe you should tell me already."

"I just got off the phone with Stan. Yesterday, there was a meeting with Peyton's caseworker, his child advocate, and a few others. They're going to let you take Peyton, Alden. It's going to take about a week for all of the paperwork to be done, so you can't leave the state with him yet, but as of today, he will be in your care. You have a few less steps to take since you're his brother and not some random person, but the actual adoption process will still take several months."

I dropped down onto the couch like a pile of rocks, in a complete state of shock.

"How?" It was the only word I could manage to say.

"Not exactly sure. Stan says it came from high up. Who cares how? Peyton's yours."

Peyton is mine. That was all that mattered. I was so fucking thrilled that I could barely stop and listen to all of the shit I needed to know.

As soon as I hung up with Rick, I called Noa to tell her the news. She had reacted the way I imagined she would – she squealed and fired off ten thousand questions. She was genuinely happy and excited for Peyton and me.

And still… There was something not right.

I figured things would feel right again when I saw her in L.A. Maybe the only thing wrong was me. I wasn't used to all of those heavy ass emotions. Before Noa, I never got emotionally involved with women, except maybe Trish. Even then, it was more of a mutual respect than anything else. I *cared* about her and I liked spending time with her, but I didn't love her.

I didn't leave myself much time to think about what was going on with Noa. I had a lot to do to prepare for Peyton. I had to hire a tutor and maybe a nanny to keep an eye on him while I was performing or even just immersed in the business side of things. I had to make sure the bedroom I had allocated as his in L.A. was clean and ready. I had to make appointments to meet with the child welfare people in California and a dozen other things.

When Peyton arrived later that afternoon with all of his belongings – most of which I had given him – the kid had launched himself at me, wrapped his small arms around my neck, and cried. It fucking killed me. Literally fucking killed me. I don't cry. I don't ever fucking cry, but I had to fight tears away and swallow repeatedly until the lump that had formed in my throat became manageable.

When he pulled away, wiping his eyes and snot with his sleeve, he puffed out his chest and announced, "I wasn't crying or anything. I had something in my eyes."

I knelt before him with my hands on his arms. "Peyton, it's okay to cry. I'm not her, okay? I'm not Tammy. I won't hit you or yell at you for crying, especially when you're crying because you're happy."

His chin wobbled as he nodded. Seconds later, more tears streamed out of the kid's eyes that were just like mine. "I wasn't allowed to cry after my dad died," he whispered. "She would get so mad and…and…"

Revulsion flooded my body. "You don't have to tell me what she did if you don't want to. I had to live with her, too. I know how she is. If you want to talk about it, you can. If you don't, that's okay, too. But just know this, Peyton, she doesn't have a place with us, okay? We can be miserable and sad people because of her, or we can piss her the fuck off and be the most incredible, badass, awesome motherfuckers out there."

He sniffled as he thought about that.

"I want us to be badass, awesome motherfuckers," Peyton said few seconds later. He stood up a little taller.

I stood up again and put my hand on his back to guide him into the living room.

"Good news then, bro," I said with a grin. "We already are."

twenty-three

Someone must have really loved me in Minnesota, because the paperwork that should have taken days was finished by late Friday afternoon. I called Noa as soon as I knew when we would be leaving.

"Hey, we're heading home tomorrow afternoon," I told her after she answered. "When the fuck are *you* going to be on your way home?"

"Is that your way of asking me to move in?" she asked groggily.

"I'm not asking. I'm telling. Pack up your shit and get on a plane and meet me at *home*."

"I can't move in with you, Alden," she said on a sigh.

"Why the hell not? We've been practically living together for weeks."

"That's different, and you know it is. Our relationship is still very new. I don't want to be put in a situation where I am completely dependent on a man again. It's not because of you, but because of me. It just…it scares me to put myself in that place."

My heart was beating too fast. Peyton watched from his seat across from me. I put on a smile for him, though inside, I had that fucking feeling again. The feeling that something was wrong, that Noa was, I don't know, hiding shit from me or something. That's how I felt for weeks after that day in New York that she had lunch with Sahara. I knew something was wrong, that she wasn't telling me something, but I couldn't figure out what.

"Okay," I said patiently. "Okay, I get that, so what the fuck happens now? You don't want to do that, but are you not…" Fuck. I almost couldn't finish the sentence. I swallowed and said, "Are you not going to meet me in L.A.?"

"Oh! No, no, no! I'm going to L.A., Alden, I promise. I bought my ticket after we hung up last night. I'm flying out Sunday evening. I'll text you all of my flight details so you can pick me up, you know, in the Bugatti," she teased. Some of the tension in my chest loosened. "Do you really have a Bugatti or did you just say that to try to impress me?"

"I'm Alden Motherfucking Badass Breck," I said with a wink at Peyton. "Little Noa, that alone is impressive. I don't need a car to impress you."

She snorted on the other end. "Yeah, you'll need like an army of Bugattis to make up for my lack of being impressed by Alden Motherfucking Lameass Breck."

I laughed. I loved that my Little Noa didn't make it easy for me. I didn't think that she'd ever stop challenging me and I didn't think I'd ever stop liking it.

"We'll talk about the future in a couple of weeks, after your meeting, after the gala, you know, after everything starts to settle down," she said quietly. "I wasn't really expecting to fall in love with a rock star that lives on the other side of the country."

"I wasn't expecting to fall in love like ever," I said.

"Well, it's because I'm Noa Harlow Motherfucking Kickass Eddington," she said in a macho voice.

"Fuck yeah," I agreed. "I'll call you after we land. Stay safe, Little One. You got two more days. Don't let anything bad happen to you or I'm going to be pissed."

"I will be shipping some of my things out there today, just some little reminders of home, and then I'm going up to the penthouse since I'll be flying out of LaGuardia. Once I'm there, I'll stay there until it's time to leave for the airport. Okay?"

I liked the idea of her being in my penthouse, but she was still going too close to where Larson lived, worked, and played. Oh yeah, I learned a lot about that asshole since Noa told me about him stalking her.

"Please, just be careful," I said, pinching the bridge of my nose.

"Promise," she said. "I love you. Tell Peyton I'll see him soon. I can't wait."

"I love you, too, little kickass."

She snickered and then the call ended.

That went well.

But the growing sense of doom hung over me like my own personal dark cloud.

***

Sunday afternoon was the beginning of a shit storm. I should have already had my shit storm umbrella, since my instincts warned me a storm was coming.

I was hanging out at my pool with Peyton, James, his pregnant wife, Linda, and their two kids, Hash, and *finally,* Doctor Greg, who had finally detached himself from Sahara. The only person missing was my girl, but she would be there later that night after everyone was already gone, which was fine with me. I'd have her all to myself.

"I still can't believe you have a girlfriend," Linda said, shaking her head. "A real girlfriend, like it's mutual on both sides and not some delusional fan."

I had known Linda nearly as long as I'd known James, for well over thirteen years. She was one of very few female friends that I had.

"I still think he's using some kind of mind control," Hash joked. At least I thought he was joking. "That girl hated him from the moment she laid eyes on him, and now she's fucking in love with him? Definitely something wrong there."

"I really like Noa," Greg piped in as he played with his phone.

"You're just saying that because you're screwing one of her best friends," I said with a snort. "By the way, are you done with that yet? Because my girl that you like so much doesn't quite have the same bedside manner as you do."

"Like when you had the sniffles a few weeks ago and you were crying like a little bitch and she yelled at you to man up?" James laughed.

I scowled. "I had a head cold! My sinuses hurt!"

"I think I like her already," Linda said as she laughed with everyone else. "She doesn't take any of your shit, huh?"

"Not even a little bit," I beamed.

Greg stood up suddenly, his face bleak as he stared at his phone.

"What's up, Doc?" I asked as I threw a wayward water football back into the pool. Peyton and James' kids were all getting along great, splashing around in the pool.

Greg's eyes met mine, and I was suddenly aware of my personal doom cloud again.

"I need to talk to you in private," Greg said solemnly, and without another word, he went inside the house.

The others looked on with curiosity, but they didn't ask any questions or follow me inside as I followed Greg. I was surprised when he kept walking through the kitchen, through the living room, and then continued to walk.

"Where the hell are you going?" I asked.

"To the music room," he said flatly.

"Umm, why?"

"Because it's soundproof."

That wasn't a good. That meant that whatever he needed to tell me was going to piss me off, bad enough where he wouldn't have wanted Peyton and the kids to hear it. I put my hand in my pocket and pulled out my own phone to check the time. Noa should be getting on her flight in a matter of minutes.

Once we were inside the music room, Greg closed the door and took several steps away from me before speaking.

"Have you been on Twitter today?" he asked.

"Well, I'm not sure why you needed to bring me all the fuck out here to ask me that question, but no, I have not been on Twitter today." I usually tweeted a few times a day, just to give my fans something to read and retweet, and do whatever the hell else they do with it, but I had been just relaxing with my friends and family and didn't care about social media, at least for a little while.

"Go to your Twitter app," Greg said and crossed his arms. He looked uncomfortable. Really uncomfortable.

I sighed and opened the app. "Now what?"

"Look for hashtag Breck's bed hopping boo."

"Is this another Trisha story?" I asked as I searched for the hashtag. "I haven't even spoken to that chick since that night in the alley."

It took me a minute to see what was going on, to see why #brecksbedhoppingboo was trending on Twitter. There were several links to pictures and links to websites. I clicked on one, holding my breath. It led me to a gossip blog, a somewhat reputable gossip blog, if that made any sense.

#brecksbedhoppingboo

Whose bed has N.H. Eddington hopped into?

N.H., or Noa, as she is known by her friends, has been traveling with Friction, pop star Jade Deeana, and a few other performers for a fundraising tour that raises money for the charity Packs for Kids. When Friction front man, Alden Breck, and Miss Eddington were first seen out in public together, Breck's publicist had shot down any questions about whether or not the pair were dating. "Mr. Breck and Miss Eddington are just good friends that are pulling together for a great cause." But after the second gala that took place in Manhattan, pictures of the "friends" hugging and kissing intimately began to circulate the internet. Soon thereafter, while in Miami, it was confirmed that they were indeed an item.

Alden Breck is known for his philandering, flirting, and sexing up his fans. In the 2013 web-based mini-series entitled, Friction, I'm With the Band, *which had reached millions, Breck admitted in a candid, but rare and soft moment that he was incapable of falling in love. "There's something hard and cold inside of me," Breck had said, looking troubled. "No one can get in and get past that, and no one ever will. Maybe it makes me an asshole to admit that I'm incapable of falling in love, or that I don't want to fall in love, and that I'm going to keep on fucking who I want and when I want. Maybe I'm an asshole, but I'll take that. At least I'm being honest, with you, and with myself. I can't love."*

Wrong, Mr. Breck. You can, and you have. Alden fell hard for N.H. Eddington. Sources close to the couple said that Alden was hopelessly romantic and soft when it came to Noa, but that the bestselling author seemed a little cold and distant in comparison. It was suggested that maybe Miss Eddington wasn't in it with a full heart, if with any heart at all. She had nothing to lose by hooking up with Alden Breck, and that has been proven in her book sales over the past several weeks. Her sales have spiked to an all-time high, just from the press she gets from being with a superstar.

Now we are all beginning to wonder if Noa ever had any real feelings for Alden Breck. There seemed to have been some, ahem, friction *between the two at times, and just recently, Noa took off for the east coast while Alden returned to L.A. with a child, who is rumored to be either a brother or a love child from some random groupie. Many found this perplexing since Noa has said herself that she would be sticking with Friction throughout their charity tour, but it appears that Miss Eddington has found someone else's bed to keep warm:* married, *U.S. Senator of North Carolina, Todd Canyon.*

Senator Canyon and N.H. Eddington were first spotted together in the early morning hours Monday leaving a townhouse that the Senator owns and usually uses as a guest house for his friends and family when they are in town. However, the source that spotted the couple did not realize it was Miss Eddington at the time, so no one cared to report it. Today, photographs are surfacing of the couple leaving a downtown D.C. hotel together Friday evening, and climbing into the back of a waiting limo owned by the Senator. More photos have come out in recent hours of the two locked in an embrace inside the hotel's lobby, and the senator's lips were definitely on her face (see photos below).

So, what do we make of this? What does Breck have to say? So, far, no one has heard anything from the rock star, but the evidence is pretty strong against Miss Eddington. Is it true? Has she given up the man who was recently voted one of the #sexiestmenontheplanet to be with a married, yet sexy in his own right, senator?

#brecksbedhoppingboo #aldenbreck #cheatersgonnacheat #staysinglebreck

With trembling fingers, I scrolled down to the posted pictures. There were eight or nine of them, but only two were really incriminating. His hands were on her face as he leaned in close to her in the hotel lobby, and her hands were on his hands as she looked into his eyes. I couldn't read the look on her face, but it didn't matter. Didn't have to. The physical contact was enough.

In the second incriminating photo, they were still in the lobby, hugging, and though from the angle the picture was taken, I couldn't see exactly *where* his lips were, they were definitely *on* her – maybe her cheek or her ear. Her eyes were closed, but she was smiling. *Smiling* like she was enjoying it.

Greg was right to take me into a soundproof room.

My shouts of anger and indignation bounced off the walls like ricocheting bullets.

Noa

I don't know what was wrong with my brain. I made it all the way to New York, got settled in at the penthouse, and as I was going through my pocketbook looking for Chapstick, I realized that I didn't have my wallet. No credit cards. No checkbook. No ID. All of those things were needed for me to board my flight the next day.

After I had found some edible food in the freezer and cabinets, I decided that my wallet could wait until morning. I had EZ-pass for my car and fortunately, I had filled the tank just before leaving Philly, so at least I didn't need money for that.

I spent that Saturday lounging on the couch, even though I would have rather been out walking about the city, but I didn't have any kind of currency on me, and I still harbored a small fear that I would bump into Larson.

It was strange. I hadn't heard from him in a few weeks. No random messages or anything. Even though I had told Alden that I didn't expect him to show up at my apartment, I honestly wouldn't put it past him, and worried that he would my entire time back in Philly. But he didn't. I had to wonder if he had finally given up, but then again, more than a year had gone by before he had even contacted me. Another year could go by before he tried to contact me again for all I knew.

I pushed Larson out of my mind. I was excited about going to L.A. Alden had Peyton! That happened much faster than I could have anticipated. I was expecting at least a few more weeks of bullshit, but I was more than pleasantly surprised by the quick turnaround. Alden was so happy, so ecstatic. He sounded like a little kid himself as he told me about it over the phone. I was sorry that I couldn't have been there to see his face when he found out, but I was also glad that he and Peyton got to have those first few hours together, knowing that their lives were changing from that point forward.

Sahara came by with dinner later that night, taking pity on my idiocy. We ate and drank a couple bottles of wine while chatting and laughing. I got the scoop on her Doctor Greg and told her my indecision about moving to L.A.

I went to bed early since I had to drive all the way back to Philly first thing in the morning. I talked to Alden for a little bit on my way there, but I didn't want him to worry. So, I didn't tell him where I was going. I would be back before my flight and that was all that mattered.

Amazingly, there wasn't much traffic going down. I parked on the street instead of using the garage I used to rent a space from. Since my car was going to be stored in Alden's garage in New York, I canceled my account. Fortunately, there were a few spaces open almost directly in front of my building. I took the elevator upstairs, let myself into my apartment, and went into my bedroom where I knew I had left my wallet on the bureau.

"Gotcha," I whispered to it as I snatched it up.

I was looking down, making sure everything I needed was in it and I wasn't leaving anything else. The shades were drawn and only a couple of soft lights were on in the living room, so the burst of bright color coming from my small dining table drew my eyes up and away from my wallet.

Sitting in the center of the table was a vase filled and overflowing with bright yellow daffodils.

***

My first instinct was to wildly look about to see if the delivery man was still in the apartment. My heart was beating so loudly it was all I could hear, and I desperately needed to hear whether or not there was someone in there. Obviously, he wasn't in the living room, kitchen, and bedroom, all places I was able to see from where I stood, but that didn't mean that he wasn't in the powder room, the closet, or the master bathroom.

"Hello?" I called out tentatively, hating the tremor in my voice.

No one answered. There wasn't a scuffle or creak or any indication that anyone but me was around. Shaking so badly I was barely able to walk, I walked slowly to the table. The scent of the flowers hit my nose and I gagged and just barely held back my coffee and bagel I had grabbed on the way down. Covering my nose and mouth with my arm, I stared at the clusters of flowers and the blue vase they were in.

I was scared. Larson had gotten into my apartment. I had no idea how, but he did it. Not even locked doors could keep him out. I knew that I might have been able to get rid of him once I went to California, but I didn't know for how long. I didn't know if he would find a way to reach me there, or if he would be waiting for me when I returned.

I was terrified, but…

Something else was uncoiling inside of me and rapidly snaking its way through my veins.

With a frightened and *furious* blood-curdling scream, I swiped the entire floral arrangement off the table with such force that it flew into the kitchen and shattered on the floor. I wanted to be sick as I looked at the water, pedals, stems, and glass on the floor. In my memory, I saw me on the floor with it.

With another scream, I kicked at the mess and nearly fell into it as I smashed through it and out of the kitchen. With my wallet and keys in my hand, I left my apartment, locking the door behind me, even if it *was* pointless.

I didn't have the patience to wait for the elevator. I knew it was possible for Larson to be lurking on the stairs, that's where I would put the bad guy if I had been writing my story, but I felt rather reckless and slammed the door to the stairs open and started to descend.

I reached the small lobby without being ambushed. I wanted to stop and tell the guy at the front desk that he sucked at his job, but I kept moving. I looked around as I made my way across the street to my car, but saw nothing unusual, but I must have been looking for the wrong things, because just as I pulled my door open, a big hand slammed it shut. I spun around and Larson stepped up close to me and caged me in against the car.

***

I wanted to scream, but I couldn't find my voice. Why couldn't I scream? All I could do was gasp for air.

"I was disappointed to hear that you are going away for an extended period of time," he said conversationally. "I was going to throw the flowers away, but once I was inside and had a look around, I saw that you had left your wallet. I knew you would be back for it. Did you like the flowers, love?"

"Go away," I whispered. "Leave me alone."

"I've missed you," he said as if I hadn't spoken. His eyes skated over my face, lingering too long on my mouth. "I don't understand what you see in Breck, Noa. You are still with him even after you know that he had oral sex with that actress in the alley. Why?"

"He didn't," I managed. God, why was my mouth so dry? Why was my heartbeat so loud?

I shook violently, so bad that my keys jingled in my hand.

"So he says," Larson said, frowning. "Noa, I said I wouldn't come and collect you, and I'm not, but my patience is gone. You need to make the decision to come back."

That thing that had uncoiled inside of me in the apartment was beginning to awaken again. It was struggling to push past my fear.

"I will never come back," I said in a voice that was a little stronger.

"Don't be so sure. Have you seen what's trending on Twitter today?"

I was thrown off by his random question. Why would I care what was trending on Twitter? Unless, it was a story about Alden…

Seeing the question in my eyes, Larson nodded once. "You should take a look."

His hand drifted down my side, across my upper thigh and to my ass. I cringed, and again, had to struggle to keep down my morning meal. His fingers inched into my pocket and a second later, he produced my phone and offered it to me. He gave me very little room to maneuver, but I took it from him, feeling uncertain about him, about everything.

"Go on, and take a look," he said patiently.

With trembling hands, I unlocked my phone and found the Twitter app.

"What am I looking for?"

"Hashtag Breck's bed hopping boo," he said with a satisfied grin.

With great apprehension, I searched the hashtag. It only took a few seconds to see what he wanted me to see. Pictures of me with the senator.

Oh, god! What if Alden sees these? I need to explain.

"Why are you showing me this?" I asked Larson as I scrolled through the tweets.

"Well," he started and waited until I met his eyes. He did not like speaking to me if I was not looking into his eyes. "This can be the worst of it, or I can add fuel to this fire."

I gave him a doubtful look. "By doing what?"

He smiled. It was like knives stabbing me in the face.

"Not everything you think you've lost is gone," he said in a deceptively soft tone.

My fury was getting the best of my fear. I was glad. I needed fury. I was tired of fear.

"How cryptic of you," I said bitterly. "Why do you want me back, Larson? You can't find another willing participant to be your punching bag by night and still look pretty by day?"

"Oh," he breathed almost reverently. "There's that sarcastic woman I met many years ago."

"The one you nearly *destroyed*!" I shoved him hard on the last word. I shoved him again and again until he was stumbling back against the building behind him. He looked shocked, like he couldn't believe that I stood up to him. Hell, I was shocked. Scared shitless, but *so* angry.

"I don't want you, Larson!" I shouted. "I will never want you again. I would rather die than to go back to you!"

"Stop yelling," he growled, taking a menacing step toward me.

"Or what? You'll hit me? Right here on the street? Why would you think that I would want to go back to *that*?"

A vein popped out in his forehead as he snarled at me. "You were on the verge of falling back into darkness. I *saved you*! If it weren't for me, you would be dead somewhere, overdosed on too much cocaine and self-pity. You need me, Noa. You need me to keep you in line."

I stared at him with an open mouth for a long moment before speaking.

"You did save me from one death and gave me another," I bit out. "I'd rather die from a drug overdose than by your hand."

I pulled open my car door. When he started toward me again, I screamed, "Stay away from me!"

"If you leave, I will undo you," Larson promised. "I will undo you, and you will come back to me anyway, because you won't have a choice."

I shook my head at his madness.

"You are a psychopath," I growled. "You are incapable of compassion and love—"

"I had compassion for you when I picked you up off of the street!" he grounded out. "I love you and that is why I want you to come back and let me care for you."

"I don't want you!" I screamed, knowing people were watching. "I don't want you, I don't love you. I *hate* you. There is nothing in this world that can make me come back to you. Nothing. Leave. Me. Alone."

I got into my car, locked the doors, and fumbled with the keys to start the ignition. Ignoring Larson fuming on the sidewalk, I pulled out of my parking spot and sped away.

***

I called my brother as I headed back to New York. I had to tell him about Larson. I was trying to be more proactive about keeping him in the loop that was known as my life. After he had a meltdown and threatened Larson's life at least five times, I asked him to get my locks changed at my apartment. Then I told him not to tell Alden. I didn't want him worrying any more than he was. He was with Peyton and I wanted him to just be happy about that. I didn't tell Warren about the Twitter thing. That would have been another conversation we'd have to have and I just wasn't up to it.

I drove the rest of the way on autopilot, my thoughts still stuck out on the sidewalk in Philly and on the flowers spilled all over my kitchen floor.

It took me a long time to stop shaking. I wanted to believe that was the end of things with Larson, but something he said was nagging at me.

"Not everything you think you've lost is gone."

What did that mean? I didn't understand. I wouldn't understand for hours to come.

Later, with only minutes left before boarding my flight, Alden called me. I was just about to text him to tell him I was about to board.

"Hello," I answered.

"What the fuck is going on, Noa? There are pictures all over the internet of you and some senator!" he roared over the line.

"Um," I started, trying to find my words. Trying to test out my tongue. "I…it's not what it looks like. I promise you it's not what it looks like."

"Then *what* is it!" he demanded. "What the fuck is it then?"

"It's not what it looks like," I repeated. "I'll tell you all about it when I get there. I'm getting on the plane and I have to turn my phone off. I promise you I'll explain everything. I have to go. I love you."

I ended the call and turned my phone off. He sounded pretty upset, but I was sure that once I explained everything to him, that he would understand.

I closed my eyes as we started to move down the runway, and I didn't open them again until I landed at LAX.

While I waited for the luggage to come through, I went to the bathroom, splashed cold water on my face, and tried to hold myself together.

By the time I walked out, Greg was standing near the conveyor, holding the handles of my suitcases. I was surprised to see him, but it was late. Alden was probably at home with Peyton. I offered Greg a faint smile, but he looked grim.

"I know," I said, waving an arm. "The Twitter thing. I can explain."

He breathed deeply and closed his eyes for a beat. "Noa, it's worse than that. You don't know because you were in the air all day."

"I don't know what?" I asked, feeling something like alarm.

"About the video," he said.

Oh, I thought. *The video.*

I laughed.

Until I cried.

Larson

It was snowy and icy that morning. Many of the businesses on the street tried to clear the sidewalks before the start of the day, but there were still some icy patches. I was only two buildings away from mine when I saw the woman slip on a patch of ice and hit her head on the cold concrete. The contents of her purse and backpack scattered on the sidewalk and into the street.

I rushed to her, helped her sit up, and assessed her head. Her eyes were dilated and unfocused. I didn't know at the time that it was a result of a morning hit of cocaine. I thought she had seriously injured herself. I made her sit while I dialed 911. I made her talk to me while we waited. I asked her name, how old she was, if she was in school, what was she taking. Her name was Noa. What an unusual name. She was pretty. No, she was more than pretty. She was striking, but she didn't seem to know she was striking.

While we waited, I began to gather her possessions. I carefully put them into her backpack and purse as I continued to ask her questions. The paramedics appeared just as I picked up a flash drive that had clearly been run over by a car. Absently, as they asked me questions, I put the broken device into my coat pocket.

I rediscovered it later that evening. I didn't see any point in returning a broken flash drive to Noa, so I plugged it in first to see if it still worked. It didn't, but I knew someone who could recover the data for her. I had taken it to the office the following morning with the intent of handing to a tech, but I had put it in the back of my drawer for safe keeping when I became busy. I then forgot about it, and did not remember even after I had taken Noa out for lunch a week later.

It was two years later before I found the flash drive again, somehow wedged *behind* the drawer I had left it in. I did take it to one of my techs this time and sat beside him as he recovered the data without opening any of the containing folders, and put it on a new flash drive. Noa and I had been together for nearly two years by that time. There were no secrets between us, no walls, and no boundaries. I plugged the flash drive into my computer in my office without a second thought. It was my right to do so. She belonged to me, therefore, anything she owned belonged to me.

There were a few documents for school, a couple of short stories, and a video. I looked through each item, saving the video for last. I was shocked by what I saw on the screen. Infuriated at seeing another man touching what was *mine*, *my* property. Strangely aroused…

I watched it again, and then twice more before I left my office that day, furious and hard with excitement. It felt…exhilarating to enter her violently with my fingers wrapped around her graceful neck that night. She had been entirely ignorant of what had incited my sadism that night.

I never told her that I found and restored the flash drive, and the sex video that she had made with the man who later became a US Senator.

Noa

Greg led me into the silent house. He explained that the house had been full of people all day, but all of Alden's guests were gone. Peyton had passed out in his new bedroom.

"Where is he?" I asked Greg as my eyes took in the large house.

"In the music room," he said and began to lead me there.

I would have loved time to explore the house. I wondered if the décor was like the New York penthouse, or if this was different because it was his full-time home.

"Is Peyton okay?" I asked Greg in a hushed tone.

"Yes," he said with a faint smile. "He is adjusting so far. He's made friends with James's kids. I think he has a pretty good head on his shoulders. I believe he'll do well."

We fell back into silence. I didn't like the silence. All I got from Alden since landing was silence. I had tried calling him from the car, between answering calls from Kristy, Tucker, and Warren, but he never answered. Then my phone eventually died. I knew he must have been pretty angry if he wasn't answering my calls. I had to explain to him…

I had to tell him that I didn't cheat on him with Todd. I had gone to meet him to ask him for a favor. I didn't think it was fair that Alden and Peyton were suffering, unable to be together because of the gossip about the rock star. Very rarely were any of the stories spot on, at best a mixture of truth and falsehoods. The people that had the power to give

Alden his rights to his brother were holding him at a higher accountability than any other perspective adoptive parents. So, I asked Todd if he could speak to someone in Minnesota since he was good friends with the governor there. I didn't know if it would work, but I didn't tell Alden what I was doing in case it didn't. I didn't want him to be any more disappointed than he already was.

The pictures were misleading. Todd and I had embraced, that was true. Maybe we held on a little too long, but it wasn't because we were doing anything pernicious. In one photo, it looked like he was kissing me, but he was really speaking into my ear. He was apologizing to me for what happened between us when I was younger. He was my professor, my *ethics* professor, and he was thirteen years my senior, old enough to know better. I was rather lost when we met, and I think I had hidden daddy issues. I think he took advantage of that. During our yearlong affair, he gave me the affection and attention I had never received from a male. I latched on to him and greedily accepted whatever he could give me. It wasn't just sex for us. I'm not sure what I was giving him that he didn't have at home. Maybe the same things he was giving me. I didn't love Todd, but it was probably pretty close to the emotion.

Todd also took care of my financial needs. He paid my rent, bought my groceries, and there was never a shortage of cocaine between us. That was another thing he was apologizing for, this time in the picture where he held my face in his hands. I had already dabbled in the white powder before I went to college, but it was Todd that made me dependent on the drug, and therefore dependent on him. That is how the video came to be. We were both high, and not at all considering the consequences of filming ourselves snorting coke and having sex. That video was made just a couple of months before I began to spiral out of control, if I ever had any control at all. Todd tried to help me, but it was the drug addict leading the drug addict. It didn't work. In the end, it took my arrest and Tucker's compassion to set me straight.

I won't lie. Cleansing myself of Todd was just as difficult as cleansing myself of the cocaine.

I had saved the video to a flash drive after we parted ways. I had held on to it to remind myself of where I had been and where I needed to go. I did eventually realize the harm in keeping it. I was going to get rid of it, but then that morning after I hit my head and Larson came to my aid, I thought that it was gone. I thought that it had fallen into the street and been run over by a car or fallen into the sewer. But I was high that morning. Larson had been right about that, I had been on my way back into badness. I had fallen off the cocaine wagon and I was losing control again.

Larson. He had the video the entire time. Why? What did he do with it? Why did he keep it? Why didn't he tell me?

God, I must have *really* pissed him off if he saw fit to release the video while I was in a position where I couldn't even defend myself.

Greg stopped outside of a door and paused, bringing me back to the present.

"He loves you," he said quietly. "Just remember that the depth of his anger is the depth of his love for you. I'll be in the living room."

I was really slow that day because it took me until then to realize that we never got my bags out of the car.

Oh. This isn't good.

Greg pushed the door open and let me walk past him into the music room.

The music room was aptly named. It was enormous. I later found out that the room was originally an attached garage built to hold up to ten vehicles, but Alden had another garage built for his cars and bikes. He renovated the space with soundproof walls and floors, and stocked it with every musical instrument I could think of. In a few glances around the room upon entering, I noted the large, black, and shiny piano, two drum sets, and a wall of drumsticks on special displays. I saw a plethora of guitars, some on stands on the floor and some hanging on the walls. Gold and platinum records were on display on one wall, Grammys, American Music Awards, MTV awards, and others sat neatly in large, lit display cases.

My eyes floated to the center of the room. Alden sat on a stool, looking down at his phone. I paused a couple of feet inside of the room when he didn't look up. I looked over my shoulder at Greg, but he sighed heavily and walked out of the room, closing the door behind him. I felt like he was leaving me to my doom.

I had taken a few more tentative steps toward Alden before I heard it. My own voice, laughing, talking, and then moaning. Moaning and more moaning.

He was watching the video. The video that had gone viral while I was hanging thousands of feet in the sky.

"You missed the part where you snorted cocaine while pleasuring yourself," Alden said conversationally, keeping his eyes fixed on his phone. "And you missed the part where you guys got into an argument over a grade he gave you on an essay." He laughed without humor. "That is just hilarious, because he was an *ethics* professor snorting coke with and fucking his young student while his wife and children were at home."

I stopped about ten feet away from him, shaking.

"Alden," I said his name so softly, I wasn't sure if he had heard me.

"What is it?" he answered unconcernedly without looking up.

The sounds of my own moans and Todd's grunts were killing me. I wanted to jam a pair of drumsticks in my ears.

"That video is…it's not recent…" I thought I should explain it to him, just in case he missed the fact that I didn't have my tattoo yet in that video, and my hair was a little longer and a whole different color. I went through a punk phase in my first year of college. My hair was purple and black in the video.

"Did you make a new one when you went to meet him in D.C.? Maybe you made two – one in the townhouse and one in the hotel."

"No!" I gasped and began to rush forward, but then he *did* look up. I froze in place.

His eyes reflected many emotions. Disappointment. Devastation. Fury. Pain. A lot of pain.

"I don't know if I can believe anything you're about to say," he said quietly. "I want to, I really want to, but you lied to me. Worse yet, you didn't tell me about the video. Don't you think that's something I would need to fucking know – not just because we love each other and we're supposed to share shit, but because it could have adverse consequences on the ground I *just* gained to have Peyton?"

I had not thought about that, about how the video could affect not just the adoption, but Peyton's placement with Alden. I wasn't the one seeking custody of Peyton, but if I were going to be spending a significant amount of time with him, it could very well have a negative impact.

"I hope it was worth it," Alden said, getting to his feet.

The video was still playing. Why didn't he shut it off? I heard myself moaning still as Todd said dirty things to me. It got louder as Alden stalked toward me. He reached me in a few strides and stopped inches away from me.

"Was it worth it, Noa?" he asked as he glared at me.

"Alden," I started, but he cut in before I could continue.

"Did he fuck you the way you like to be fucked?" he spat out at me. "Did you sit on his dick and ride him hard? My dick is bigger than his, so maybe you didn't enjoy it quite as much."

My vision blurred as tears filled my eyes. "Alden, I didn't—"

"I was so worried about you," he said in a soft, tortured voice. "I was so worried that Larson would get to you and hurt you while you were gone. I was *sick* with worry, Noa. I couldn't fucking sleep, could barely fucking eat. I had to play it cool for Peyton's sake, but I was going *crazy* worrying that motherfucker would harm you, and you…you were with another man. You lied to me about where you were going and what you were doing, worried Tucker and your brother when you did your disappearing act, and you were with another man all along. Why should I believe anything else that comes out of your mouth?"

"Let me explain," I sobbed softly, but he was already speaking before I could finish my last word.

"The video explains enough!" He held up his phone, shaking it close to my face. "You promised me that you wouldn't hold shit back from me again, Noa! It almost doesn't matter what the fuck you were doing, who the fuck you were doing, or why the fuck you were doing it, you broke the promise!"

"You don't understand," I tried to say.

"My attorney wants me to send you home," he announced as if I hadn't just again tried to speak up for myself.

I stood still as I watched him take a few steps back from me. He finally turned the video off before reaching into his back pocket for something. He produced a pack of cigarettes and a lighter. I had only seen Alden smoke a handful of times since meeting him. It was always when we were having drinks with other smokers, and I had tasted it and smelled it on him a few times.

"He thinks if you stay anywhere near here, it will be problematic," he said after inhaling a few puffs of smoke. He was no longer even looking at me. Instead, he looked to the floor at his feet.

He put a hand in his hair and tugged hard.

"I know he's probably right, but I don't know if I can do that," he said, his voice strained and quiet. He looked up at me again, and his expression was a tortured one. "I don't know if I can send you away. Despite all of this fuckery you've caused, I don't know if I can just let you go like that. What am I supposed to do, Noa? What the fuck am I supposed to do?"

Wiping tears off my cheeks, I bitterly replied, "Oh, am I allowed to respond now?"

Alden took a few angry steps toward me, pointing with his cigarette hand. "You don't get to be angry," he growled. "You caused this shit."

"You won't even give me an opportunity to explain anything to you!" I shouted.

"You lied!" he shot back. "You snuck off to be with some other dick! The proof was in the pictures and the fucking video, Noa! It sure as hell didn't look like you were just having tea and discussing eco-fucking-nomics! Hell, maybe you were having a great time laughing at his lack of 'ethics' while you were screwing him."

"When you were caught with your zipper down and Trisha Livingston kneeling before you ready to suck your dick, I was angry and I was hurt. But I listened to you, I let you explain yourself, and even though *that* was far more proof of wrongdoing than a seven-year-old video and a couple of pictures of me hugging someone, you still won't listen. I'm *not*"—my voice cracked—"going to beg you to listen, Alden. I haven't begged a man since the last time I pleaded with Larson not to beat me. You haven't raised a hand, but the irrationality and subsequent damage are the same. I will *not* beg you."

I turned away from his surprised expression and walked out of the door.

***

I found a bathroom just outside of the music room. I stood in there, staring at my harsh reflection in the mirror, willing my tears to stop. I hate tears, and I especially hate them on my own face. My mother used to use tears as a weapon. She would scream and bawl about how miserable her life was, how it had been ruined by the birth of two ungrateful children, my birth in particular.

Larson used to taunt me for crying, but withholding my tears only made him crueler. I learned to cry just enough to satisfy his sadism, but I did my hardcore weeping when I was alone.

I had every right to cry, though. Larson, the Twitter trend connecting me to Todd and labeling me as a slut, the damn video, and then Alden. I expected him to be upset, obviously, but I also expected him to *listen*, to *want* to listen.

Stupid, Noa. Stupid. You deserve to be hurt for that expectation.

I washed my face and used my fingers to try to release some of the tangles in my hair. I was going to ask Greg to drive me to a hotel since it was obvious I wasn't staying at Casa de Breck. I didn't know what my next step would be. I had no idea how bad things were, how Todd and his team were reacting, or even what Alden's people would be doing. I didn't have their resources either. I had no team or anyone but my friends and brother to direct me.

I stared in the mirror again, wringing my hands anxiously as I thought about how I was going to handle all of it, *if* I could handle it all. But I knew the world wasn't going to stand still while I tried to figure it out in Alden's bathroom. So, I turned the light off on my reflection and left the false security of the powder room.

I found Greg sitting at the bar in the living room, nursing a clear drink in a glass. He looked up at me with concern creased in his forehead.

"How did it go?" he asked.

I answered him with a question of my own. "Can you drive me to a hotel? Preferably one near the airport."

He looked saddened by question as he stood up. "Noa, I'm sorry."

I shrugged rather jerkily. "I just want to get out of here."

Greg started to lead me away. He pulled the front door open, but paused when something over my shoulder caught his attention. I could tell by the sudden tension around his eyes that Alden had entered the room.

"What are you doing?" Alden demanded.

I didn't look at him when I spoke crisply over my shoulder. "I'm leaving."

"Are you fucking kidding me?"

"A little space probably will not hurt," Greg said quietly. He put his hand on my back to guide me out of the door, but Alden grabbed my arm to restrain me.

"Fuck, Noa, if you want me to listen, I'll listen," he said, aggravated.

"What?" I stared at him incredulously.

"I. Am. Listening."

Maybe it was his dispassionate attitude, like he was only going to listen to appease me, not because he *should* or *wanted* to. Maybe it was a culmination of the whole day finally crashing into me, but something *snapped*. I snatched my arm out of his grasp and shoved him away from me.

"Fuck you."

He had the nerve to look surprised that I had shoved him. Just like Larson had been surprised when I shoved him. They both thought that I was just going to curl into myself, whimper, and beg.

That thought made me even more violent. I shoved him again and again until he was against the bar.

"Fuck you! Now you want to listen? You didn't want to listen to anything I had to say earlier when *I needed you* to listen!" I shoved him against the bar. "I needed you!"

I hated that I had to admit that aloud. I hated that I needed him at all. It was the truth, but I hated it. I hated to need people more than I hated to cry, and I was doing both. Tears had blurred my vision as I shoved him again.

"*My* name and *my* face and *my* privacy have been smeared across the fucking internet and gossip magazines and news shows," I wept as I shoved him weakly. "Not yours. My career could be irrevocably damaged, *not yours*." Another weak shove. "And it was all because I went to visit Todd to do something for *you*, and you wouldn't even fucking listen to me!" I shoved him hard again.

When I went to shove him again, Greg caught my arms from behind and began to pull me away from a flabbergasted Alden. I let Greg turn me toward the open door.

"Noa," Alden said my name with disbelief and remorse. Then again with a little desperation. "*Noa*."

I turned to face him at the threshold. He still stood against the bar, but he looked like he was just waking up from whatever haze he was in. It didn't matter. It was too late.

"You're listening too late, Alden. I'm finished talking."

"*Noa.*" That same, pathetic plea.

I turned my back on him and stepped out into the dark.

"Seven years ago I had an affair with my student Noa Eddington. My former recreational drug use is not a secret. As many of you know, I played an integral part in the opening of several drug rehab centers in the state of New Jersey and here in Washington, D.C. I have shared my experiences several times with the residents of these centers. Therefore, my former habit was not widely known, but it was not a secret. As for my relationship with Miss Eddington, it was highly inappropriate. My wife and I have long ago *privately* dealt with my illicit behavior. Not only are we obviously still together, but stronger than ever. Miss Eddington and I have also come to terms long ago, as well as Miss Eddington and my wife. I apologize that this video has taken time and energy away from important issues, but it has been seven years. My family and Miss Eddington let it go a long time ago, and now it is time for the American people to do the same."

Todd pointed to a female reporter at the front of the crowd.

"Senator Canyon, do you have any comment regarding the pictures of you and Miss Eddington that were trending on Twitter? Are you again having an affair with Noa Eddington?"

"I would hardly qualify any of those pictures as proof of an affair. I again apologized to Miss Eddington for my past behaviors and expressed how happy I was that she was able to break free of drugs and live a healthy life. Next question."

"Why did you meet in the privacy of your townhouse and then later a hotel?" Another female reporter questioned.

"I hadn't spoken to Noa in a long time and I didn't want our reunion to be public. My wife was aware of where I was going and whom I was meeting when I left my home that night. Miss Eddington was staying at the hotel and I went inside to retrieve her for dinner at my family home with my family. I simply picked her up on my way home. I'll take one or two more and then I have to move on."

He chose a balding middle-aged male reporter. "What was the purpose of Noa's initial visit?"

Well, hell, you are some nosey bastards, I thought, shaking my head. I already knew what he was going to say. Todd had made it clear when he caught up with me on the phone before I flew back to New York that when he was ready to talk, he was going to tell all, that he had nothing to hide. Even though I wasn't talking to Alden, I was worried that if he told the world why I met with him, that it would jeopardize Peyton, but Todd assured me that all legal avenues were followed. He and his friend only gave it a little push.

"Noa was dating Alden Breck, who was tied up – quite frankly – in legal BS in his efforts to adopt his younger brother, who was in the Minnesota foster care system. Noa felt that Mr. Breck was being held at a higher accountability than most because of his celebratory status. She asked me to speak to my good friend Governor Stomore about the situation. It did not take long to find that Miss Eddington's suspicions were correct. It didn't make sense. Mr. Breck, while a little on the wild side, is perfectly capable of emotionally and financially supporting a child and providing a stable environment, as many celebrities in his position already do. In addition, since the young man was Mr. Breck's natural half-brother, the process should have been a little easier than had he been a complete stranger. No one is in trouble here, but this simple inquiry by Miss Eddington has shown that there are some major flaws in the foster care system, nationwide. With that said, Governor Stomore, Governor Mato of New Jersey, several other politicians, and I have decided that there need to be some changes to ensure the safety and well-being of our nation's foster care children.

"Thank you for your questions," Todd said abruptly. He waved to the crowd, flashed his big toothy smile, and walked away from the podium, taking his wife's hand before being ushered away.

***

Todd's news conference was the Wednesday after Larson leaked the video onto social media. Two days after that, Alden called me. I had not spoken to him since the night I left his house. I almost didn't answer, but there was still some unfinished business, and I wanted to be sure that Peyton was okay. I was very disappointed that I had left L.A. without seeing him again.

"Hello," I answered cautiously.

"I didn't think you were going to answer," he said as he let out a harsh breath.

"I had to think very hard about it."

"You have no fucking idea how good it is to hear your voice, Little One."

I couldn't return the sentiment and I didn't want to encourage him, so I changed the subject.

"How is Peyton?"

There was a slight pause before he answered. "He's good. He's upset that he didn't get to see you."

"He can call me anytime," I said quickly. "I don't want him to think that I don't want to talk to him." It went without saying that it was Alden that I didn't want to talk to.

"Okay," Alden said quietly. "I'll let him know."

"Thank you."

"I saw Todd's press conference," he said gingerly. "Fuck, Noa," he sighed. "I blew that whole thing way out of proportion. I'm sorry I didn't listen to you. That's all you wanted me to do was to shut the fuck up and listen and I didn't do it. I promise when you come back, I'll be all ears."

Resentment resonated in my bones. "I see," I said bitterly. "You didn't want to believe me, didn't want to hear me, but Todd gets on national television and tells *the world* what happened and you believe *him*."

"I understand you're angry, but you can yell at me all you want when you come back. I gave us each a few days to cool down, but—"

"I'm not coming back," I said curtly.

"What do you mean you're not coming back," he demanded.

"I mean I'm not coming back. I meant what I said when I compared you to Larson. You can't talk to me that way and—"

"You have been talking to me like that from the moment you met me," Alden quipped.

"All the more reason why I shouldn't return," I snapped. "God, Alden. You don't get it, you don't see why the way you reacted is just so…" I made an exasperated sound.

"It's so what?" he demanded. "For fuck's sake, just say what you want to say."

I closed my eyes and rubbed my forehead with my fingers. "Larson used to take the most innocent circumstances, twist them into something else, and then throw accusations in my face. He never allowed me to explain. He would just yell and say vicious things. I think he got off on it."

He made a sound of disbelief. "You think that I…you fucking think that I *got off* on that?"

"Not necessarily, but…that's how it started to feel. I don't ever want to feel that way again."

"I'm *not* like *him.* I would never purposely do anything to hurt you."

I almost laughed. "Alden, I can't believe that. Remember when you slept around to try to hurt me?"

"That was just an immature, fucked up thing, and we weren't even together then."

We could sit on the phone all day disputing whether his behavior was intentional, but it wasn't going to get us anywhere.

"I have to go," I said abruptly. "Text me before Peyton calls to give me a heads up."

"Wait, Noa," he said with a hint of desperation. "You have to come get all of your stuff eventually. We'll talk then."

"You can get rid of it all. Donate it, trash it. It doesn't matter. I'm not coming back for it."

"Little One, don't…don't do this," he pled softly. "Don't fucking do this. Please."

Blinking back tears, I whispered, "Bye, Alden."

I ended the phone call and officially ended us.

***

Saturday morning I went out to get a few groceries at the market a few blocks away. Most of the plethora of reporters and paparazzi that had been lingering outside of my building had gone away. Only a small handful remained to throw invasive questions at me or to snap my picture. I ignored them and hopped into a taxi. I could have walked the three blocks, but I didn't want any of the gossip hungry ingrates to follow me. I didn't drive my own car because it wasn't worth losing my parking spot on the street for a trip a few blocks away. That was another loss due to my breakup with Alden, my precious garage parking space. There was always a long waiting list, and I was at the bottom of it.

I had taken something similar to Todd's approach when dealing with the media; that is I went on with my life as if there had never been a political sex scandal. I didn't have a press conference, but I didn't stay holed up in my apartment waiting for the scandal to pass over either. If I needed to go somewhere, I did. I didn't walk like I was ashamed or humiliated – and I was totally humiliated – but I went on as if life was normal. I felt anything but normal...but the reporters and paps didn't know that.

It was gala day in Los Angeles. It was the biggest one of them all, jam packed with celebrities and the shenanigans they get into. Some of the biggest names on screen and in music were attending, in addition to several politicians. Unlike the others, there was also an after party, because celebs love their after parties. The beautiful pale yellow gown I was supposed to wear was probably hanging up in a closet somewhere in Alden's house. I had been looking forward to going, not necessarily because of the crowd that was attending, but because it would have been the end of one stage of my relationship with Alden and the beginning of another. Without the galas and with the nearly three month stretch without any performances, we would have been able to explore our relationship. We would have had some normality in our lives, especially with Peyton.

But that was all over. Alden would be going to the gala alone, or with someone. I didn't want to think about that. He would go home alone and plan out his days with Peyton that didn't include me. That was what I wanted, though, right? He had been so much like Larson when we were in the Music Room that it scared me, and angered me. I was always dismissive of Alden's dominant traits and had taken for granted that I had free reign of my voice while with him. That night as he hammered me into the ground with his words and venomous attitude, I had begun to feel as small as Larson has ever made me feel, and I had wondered how I had not seen it coming. As children, our teachers and parents had lied when they said that words didn't hurt. Words hurt more than anything.

Since I obviously wasn't going to the gala, I decided that I would have Warren and Tucker over for dinner that night. I would cook a hearty meal for them and drink wine until all was blissful. As I walked through the market selecting various vegetables to go with dinner, I realized that was another thing I was losing with Alden. There had been a few times over the weeks that I was able to cook for him, but I had been looking forward to doing it in place to call home, not on some hotel stove. Having the overactive imagination that I do, there had been many daydreams about living a domesticated life with an untamed rocker.

Loaded with a few heavy bags from the grocery store, I went inside of my apartment building and got all the way to my door before I realized I had left my keys inside. I scolded myself under my breath as I carefully put my bags down at my door and walked a few doors down. The old lady that Alden had captivated with a salacious twist of his hips was my key master. She was the one person in the building I entrusted with a key to my apartment in the event that I did lock myself out.

I knocked loud on Mrs. Q's door to compete with the ear splitting volume of her television. It only took two good pounds before I heard her on the other side of the door.

"Yes, who is there?" she asked in a shout.

"It's Noa, Mrs. Q," I announced. "I locked myself out."

"Again?" she asked as locks clicked on the door. She pulled the door open and the blaring sounds of some old movie invaded the quiet of the corridor. She smiled at me with a soft grandmotherly smile. "I can't give you the key. You haven't returned it yet. How does someone lock themselves out twice in one morning?"

I blinked and then inclined my ear in her direction. "I'm sorry?"

"I *just* gave your boyfriend the key about twenty minutes ago, silly girl. What did you do with it? Did you lose *both* keys? You should really be more careful, Noa," she said shaking her head with disapproval.

I looked down the hall to where my apartment was with a sickening feeling in my gut.

"How do you know he was my boyfriend, Mrs. Q?" I asked in a hushed voice without taking my eyes off my groceries in front of my door.

"I'm old, but not stupid, Noa Eddington," she admonished with a hand on her hip.

"No, you're both old and stupid," I almost snapped at her, but I bit my tongue. It was my fault for entrusting the key to an eighty-year-old woman who could be easily charmed by Larson's big smiles. I finally understood how he had gotten into my apartment that day. It was time to move, time to take better care of my keys, and definitely time to stop leaving them with clueless, sweet, old ladies.

"Thank you, Mrs. Q," I said, forcing a smile in her direction.

"Well, don't forget to return it so that it is here if this happens again. It probably will, no doubt, since this is the third time in a week."

I gave her a wave and began the walk back to my apartment. I stopped in front of my door and looked at it with apprehension. I probably should have called the police, or in the very least Warren, but besides annoying the Philadelphia P.D., I wouldn't accomplish anything. It would be hard to prove that he entered without my permission, and even if I managed to do that, not much would happen to him.

Resigned, I raised a shaky hand and tested the handle. It was unlocked. I took a very deep breath and pushed the door open to face Larson once more.

He sat in the middle of the room, looking perfectly at home with his ankle propped on his knee and arms spread along the back of the couch.

"Get out," I said without preamble.

"How is that fire feeling?" he asked with a smirk. Of course, he was referring to the Twitter fire he fueled with the video.

"Feels delightful," I said haughtily. "I enjoy the heat. Now get out."

"You're back here and not with Breck, so I am assuming he did not take it too well. I cannot say that I blame him. The first time I saw the video, I too was infuriated, but then I learned that I had voyeuristic traits. It was extremely arousing to watch you with the professor, but still infuriating."

I crossed my arms and tilted my head to one side. "How does it feel to know that no matter what you do, I don't want you? It must really sting to know that even with your good looks, intelligence, and money that you still can't have what you want."

"I will eventually-" he began, but I cut him off.

"Not eventually. Not *ever*, Larson. No matter what you threaten me with, no matter what you throw at me, you'll *never* have me. Now get out of my apartment."

I stood aside and gestured to the door. It took him a moment, but he finally got to his feet and slowly made his way across the room. The closer he got to me, the more nervous I became, but I refused to cower. I was done with cowering.

He stopped directly in front of me, too, too close to me.

"Do you know what is interesting, Noa?"

I sighed disinterestedly. "I suppose you are going to tell me, Larson."

He moved so fast that I had no time to react, no time to brace myself. One hand closed over my mouth and the other closed painfully around my arm while he slammed my door shut with a kick of his foot.

"It is really interesting that you thought that you could continue to speak to me that way," he growled.

With my free hand, I pulled on his thumb until his hand slipped. Without thought, I sunk my teeth into the meaty part of his palm. Larson cursed and released my arm to hit me in the face, but I had released him and turned my head just in time so that his hand landed on the side of my head instead. I stumbled from the blow and during that second of vulnerability, he grabbed a hold of my hair and threw me to the floor. I knew what was coming next. It was one of his favorite things to do while I was on the floor. I rolled away just before his foot made contact with my ribs, but he still managed to get a kick into my back before I could begin to crawl away.

I always took his brutality with the least amount of noise possible because any kind of outcry used to make him come at me that much harder, but I wasn't playing by his rules anymore. I started to scream for help at the top of my lungs.

"Stop screaming," he growled as his arm snaked around my neck from behind.

He pulled me to my feet and I instantly lashed out. I swung my foot to kick behind me and made contact with his shin. He cursed as his hold on me loosened enough for me to twist away from him.

"Someone help me!" I screamed repeatedly as I struggled to stay out of his grasp.

I clawed at his hand as it once again closed over my mouth. He lifted me with his other arm and started to carry me into the bedroom. No amount of kicking and thrashing seemed to be enough. I was terrified of what would happen to me in that bedroom. He could kill me, but there were things worse than death.

I was beginning to lose hope when my front door was thrown open and the men who worked security downstairs (ironic, right?) rushed in and forced Larson to the ground.

Everything was a blur of activity after that. The police came. Larson was taken out in handcuffs. Paramedics were called to look me over. I had some bruises forming on my back and arms, and a few minor scratches. I was lucky that was the extent of my injuries because I had experienced much worse at Larson's hands.

Someone had called Warren because he arrived not too long after the police carted Larson out. He was in such a rage that the police threatened to handcuff him and stick him in the back of a cruiser unless he calmed down. Tucker showed up just before we left for the police station. I had to go make a formal report and file for a restraining order against Larson. They found a judge to approve it right away.

When we returned to my apartment later, there were more reporters and photographers than there had been that morning. Hanging outside of my building had won them first dibs on the story about Larson. I didn't give them any comments, but they were probably able to deduce what happened on their own until the police were ready to release a report.

Tucker went home after we decided that I was going to stay with Warren for a while. Staying in the apartment was not an option. I would stay with Warren until I was ready to find somewhere new and more secure to live.

It didn't take long for news to travel to the west coast. Kristy called me first, bawling and cursing viciously. It took me a half hour to get her off the phone. Alden called me in the afternoon as I was packing up some of my things.

"Hello?" I answered on the second ring. My voice was raspy from screaming earlier and then all of the talking I had to do with the police.

"Noa!" Alden exclaimed. "Are you okay? Please tell me you're okay!"

"I'm okay."

"Are you just saying that to appease me? I want to know the truth. Are you hurt?"

"I'm a little banged up, a lot of pissed off, but otherwise okay."

I heard his heavy sigh of relief. "I saw that asshole in handcuffs. There are pictures and video all over the internet. Now maybe people will see him for the abusive psychopath that he is. I wish I were there. I would fucking kill him."

"Get in line, Breck. I'm first."

"Obviously. Tell me what happened. How the hell did he get into your apartment again?"

"He sweet-talked Mrs. Q, you know the old lady you pelvic thrusted? He showed her pictures of us, they were old of course, but she didn't know that. She just assumed he was my boyfriend and gave him the key."

"Do *not* give that old bat any more spare keys! I know she's old, but is she stupid, too?"

I almost snickered because his thoughts were similar to the ones I had earlier.

"Well, I'm moving out. I'm going to stay with Warren for a little while. So, I don't have to give the old bat any keys."

"What happens when he gets out of jail? How are the police going to protect you? How is Warren going to protect you? You know what? I'm coming out there. I can be out there by tonight. I need to see with my own fucking eyes that you're okay and I'll feel better about your safety."

"You can't come out here," I said on sigh. "You have the gala tonight."

"I don't give a fuck," he said belligerently.

"Yes, you do give a fuck! You give millions worth of fucks. I'm fine. You need to be there at the gala and you know it."

"I do whatever the hell I want to do. It's my damn party."

"Which is why you should be *there* not here. Besides, what are you going to do with Peyton? Bring him out here and possibly put him in harm's way? No, I don't think so."

Alden sighed heavily again. I could almost see him dragging his fingers through his hair. "I am going to go fucking crazy with worry, Noa."

"Well, don't," I said. "I'm fine. I'm safe. Listen, I have to go. I have to finish getting some of my things together."

"I hate this," he said quietly. "I fucking hate this. I hate that we're…if you were here, this wouldn't have happened. I'm not saying that to pass the blame onto you. It's my fucking fault."

I swallowed hard and pushed a loose strand of hair behind my ear. "Listen, it's Larson's fault. No one else's."

"Yeah," he said, unconvinced. "I know you don't want to talk to me, but can I call you to check on you later tonight and tomorrow? Please, Little One."

"Yes," I said softly.

"Thank you," he answered just as softly. "I love you, Noa."

I couldn't say it back without crying, so I simply ended the call.

Warren watched me warily from the doorway to my bedroom.

"Why did you break up with him?" he asked. It was the first time he outright asked the question since I returned from L.A.

"While I was trying to give him an explanation on the video and the Twitter feed, he wouldn't let me answer. He just kept accusing me of cheating and lying and holding things from him. He reminded me so much of Larson," I said, shaking my head. "I just didn't want to miss the signs again and end up…well…here."

Warren was quiet for a long time as I moved about my room. I knew he had something on his mind, but I was going to wait for him to say it without me having to prod him.

He didn't disappoint.

"I am not Alden Breck's number one fan or anything," he started, moving into the room, "but I don't think he's anything like Larson."

I shook my head. "You weren't there. His temper…" I continued shaking my head.

"Did he give you the impression that he was going to hit you or push you or do anything physical to you?"

I thought about it. He had gotten in my face a couple of times, but I hadn't been afraid that he would hurt me.

"No," I said slowly. "But he was clearly trying to intimidate me. That is such a Larson thing."

"Noa," Warren said on a sigh. "Maybe he wasn't trying to intimidate you at all. Maybe he was just pissed the fuck off. First, he had watch social media explode because of the pictures of you and the senator. Then, before he could even begin to deal with that or talk to you about it, the video popped up online. You *did* lie to him, even if it was for a good reason. He probably sees that now with a clear head, but I know if I were in his shoes, I would probably react the same, if not worse. I don't know any one, yourself included, who would handle it much differently. Has he given you any other reason to believe that he's an abusive asshole?"

I thought about it. Something did come to mind, but even as I was saying it, I realized how lame it sounded. "Before we were official, he was banging girls because he knew it hurt my feelings."

"Oh, the whole jealousy routine." Warren nodded with a smirk.

"Excuse me?"

"He wanted to make you jealous. I've done that before."

I wrinkled my nose. "That's disgusting. And stupid."

"It's very stupid," Warren agreed. "But that's not the same as hurting you the same way that Larson has. And you know what? Breck is so upfront about who he is, flaws and all. Larson isn't. Larson is a nice guy on the surface and brutal on the inside. Alden doesn't try to hide behind anything."

I raised an eyebrow. "If I didn't know any better, I'd think that you *like* Alden Breck, Warren."

He sighed. "Let's not get carried away here."

A faint smile pulled at my lips as I thought about what Warren had said. Alden did have the right to be furious the day that everything went down. I had to see things from his perspective. What if I got that picture of Trisha while Alden was unreachable? What if before I could even really begin to deal with that, a video was released of the two of them having sex? I had barely been able to keep calm long enough to let him explain the photo. In fact, I had still been very argumentative and disbelieving. The video in combination with the hashtag was so much worse. I should have given him time to calm down and process everything and then waited until he was ready to hear me.

"You know," I said, "he's an arrogant jackass, but besides the whole wanting to make me jealous thing, he hasn't really *hurt* me. And that *was* before we were an official couple, and it is more juvenile than malicious."

Warren nodded absently as he looked at something on his phone. I didn't think he was listening anymore until he said, "So, if you don't mind leaving within the next ten minutes or so, there are three seats left on a 4:45 flight to LAX. That will get you in L.A. around eight. The gala starts at 7:30. You could get there around ten, before Friction takes the stage."

My heart pounded with excitement, but I was reluctant. I had spent a lot of money flying around over the past two weeks. I made good money, but I didn't have a never-ending supply of it.

"I'll pay for your ticket," Warren suggested.

"If I didn't know any better, I would swear that you're trying to get rid of me, Warren," I said through narrowed eyes.

"You deserve to be happy, Noa. What kind of big brother would I be if I didn't do the best I could to make sure you were happy? Now stop dragging your ass. Come on. We have to get to the airport."

twenty-seven

To save time, Greg reserved a hotel room for me not far from the airport. It was there that I showered, pulled my hair up into a twist, and pulled on my pale yellow gown and silver sandals. I had no idea what had happened to my gowns and other belongings that I left at Alden's, but Greg was able to figure it out. With a little help from James' wife Linda, someone delivered everything I needed to the hotel room. Greg even convinced Alden's driver, Al, to come pick me up and drive me to the gala. By the time we pulled up outside, it was a few minutes after ten.

As I walked inside, reporters called my name and I stopped three times to pose for photographers. My anxiety level was so high that I was worried I would start to hyperventilate. There were familiar faces everywhere I turned, except for the face I *wanted* to see.

"Hey, you made it," Greg said when he found me a few minutes after my arrival. "Are you okay?" He did the doctor thing and looked closely at my eyes, put his hand on my forehead and assessed me head to toe before I could even respond.

"I'm just very nervous," I said. I held my clutch in a death grip to keep my hands from shaking. "There are *a lot* of people here."

Greg gave me an empathetic pat on the arm. "The Hollywood scene can be rather overwhelming, but just remember: they're just people."

"I feel like everyone is looking at me. It is more than overwhelming to know that probably more than half of the guests have seen me naked and snorting coke."

Greg smiled impishly as he leaned in conspiringly. "Well, then you fit right in because I am pretty sure that I have seen more than half of this room naked and behaving badly."

I snickered. That was true. We were standing four feet from an actor who was caught picking up a transvestite prostitute last year, and standing by the stage was a young singer who had been filmed on multiple occasions doing outrageous things while drunk and high.

"She made it!" a tall, beautiful, pregnant redhead cried out as she stepped in front of me. I recognized her instantly as James' wife, Linda. I had seen many pictures of her over the weeks. "Oh, my god, I'm so excited," she said, bouncing a little on her toes. "It's like a movie! Or a book! This is so romantic! He has no idea that you're here, none at all!"

To my horror, Linda began to cry. "I never thought I'd see him fall in love. Like ever. We had all just resigned ourselves to the fact that he was going to be a slut for the rest of his life. I knew it was real once I saw his pain this past week. He put on a happy face for Peyton, but…" She wiped at her tears and shook her head.

"But you're here now," Greg said and gave Linda a pointed look. "That is what is important."

Linda laughed. "Oh, god, I'm sorry. Pregnancy hormones. I don't usually cry."

"They're backstage getting ready. They'll be going on any minute now."

Right on cue, the lights dimmed and the stage began to come to life. The spotlight landed on Hash first as he beat out a cadence on the drums. Then James as he began on bass. Finally, the spotlight illuminated my rock star as he walked on stage, guitar in hand. He didn't do his usual entrance, waving and jumping around. I knew that was my fault. He had tried to call me only minutes before I arrived at the gala and I had ignored the call. I didn't want to give myself away, but he probably thought that I didn't want to speak to him.

I watched most of the performance from a dark patch in the enormous room where he couldn't see me. Greg was going to take me backstage before the band finished, so that I would surprise Alden as he came offstage. After their fourth song, Alden addressed the crowd as he always did. I knew it would be a little different since it was the last gala, but I was entirely unprepared for just *how* different it would be.

"I want to thank you all for showing up to our little party. Your generosity will help millions of kids in the foster care system across the nation. I know it may sound like bullshit, but I'm not sure if I would be here today if I never received those two sacks with everything in them from tighty-whities to this guitar right here. To this day, I don't know who it was, but thank you, whoever you are." The crowd cheered and clapped for a good half a minute before Alden was able to speak again. "As you all probably know, I recently got custody of my little brother, Peyton. He was in the foster care system, and someone also gave him one of these bags, though his wasn't as cool as mine." The crowd laughed. "But I want to thank that person, too, for helping out my kid brother."

Everyone clapped. Beside me, Greg gestured that we should head backstage, but Alden's next words kept me rooted to the ground.

"Maybe you know, or maybe you don't know, but I've had simultaneously the best and worst week of my life. The best and most important thing is that I got my brother. He's an incredible fucking kid. He's smart and sensible and he has my good looks."

Everyone laughed except for Greg and me. We knew what the worst part of his week was. Me.

"Other very good things happened this week for Frictitious. I can't really talk about it publicly just yet, but amazing things are happening with the label and I'm really excited about that."

The crowd applauded politely.

"So, now on to the bad shit. It's no fucking secret. You all know what the fuck I'm talking about and probably at least half of you would be lying if you said you didn't see the video or the pictures. I don't blame you, because she's smoking hot, right? Why wouldn't you want to see that?" He grinned. Actually *grinned.*

There were several catcalls along with some comments about my body. I almost melted into the floor. Like, became *part* of the floor.

Alden pointed to someone in the audience. "Watch your mouth before I break your pretty face, handsome." More laughter. I did not want to know what the person had said.

"I need a table to crawl under," I said to Greg.

He sighed in response.

"Anyway," Alden continued. "I, of all people, know that this shit happens. It's happened to the best of us. Shit we thought was personal becomes the whole world's fucking business, but I was an asshole, a bigger asshole than usual, I have to tell you guys. I was jealous and unreasonable and I drove away the one girl I ever truly loved. That was the worst part of my week, maybe of my entire life. But…"

But?

I glanced at Greg and Linda. They looked just as confused as I was. They had no idea where this was going either.

"But…" Alden said again. "My week is closing out on a high note. Despite the bad shit, this is still the best week of my life, because my girl..." He looked in my direction. No. He looked *directly* at me.

Impossible!

My mouth dropped open wide as his gaze settled on me.

"My girl came back. She thought that I wouldn't see her standing out there in the dark, but she doesn't know that I can find her anywhere, in any fucking crowd. I saw her halfway through the second song. I had no idea that she would come. You all have no fucking idea how good this feels."

All eyes were on me now. Well, yeah, because there was also a *spotlight* on me!

"Oh, my god," I breathed, putting a hand up to my face to try to block out some of the gazes.

"Yeah, don't be shy, Little One. Everyone sees you now in your yellow dress."

If they didn't before he said that, they did afterward.

"Isn't she beautiful?" Alden asked, and was once again rewarded with catcalls, applause, and more comments. "I can't wait to get her out of that dress, but don't get too excited, you perverts. This one ain't going on video."

"Oh, my god," I said again, shaking my head. "Oh, my god."

"My last song is a solo," Alden said as someone handed him his acoustic guitar. He looked over his shoulder at Hash and James. "I hope my brothers from other mothers don't mind."

Both guys grinned and gestured for him to continue. Of course, Hash had to say something, though.

"Your girl's boobs look great in that dress!"

"Hash, later remind me to put my fist in your mouth," Alden said, adjusting the strap on the guitar. "I started to write this song only days after meeting my one and only. I knew she was extraordinary from the beginning. I am not a guy that knows anything about romance and writing love songs – I leave that to James, but I took a shot. This is called 'Know You.' I hope you love it, Noa, even if you think it's lame. This one is for you. "

Excuse me Miss, but have we met
Let me introduce myself
I'm Alden Breck
Maybe you've seen my name in lights before
Honey come talk to me
I want to know you more

What's your name
And do you have a man
Girl don't be mean but try to understand
I never felt this way before
Honey come talk to me
I want to know you more

I want to know your story
Can we turn the page
I want to read you deeper
And know your ways
I know you're scared and unsure
But come talk to me
Let me know you more

Let me touch you there
Let me kiss you here
Let my fingers explore you
And stir your desire
Baby come for me
And let me give you more

Now you know my name
Now you know my song
Now you have my whole heart
As long as it beats on
You came and talked to me
You changed my whole life
Little Noa come here to me
And be my wife

I hate tears, but I openly cried and I didn't care who was watching. I only had eyes for Alden as he discarded the guitar, jumped off the stage, and made his way to me through the parted crowd. I barely registered the thundering applause and the cheers or the flashes from cameras.

No words, no hesitation. Alden put an arm around me and pulled my body into his as one hand wove into my hair and his mouth met mine in a heart-swelling kiss that made everything inside of me tingle. His tongue was warm and sweet, his lips soft but punishing, and I could not get enough. My fingers laced behind his head as I pulled him closer, closer, until the kiss was so deep that it was invasive.

When the kiss finally ended, I was breathless and my whole body was on fire. He gazed down into my eyes as if the rest of the world wasn't there, like we weren't being watched by hundreds of pairs of eyes.

"Do you want to go backstage and get fucked by a talented, incredibly good-looking rock star?" he asked, boldly grinding against me.

"Yes," I whispered breathlessly. With my lips touching his, I asked, "Is Jared Leto back there waiting for me?"

Alden growled. I laughed.

And then he took me backstage.

***

There were a few people in the dressing room when we went back, most of them worked for Friction, but Alden said one word and gestured toward the door with his thumb.

"Out."

They left without question, though they gave knowing smiles and glances.

As soon as the door closed, Alden locked it and then lifted me into his arms to kiss me again.

"Fuck, I've missed you," he said when he put me down.

"I missed you, too."

He led me to one of the leather couches and sat down. He put his hands on my hips and guided me to stand between his open legs. Slowly, he began to ease my dress up my legs.

"I hate to think how many other people have done what we're going to do on this couch," he said.

"I don't know, but I'm sure none of them have done it like Alden Breck will do it," I said, feeding his ego.

He kissed my thigh and grinned up at me. "You're fucking amazing, you know that?"

"I would have to be fucking amazing to put up with your bullshit." I gently pushed my fingers through his hair.

His eyes closed and he rested his head against my belly.

"I thought I lost you, like really lost you," he said softly. "I was trying to play it cool for Peyton's sake, but I was fucking dying inside. I was all knotted up and twisted and there was nothing I could do to relieve the pressure. I hope you forgive me, Noa."

"Hey," I whispered, gently tilting his head up. His eyes opened and met mine. "We both made some mistakes, okay? We'll be making many, many more, I am sure of it."

"But—"

"Ssshhh." I stroked his cheek. "Let me make you feel better, baby."

I dropped to my knees before him, being mindful of my long gown. Alden watched me with curiosity, but I could see the torture that was lingering in his eyes.

"Sit back," I said, giving him a gentle push. He obeyed without question and pushed back until his back was against the couch.

I undid the buttons of his coat and pushed it off his shoulders. He pulled it off and tossed it aside as he continued to watch me with interest. I released the catch on his pants and slowly pulled the zipper down before putting my fingers under the elastic of his boxer briefs and tugging them down. Alden lifted his hips to aid me, but otherwise didn't move, or maybe didn't even breathe. I pulled his pants and boxers all of the way off, removing his shoes in the process. I left everything in a pile on the floor and positioned myself between his legs.

His cock stood at attention against his belly when I reached for it. The bulbous head was big, thick, and droplets of semen made it glisten in the soft light of the room. The shaft was so thick that my hand appeared small and dainty wrapped around it.

After some admiration (and fear), I looked up into his eyes as I moved to take him in my mouth.

"Wait," he said, putting a hand on my forehead to stop me.

Seriously? Really?

"What?" I asked, surprised.

"You don't have to do this," he said, and it looked like it pained him to say it. "You don't owe me this, Noa."

"Alden?"

"Yes, Little One?"

"Shut up," I said huskily.

Before any more words could be uttered, I sucked the head of his perfect cock between my lips.

"Oh, shit!" Alden hissed as his hips came off the couch, pushing his cock deeper into my mouth. His eyes had closed on their own accord, but now he looked down at me with his dick in my mouth. It was like he completely forgot that he just tried to stop me. "Suck me, Noa."

Wrapping both of my hands around his shaft, I eased more of him into my mouth until I could feel that sticky head *past* my tonsils. I resisted the urge to gag as Alden groaned my name. I hollowed my cheeks, creating as much of a suction as I possibly could before I slowly pulled back until just the tip was in my mouth. I eased him back in a little faster this time. Then I was moving, pumping him as I sucked his cock in and out of my mouth.

There were moist suctioning noises mixed with Alden's moans and mutterings. My saliva mixed with his pre-cum as I sucked him with a growing animalistic zeal. I moaned as I pumped him and took him deep into my mouth. His fingers knotted tightly in my hair and his hips rose off the couch, forcing his large erection deeper. I cupped his balls in my hand and massaged as I orally pleasured him.

"I'm getting close," he grunted. "I want to be inside of you when I finish. Noa…fuck…stop."

Reluctantly, I eased away from him. His dick fell from my mouth with moist sound. Alden leaned forward, grabbed the back of my head, and kissed me. It was a sloppy, wet kiss with more tongue than lips and I loved it. It was erotic and made me want him even more.

"Get your hot ass up here," he groaned, pulling me off the floor.

He held my dress up as I stepped out of my panties and straddled his thighs and eased down onto him.

"Oh shit," I gasped as his heavy cock reacquainted itself with my vagina.

"Baby, we fit so well together," Alden moaned against my neck.

His hands found my hips and he began to rock into me. I cursed under my breath and licked my lips as I looked into his hazel eyes.

"I can't wait to come inside of you again," he groaned. "Can't wait to feel my hot come spurting inside of your perfect pussy."

A hole appeared in my sexual fog, leaving a small space for clarity. Something dawned on me.

"I didn't take my pill," I blurted out, trying to still myself on him, but he kept moving me and moving inside of me.

I groaned and said, "I haven't taken it all week. Alden! Are you listening to me?"

He nipped at my bare shoulder and then looked up into my eyes.

"Yeah, I heard you and I don't care."

"What?" I surely didn't hear him as I thought I heard him.

We never talked about having babies, not exactly. We talked about future, hypothetical children, but not really *our* children. When we first started fooling around, I was less concerned with pregnancy than I was about getting some sexually transmitted disease, but Greg made all of the guys get tested regularly, and Alden claimed to have always worn a condom with everyone before me. I wasn't so worried about diseases by this point, but I should have definitely been worried about getting knocked up. Right?

"I said I don't care," Alden repeated. "I want everything with you, Noa. Everything I never thought I wanted before. Marriage." He kissed my left ring finger. "A home." He kissed my lips. "A family." He thrust gently inside of me. "I told you once before that you are magical, Little One. Why wouldn't I want to create more magic with you?"

I'm not going to cry. I'm not going to cry. I'm not going to cry.

I cried. And kissed him. And rode him with desperation.

Moments later, we exploded together, cursing and groaning. I clung to him, burying my face in his neck as we tried to catch our breaths. After a few minutes, he pushed my hair away from my face and gazed lovingly at me.

"I'm so glad that you fell on your face at that concert," he said, caressing my cheek with his thumb.

"You mean you're so glad that you almost killed me with your pelvic thrusting," I corrected.

"What can I say? Chicks dig a good pelvic thrust."

I rolled my eyes. "Jared Leto doesn't pelvic thrust."

"Then you should go marry Jared Leto."

"Can I?" I asked excitedly.

"No," he said, and kissed me. "Only me. Always me."

"Only you and always you."

Epilogue

One week after the gala, I married Alden Breck. I married *the* Alden Breck, the same man who couldn't keep it in his pants when I first met him. The very same man who had sworn to anyone who would listen that he would never, ever fall in love, never settle down, and definitely *not* get married.

Our ceremony was short and no frills. We went to the courthouse, applied for a license, and the next day, Alden had a justice of the peace come out to the house and marry us in the garden. Hash and James served as witnesses. I wore a pair of jeans and a T-shirt that said "I'm With the Band" and Alden wore an equally dumb shirt that said "I'm the Band."

I didn't want a big ceremony. I was never *that* kind of girl. I didn't want or need all of the fairytale stuff. I just wanted *him*. I did not need to prove to a big group of people that I loved the man I was marrying. I did not need to read my personal feelings aloud as proof. I only needed to prove it to Alden, and vice versa. I had nothing against anyone else who went for the frills though, like Sahara.

On the first day of summer, Sahara and Greg were married in the warm Californian sun. Sahara is an elegant woman, and Greg is a refined man, despite the rock star company he keeps. Of course, the wedding was beautiful, elegant, and refined like the bride and groom.

Alden was Greg's best man. I was proud of him for not scowling through the ceremony. As he feared, Sahara was stealing his doctor.

Greg took a position in one of New York's top-notch hospitals. Sahara had been willing to give up her position and move to California for him, but he did not want that for her. He appreciated how hard she worked to get into her corporate position, and for him, the end of an era was over. He loved Friction, and even though there was only about fifteen years between them, Alden was like a son to him; however, he was ready to move on and live his own life.

Two months after that, Peyton was officially adopted into the Breck family. We had a quiet celebration at home, just the three of us. We ate ice cream and cake and Alden gave his brother *his* guitar, the very one that he had received as a donation when he was only nine years old. Alden's name was engraved on it years ago, but he had Peyton Breck added to it just below his. I could tell that it was hard for Alden to part with the guitar, but Peyton, as young as he was, did understand the significance. He blinked back tears as he accepted the gift.

"I promise I'll always take really good care of it," he said before hugging Alden.

Peyton and I got along very well together. He was an affectionate kid, never afraid to just give me a random hug or to tell me he loved me. However, he was still Alden Breck's little brother. I often had to talk to him about his cursing and talking about what chicks dug.

"Don't worry about what chicks dig," I admonished. "Worry about school, music, and Pokemon or whatever boys your age worry about. No chicks!"

"Chicks don't dig overbearing moms," Alden had muttered under his breath as Peyton walked out of the kitchen.

I hit his elbow just as he was about to take a drink out of the glass he was holding. Lemonade splashed into his face and dribbled down onto his clothes.

"Chicks don't dig sloppy 'rock stars,' either."

"Do chicks dig sticky faces?" he had asked and chased me around the kitchen trying to kiss me with his sticky lips.

In early November, Larson Wright died in a freak accident on the New Jersey Turnpike. His car had gone off the road and wrapped around a tree. He wasn't drunk or high, nor did the autopsy reveal any other medical problems that could explain the accident. The authorities really took a wild guess when they said he probably fell asleep, as the accident happened at two in the morning.

I hated Larson for all of the things he had done to me, but death is a high price for anyone to pay. I wasn't sad that he died, but the loss of a life is always unsettling. Eerily, he left me all of his possessions. *All* of his possessions – his cars, including the Bugatti, his cabin in the Catskills, his condo and all of the contents within, an enormous life insurance policy and all of the money in all of his accounts. The total net worth was a staggering amount of money. It wasn't as much money as Alden had, maybe only a small percentage of Alden's net worth, but it was still a lot. I did not want it, any of it. Even if I was not with Alden and had to rely solely on my own resources, I would not have wanted it. I put the condominium and house in the mountains up for sale. I gave Larson's family permission to go through the homes and take what they wanted and I sold the cars.

Alden helped me to start a charitable foundation for victims of domestic violence with all of the money that was in Larson's accounts and the money that we made selling his things. The charity will help victims transition out of their abusive households by providing help with rent, mortgages, bills, childcare, and all of the other things that can make leaving a daunting prospect. There will also be counseling help and legal help, because those are just as important as the rest. I was able to enlist the help of Friction and others that I met at the gala in L.A. – actors, actresses, producers, and directors and more.

While I was busy with that and my writing, Alden was busy with Frictitious. That big meeting he had a few days before the gala was with another music label, a pretty big one. Alden bought it, but that wasn't all he was working on. He also bought a production company. Originally, he had wanted one to produce the videos for Friction and the other bands on the label, but Hash came up with an idea for a series. He wanted to do a documentary type series that followed around musicians who were struggling with a drug habit. Each one would be followed while on tour, because according to Hash, that's when he had the hardest time staying clean. Alden agreed to do it, and I had the feeling that it would open up even more doors for Frictitious.

Alden and I did create our own magic. Jeremy Breck was born nearly a year after I was trampled by tramps at a Friction concert. His father was in awe at what we created. For months, I would catch him stroking Jeremy's fingers and toes, caressing his nose, and sniffing that baby smell on his head.

"I can't believe we made him," he often says while watching our son sleep.

Sometimes life seems surreal to me, too. Alden, Peyton, and I had such rough beginnings. Our lives could be something else entirely. My life *was* something else entirely for a good while. I hate many of the events of my life that lead me here, but I have learned to embrace my past as well as my present and future. I learned critical life lessons. I know what kind of mother *not* to be, and to love and cherish my children and to take responsibility for my own shortcomings. I have learned to ask for help when I am struggling and suffering, as I should have asked my brother all of those years ago. My experiences with Todd have taught me that even the people who may care about me may not good for me. My life with Larson has taught me independence, courage, strength, and endurance.

I can choose to be weighed down by regrets, but…I have let all of my regrets go. My current regrets are nothing deeper than regretting to take a cake out of the oven so that it doesn't burn. I am not saying that I should not feel badly for some of the things I did in my past, but my end result is so unbelievably fantastic that I cannot regret those things that brought me to this place. I cannot regret the events that have led me to Alden, Peyton, and Jeremy.

"Hey." Alden waved a hand in front of my face.

I blinked and looked up at him. I was in my office, with Jeremy asleep in a baby swing in the corner.

"Hey," I said, leaning back in my chair and rubbing my eyes.

"Where were you just now, Little One?"

He walked around to my side of the desk and sat down on the edge.

"I was just thinking about everything that led me here. I have no regrets. Like, none."

"I have some," he said, crossing his arms.

"Yeah? Like what?"

"I was with a *lot* of women before you. I didn't regret it for a long time, but…especially now that we have a family, I feel like I fucked up. It doesn't make me a good role model for the boys. If we have a daughter, and she brings home someone like me, I will probably fucking kill him."

I smiled faintly. "I'm not saying that being a slut was a good thing, but if you hadn't had all of those women, you may not have been able to fully appreciate what we have. You could have been tainted by a broken heart, you could have been with someone else – the possibilities of what could have been are endless. I don't like to think about what could have been. I don't need to think about what could have been. What I *have* is exactly what I want and need."

He leaned over and kissed me gently on the mouth.

"You say pretty shit," he murmured as he stroked my cheek with his fingers. "You should be one of those romance authors."

"You're a bombastic man with a wicked pelvic thrust. You should be a rock star."

"You forgot talented and good looking and lyrical god." He shook his head in disappointment.

"Okay, get out before your ego wakes up Jem."

"Don't call Jerm Jem," Alden said, getting to his feet. "He's not all sparkly and shiny and shit."

"Interesting, because you sure are," I said sweetly and batted my eyes.

"Psh. Fuck yeah, I am. Don't forget it, Little One."

"You really rub me the wrong way," I said, turning my attention back to my computer.

I fully expected him to say something like "that's not what you said last night" or something similar, but he didn't. He kissed the baby and started out of the room. He paused in the door and looked back at me.

"It's called friction, Little Noa. And you *love* every minute of it."

I watched him walk out of the room and stared at the doorway for a long moment before snorting, "Friction. Puh."

I hid my smile, even from myself. Alden was right, of course.

I love our brand of friction, every minute of it.

The end

Special Thanks

Kristen Switzer
Arlene Babwah
Karleigh Brewster
Tina Kleuker
Marta Vilaca
Sheena Lumsden
Nikki Costello
Heather Carver
Kris Davis

You ladies and gent ROCK!

Also By L.D. Davis

Accidentally On Purpose
Worthy of Redemption
Worth the Fight
Tethered
Girl Code
Pieces of Rhys

Made in the USA
Middletown, DE
30 March 2015